mark

a novel by Adam Darby

for me

CHAPTER
one

FACT

IT WAS NEARLY DARK BY THE TIME THEY EMERGED FROM THE jungle—stepping from the shaded, muddy trail to the dry, firm ground of the tribe's village—small huts surrounding a taller, longer structure at the center of the clearing—all with reed walls and thatched roofs—open ground mostly bare, red-brown dirt—packed by billions of footsteps over thousands of years. Mark stopped when his captors stopped—looked up and saw a full moon rising through the soft sunset colors still visible—pinks, purples and oranges fading fast from east to west—first few stars blinking in the darkest parts of the sky.

The four men spoke to each other—their strange language accompanied by grunts and hand gestures—coming to some sort of consensus after a minute or two—then shoving Mark toward a small hut along the edge of the village. A group of children stopped playing and stared silently as he passed—mouths open—fear and wonder on their little faces. Mark tried to smile at them—tried to put them at ease but he felt too much pain to pretend—too much fear to worry about anyone else being afraid—walking past them with his eyes on the ground—focusing on his pace and not deviating from the path his captors were taking—keeping the wooden spears off his head and away from his sore back.

They kept Mark outside the small hut while two of the men entered and spoke with someone—voices hushed and hurried—one of them much more animated than the others. Mark waited and listened—tried to see inside but it was too dark as he peered through the open doorway.

After a few minutes the two men came out and relayed some brief commands to the other two—all four then working together to force Mark inside the small, unlit hut—pushing and pulling his arms—poking his back with their fire-hardened spears.

Once inside the dank, windowless space—once his eyes had adjusted to the darkness—it was easy to see what they wanted—the task he'd have to complete—his first taste of forced labor just a day after being taken by the tribe.

Light soon began to trickle in from a quickly growing bonfire outside—making shadows on the reed walls and thatched ceiling. A woman was laid out on the floor in the center of the hut—naked with her legs bent at the knees and spread apart—head and face resting back in the shadows—arms stretched out away from her body. Mark looked at her hands in the increasing flickers of light and saw they were covered in ocher paint—smeared as well over her breasts—a line of it going from her neck down to her waist.

Two of the men let go of Mark's arms and backed away. At the same time Mark felt spears poking into the muscles that ran along his spine—nudging him toward an older man he hadn't seen at first—kneeling just on the other side of the woman. They looked at each other and Mark saw dark lines carefully drawn onto the man's face—charcoal tracings along the deep wrinkles in his skin—his hair cut in the same shape as all the other men.

As Mark approached the older man began waving a bundle of smoking leaves and bark over the woman's body—burning specks floating down to her skin but she did not move. Her chest raised, fingers twitched and toes just barely started to curl—but the rest of her stayed firmly in place—determined, Mark thought, to remain—to endure any and all hardships for as long as she had to.

This wasn't Mark's real life—slave to a prehistoric tribe. It wasn't his life just thirty-six hours ago—before they found him wandering the jungle—the two days he'd spent lost and alone before that—or for all the weeks and months and years of his life leading up to now. This wasn't him—who he really was.

He'd known he was lost soon after leaving the outfitter's camp—had become aware of something following him two days later—something close but never seen—never heard when he stopped to listen. There was something tracking him—hunting him as he tried to find his way back.

Occasionally he would stop and stand as motionless as possible—sweating with every heartbeat pounding up through his head—watching for any movement—waiting to hear another small sound from whatever terrible thing was pursuing him.

Finally the four small men emerged from behind giant trees, tangled vines and broad-leafed jungle plants—surrounding him and slowly closing in. Mark spun around to see each man with a long wooden spear held waist-high—all pointing toward the middle of his body.

The men spoke to each other but never turned their heads or even seemed to blink. Mark slipped and stumbled as he searched for a way to escape the tightening circle—sturdy, shoeless feet of all the men shuffling in unison over the leaf-littered forest floor—working together to keep him corralled—their eyes never leaving him—tips of their spears never dropping or turning away—strips of cloth or animal skin hanging down from coarse rope belts.

As they inched closer Mark put his hands in the air and tried to speak to them—English words and phrases he hoped they would somehow understand. But the four small men did not stop moving toward him until the points of their spears touched his ribs and stomach—two of them poking at the backpack hanging from his shoulders—one even testing the bottle of insect repellant bulging from the front pocket of his pants.

They talked to each other for another minute or two—puzzled glances now traded between them as they decided Mark's fate. Then the circle suddenly broke apart—two of the men marching away single file—the other two slapping at Mark with their spears—hitting his backpack and legs—his arms and swinging for his head.

They walked for hours through the thick jungle—small bodies of the four men moving easily between the trees and dangling vines as Mark struggled to keep up. When he couldn't match their pace they stabbed at him from behind with their spears—tripped and fell and they beat him with the blunt ends of the same long, fire-hardened sticks. When he tried to escape—running off suddenly through the dense vegetation with no idea where he was going—the men would chase after him and have him surrounded within a few minutes—laughing and joking with each other as they closed in—striking him in turns before returning to the trail.

At one point they stopped and ripped Mark's backpack

off his shoulders—made him sit in the mud as they inspected its strange contents—pulling things out one by one and passing them around—synthetic sleeping bag and rain jacket and the little metal stove. Once they were through inspecting an item the last man holding it would toss it over his shoulder—discarding Mark's carefully chosen supplies and leaving them to disappear into the jungle—curiosities only useful as amusing distractions during a break in their long march.

They continued their trek into the night and through to the next morning—traversing trails Mark could not distinguish from the rest of the jungle. But he kept moving forward—tired, thirsty and sore from all the beatings—anxious to see their destination—wondering if they were taking him to some deeper, darker, even more untouched place—a cursed part of the forest where primitive tribes killed and ate their enemies and any outsiders they managed to capture. Or maybe they were delivering him back to civilization—deporting him to the outside world where something so weak, so strange and so useless surely belonged.

In the small, dark hut with the woman and the older man, Mark continued stepping forward until the spearpoints finally pulled back from the skin around his spine—flinching to a stop as he heard the blunt ends of the heavy spears tapping down onto the packed-earth floor behind him.

He was at the woman's feet now—looking down into the shadows—the older man wafting smoke into her face from the bundle he held—Mark able to see that her eyes were open—tears on her cheeks with her nostrils flared.

He stood there and watched as the older man bent down

and whispered into the woman's ear—bundle held over her abdomen—smoke drifting up across Mark's face. The older man continued talking to the woman for what seemed like a long time—eventually shaking the collection of burning leaves and bark as he spoke—Mark watching more of the gray-white particles breaking away from the bundle—some hanging in the air and rising toward the ceiling—some dancing away and sinking slowly toward the ground.

Once the older man had finished his incantations, Mark felt someone stepping forward from the doorway—rough, small hands grabbing his shoulders from behind—pulling him down to his knees—the other men then coming forward as they all began to chant—the older man standing up slowly—looking down at Mark—staring blankly at him with firelight flickering over his face—the chanting growing louder and louder.

Mark turned his head and looked out the open doorway—the rest of the tribe now dancing around the raging bonfire—chanting in time with the men inside the hut. He turned back and looked down at the woman—her head raised out of the shadows—bloodshot eyes staring up at him—shaky voice chanting along with everyone else.

A few seconds later one of the men pushed Mark down on top of the woman—her head falling back but she kept looking at him—kept dutifully chanting—Mark looking up as the older man began dancing around them in a tightening circle—wafting smoke through the air as he went—the other four men still chanting as they did the same dance.

Mark looked back down at the woman—on his hands and knees with his bottom half between her legs—feeling her smooth skin wrapping around him—her hand squeezing inside the waistband of his pants—ligaments in her neck protruding as she leaned forward—hand still reaching—searching inside the strange garment—still chanting along with everyone else.

When he looked up again at the dancing men, Mark saw spears in their hands and knew what would happen if he fought—if he protested—if he refused to do what they demanded be done.

Mark woke up in the morning with his arms still wrapped around his head. Members of the tribe had rushed into the little hut several times throughout the night to hit him with spears as he slept—waking him suddenly and laughing as he rolled away—laughing even as he screamed and eventually cried against the back wall of the hut. It started several hours after the woman left—after all the dancing and chanting and the smoking bundle of leaves and bark—after the bonfire had slowly burned itself out.

But as he opened his eyes just after the sun had risen above the tallest treetops—as he cautiously raised his head to look around—there were no spears and no one else seemed to be inside the tiny hut—morning light coming in through the open doorway—smoke from the night's fire still hanging in the heavy air. Mark blinked himself awake and turned his head away from the sun—sat up after a minute or two and scooted carefully into the shade—vertebrae popping as he moved—bruises and cuts hurting as his muscles flexed and his skin stretched—his mouth feeling dry as he instinctively began looking around for water.

"Hi," Mark said as he noticed the older man—the witch doctor with the charcoal black lines curving around his wrinkled face—sitting in a patch of shade on the other side of the hut—the two of them separated by the angled block of sunlight coming in through the open doorway—staring at each other—the older man not moving—not even blinking his eyes. "Hi," Mark said again as he raised a hand to wave—squinting and yawning—scanning the rest of the packed-earth floor—hoping in vain to see something that held water—an ancient clay pot or bowl or even just an upturned leaf. "Water," he said. "Water." Mark cupped his hands and lifted them to his mouth—pantomiming for the motionless older man.

The rain started early in the afternoon that day—Mark's first full day with the tribe after his first full moon night—not allowed out of the hut until the storm finally arrived—rain pouring down while thunder ricocheted off the thick walls of jungle that surrounded the village.

The older man stayed with him inside the hut all morning—never moving except to turn his head each time Mark ran out the open doorway—then turning again a few minutes later to watch him being shoved back inside by the same four men that had found him wandering the jungle—the failed escape attempts piling up as noon came and went—the beatings—not even able to find something to drink in one of the wettest places on Earth.

Once the rain started, however, Mark ran outside and was surprised when no one came running after him—stopped and stood there waiting for them to come—soaking wet with bare feet squishing into the slick mud—spinning around to peer inside all the huts—seeing columns of small faces staring out at him—smallest children at the bottom—then the adolescents and then a few adult faces at the top.

The rain smacked into his head and body and soaked into the pants he was still wearing—his shirt, shoes and socks having been taken from him the night before—half-naked now as he turned from hut to hut—watching the faces appear and then disappear from the open doorways—eventually spotting a puddle of muddy water near where the bonfire had been—now just a concave circle of gray ash—black and brown pieces of half-burnt wood.

Mark walked over and squatted down—tried to sweep away some of the silt from the puddle—then cupped his hands and submerged them—carefully lifting as much water as he could to his mouth. He drank twice more from the puddle—then looked back up at all the people in the doorways—rain still falling—running cool down his face and back—muddy water collecting in his stomach.

Eventually he stood up and turned toward the largest hut in the center of the village.

"I'm leaving," Mark said—barely able to hear his own voice over the rain—shattering sound of myriad drops slapping into the bare ground and the rooftops—soaking the endless jungle beyond. "Bye, everybody—hell of a party last night." His voice was shaky as he backed away—more faces crowding into the doorways as he got farther from the half-drained puddle—serious faces of men intent on keeping their captive—their soft-bellied slave.

Once he got to the trees Mark turned and started running—navigating a narrow tunnel of tropical vegetation with branches coming together over his head—broad green leaves leaning over in front of him—heavy with the afternoon rain. He smacked them out of his way and tried not to slip on the muddy trail—finally looking back to see several faces running after him—bows held out in front of their strong, slender bodies—bundles of arrows held vertical in angry hands.

Mark ran harder—heart pumping faster and lungs trying to catch up—not worrying as much about slipping or stepping on something sharp with his tender feet—few seconds later feeling a sudden bite in his leg just below his knee—then tumbling down to the mushy, decomposing leaves that lined the forest floor—rolling through thin stalks of jungle underbrush.

Once he came to a stop Mark turned over onto his back and looked down at his leg—blood leaking out with an arrow going through it—something shiny catching his eye at the front end of the lightweight wooden shaft—delicate-looking feathers attached to the back.

"How'd they—" he started saying as the pain suddenly eased—as his eyelids drooped and his hearing faded—reaching to touch the sharpened metal tip as his captors quickly approached—dead leaves clinging to his arms and back—his pants heavy with rain and blood.

Soon Mark felt the young men lifting him off the ground—raindrops hitting his eyes as he suddenly found it hard to focus—hard to see or hear or even smell anything—to distinguish the waking world from one of dreamed-up terrors.

"I think I've figured out a name for you," Mark said from his back—turning his head a few minutes after he woke up inside the same small hut where he'd spent that morning—where he'd been forced onto a woman the night before. "Splinter," he said—blinking as his eyes tried to focus on the older man sitting across from him in the dark—seeing the man's unblinking eyes and the dark tracings on his face. "Ever heard of the Teenage Mutant Ninja Turtles?" Mark was sitting up now—rubbing his forehead as he looked around and out the open doorway. The rain had stopped and all he could hear were insects and frogs. The moon was up and close to full—making the wet, bare ground outside the hut shine blue. "Didn't think so," he continued—talking to the older man as he looked outside. "There's a group of turtles in New York City—in the sewers. They mutate into ninjas somehow—then they're brought up by a mutant rat who's sort of their leader. Anyway, the rat's name is Splinter."

Nothing about the older man changed—no movements that might have signaled he'd heard sounds coming from his tribe's strange captive—from the tall slave sitting just a few feet across from him. He just kept looking at Mark—kept his hands clasped in his lap.

Mark laughed as he inspected the two wounds now bracketing his leg—pants cut away from his knee down. The arrow with the shiny, sharp tip and stabilizing feathers was gone—thick layer of green paste now covering the holes—dried blood clumped in his leg hairs and there was swelling beneath his skin.

"I guess I'll have to figure out what names to give the other four—the ones who dragged me here. There's Donatello, Leonardo, Raphael and my personal favorite, Michelangelo."

Mark touched the two wounds but couldn't feel the pressure he placed on his leg—moved his hand down toward his ankle and the feeling gradually came back—then wiggled his toes and tried to flex his calf muscle—sending a sharp, sudden pain shooting through his leg—fresh blood leaking through cracks in the green paste. He winced and looked up at Splinter but the expression on the older man's face hadn't changed.

Mark scooted back against the wall and looked around—pushed himself as deep as he could into the corner of the tiny hut—tried to ask for his shirt or a blanket but got no response—then just leaned against the wall and crossed his arms—big smile on his face so the tears wouldn't start—trying to distract himself—wondering if he'd be warmer if he took his wet pants off.

"I guess that woman last night will be April," Mark said. "She gets herself roped into helping the Ninja Turtles all the time. And I guess I'll have to be Casey Jones. He's kind of a screwup but he has fun."

Splinter sat there on the bare ground—never speaking or making any kind of gesture—Mark's silent guard for the night. Mark looked him over carefully—the deep wrinkles of his face—black eyes and lipless mouth. Then he let his eyes wander to the walls of the hut and out the open doorway—Splinter's eyes, meanwhile, never leaving his captive's face.

After some time the darkness and the quiet began to burrow deep into Mark—the solitude and the helplessness—the shock of suddenly realizing he was now a slave to a prehistoric tribe—something insignificant that would likely be discarded soon—left for the jungle to slowly swallow.

So he began to talk—to dream out loud—to pray for yesterday's yesterday and for the chance to turn back—to choose another route—to go where they would not find him.

STORY

"I have a wife, you know—and a son—little guy and his mom expecting me back home soon—probably wondering why I haven't called for a few days. Are any of these kids around here yours, Splinter?"

.

.

"No? Well, there's still time. Of course you'll have to find the right woman first—like I did. Unless you already have a wife? Or two? Was that one of them last night?"

.

.

"I don't even know if you all do the husband-and-wife thing here—wouldn't surprise me if you didn't. And I might not blame you—half the time you're miserable—another forty percent you're ignoring each other—then maybe ten percent of the time you're actually enjoying your life together—probably less than ten percent, now that I think about it. You know what I mean?"

.

.

"It was different in the beginning, of course. I met my wife along a hiking trail up in the mountains. It was early spring and there was still snow on the peaks and in some shady patches under trees. Have you ever seen snow, Splinter?"

.

.

"Of course you've never seen snow—or cars, or planes, or people over five and a half feet tall. But that's fine—it's fine. Maybe it's actually better to live that way—like you—in the dark. When you know about everything there's always something you're missing out on. Then you have to chase after it and you end up doing something stupid or going someplace you have no business going."

.

.

"But anyway, back to my story. So my wife had been out hiking with a friend and somehow sprained her ankle pretty bad. I was by myself and found them an hour or so before dark. I remember the snow on some of the peaks was colored orange from the last bits of sunset light. The sky was clear and it was cold and getting colder—probably below freezing by that time. But the snow up on the mountains looked almost like lava—sun hitting it just right.

"I was heading back to my car when I found them along the trail. My wife—or the girl who would become my wife— was sitting there on the ground holding her leg. Her friend was sitting beside her with a cellphone in her hand—trying to find a signal so she could call for help.

"But with the sun going down and the temperature dropping I knew we didn't have time to wait around. So I stood there talking to them for a few minutes—making them feel a little more comfortable with me—my wife sitting there rubbing her ankle—saying she just needed another minute or two and she'd be able to walk the rest of the way. But I could see the skin changing color already—could see her ankle swelling up with fluid.

"Finally I talked them into letting me carry her—piggy-back ride to their car or until her leg started feeling better. I gave her friend my wallet and keys and made some stupid joke about not being a serial killer. They both laughed in a nervous sort of way—looked at each other as I helped my future wife up and got her boosted onto my back. She put her arms around my neck and hiked her legs up around my pelvis. We started down the trail and I went a little faster than I should've—trying to be mister macho in front of the pretty girl, you know what I mean?"

.

.

"Anyway, we were going down the trail and I was talking to her the entire time—trying to be clever about how the snow looked like lava with the sun hitting it just right. But the trail had rocks pushing up in places and I kicked one and went tumbling down into the dirt. I put my hands down and slid a few feet—cut my palms and my knees. My wife rolled off my back and laid there grabbing her ankle and biting her lower lip. She did that a lot. Whenever she was hurt or nervous—bit her lip."

.

.

"So I got up and looked myself over. There was dirt and blood all over me—little pebbles embedded in my hands. I picked them out—blood still oozing from my palms but it wasn't gushing or anything. My legs, though, were bleeding a lot more. My pants had ripped open above my knees and I could see blood sliding down my kneecaps—could already feel it in my shoes. It wasn't spurting, though, so I figured I wasn't hurt too bad.

"But my wife and her friend looked at my hands and my legs and must've thought I had only a couple seconds to live. Their eyes got wide—my wife still gripping her ankle with both hands. Her friend just stood there with all our bags draped over her shoulders. I walked over to her and took my water bottle out of a side pouch on my backpack—poured the water on my hands first—then my knees and let it run down my legs and into my shoes. Blood kept seeping out of the deepest cuts but, like I said, it wasn't spurting.

"None of us said anything the rest of the way. I guess I was a little embarrassed. It probably only took another half hour to get to the parking lot but it seemed like a lot longer. It was dark by the time we got there and we only had a little keychain flashlight between the three of us.

"Since my wife and I—my future wife—were both injured, we climbed into her friend's car and let her drive us to the nearest hospital. They stitched me up—cleaned out all my wounds. My wife went for X-rays and I got a little worried I wouldn't see her again. After they were through with me I wasn't sure where she was so I just strolled around the hallways. I must've walked in front of the nurse's station too many times because they kept asking me if I was lost or if I needed to call someone for a ride.

"Instead of calling a cab or my mother I waited there in the lobby for another hour—waited until my wife and her friend came out. My wife was trying to figure out how to walk with crutches. Her friend rolled her eyes when she saw me but I didn't care. I said I owed them dinner and I can remember my wife smiling at me for the first time—a real smile—not the one people use when they're just trying to be polite."

.

"A few months later she told me she'd been so worried about us never seeing each other again—sitting in that hospital room as they worked on her ankle—so worried I might leave that she begged her friend to go out and walk the hallways looking for me."

"That was eleven years ago. It'll be twelve in a couple months."

SHOW

There were black curtains hanging in the middle of the large conference room—four temporary walls with bright lights and long, puffy microphones reaching over the opening at the top. Mark walked into the windowless room by himself—still slim but putting on weight fast—toughened, scarred skin losing its tan every day.

He stood there just inside the double doors—expanse of soft, patterned carpet spread out in front of him—padded chairs and folding tables stacked against the walls. It was quiet inside the huge, darkened room—no sound until a door squeaked open somewhere near the farthest corner from where he stood.

INTERVIEWER: You must be Mark it's a pleasure to meet you I can't tell you how much I've been looking forward to this your story is just so amazing.

The smiling man Mark saw marching toward him was

tall—broad shoulders slumping only slightly with age—gray hair perfectly styled with a hard, gelled wave going back and to the side. Mark had seen the famous journalist on TV many times—was surprised he looked exactly the same in person—his deep voice sounding the same as well—always speaking in long, run-on sentences that somehow made sense because he knew exactly when to pause and when to speed up and-and-and when to stutter over a word in order to allow things to sink in for just the right amount of time before he continued.

MARK: Hi.

The famous journalist kept saying how excited he was as he shook Mark's hand and then led him across the conference room—taking him through another set of double doors and down a brightly lit hallway—then ushering him into a small room with tables full of assorted snacks and large, cylindrical coffee warmers—neat rows of bottled water and colorful cans of soda. The crew members were there and the older man took Mark around to meet everyone—then guided him to an even smaller room where they had mirrors set up in front of an empty chair—large, heavy-duty black cases stacked in each corner—a young woman standing next to a small folding table—arranging brushes and spray cans and little tubes of makeup.

INTERVIEWER: Mandy will put your face on and then we'll get you to do a little paperwork and after that we'll finally start the interview I-I-I just can't wait to hear about your amazing experience, Mark.

Mark sat down in the empty chair and Mandy started tucking tissues around his shirt collar—complimenting his eyes and the bone structure of his face—gestures he assumed were meant to calm his nerves before the questions started—the poking and the prodding—bright overhead lights and long, puffy microphones—the cameras and the big-shot TV personality all working together to condense the last few years of his life down to a one-hour special—commercial breaks included, of course.

CHAPTER
TWO

FACT

THE FOLLOWING DAYS AND NIGHTS—THE WEEKS AND months enslaved—Mark worked when forced to work—slept when allowed to rest—ate whatever scraps of food were tossed his way. The Ninja Turtles took him into the jungle nearly every morning and he followed as best he could—at first choosing each step carefully on his stiff leg— never any sign of infection from his arrow wound thanks to the medicine man's green paste. His shoeless feet quickly became tender and sore as they slowly toughened with each day's punishment—thin-skinned appendages barely able to carry him back to the village in the evenings—swollen and bloody and cared for at night by the older man—the witch doctor, Splinter—washing them and rubbing the green paste into each fresh wound.

Mark worked hard each day to keep pace with the quiet line of prehistoric hunters—knowing that if he fell behind the men would strike him with one of their long bows or poke him in the back with a metal-tipped arrow. If he made too much noise while they were hunting—scaring away whatever animal they'd been stalking—they would shove him into a cluster of thorny reeds or the leaves and stalks of poisonous plants—then laugh as they watched him stumbling to his feet—digging out thorns as he hurried on or trying not to scratch a burgeoning rash.

The only relief he found from the constant toil came during heavy rains—the days of downpours when the tribe barely left their huts. There was also a bit of solace during the full moon nights when he became part of their strange rituals—forced down onto a different woman every thirty days or so—fresh ocher paint and the smoking bundle in Splinter's hands—whole tribe chanting and dancing and the big bonfire outside the open doorway.

After a few months—with his pants in tatters and the degraded fabric always catching on thorns and branches— Mark began covering himself with a dried skin and length of rope—same as all the men of the tribe—the women's coverings differing only slightly. Some of the men also tied lengths of rope around their upper arms and their elbows and wrists. One day Mark did the same but was beaten with a spear and the ropes were cut away by the Ninja Turtles— showing him clearly that they were a status symbol he had not earned—he a slave who should feel lucky to even be al- lowed to have the dried skin and enough rope to tie around his withered waist.

But he did not feel lucky. Even when he watched the men shoot a monkey out of a tree with their bows and arrows—witnessing a prehistoric scene few people even knew still existed—he did not feel lucky. And when a flock of parrots flew overhead one evening in an uncountable mass—tropical sun setting behind their brightly colored wings—another bonfire being built nearby while the full moon peeked above the eastern horizon—that wild beauty along with the knowledge he'd soon be served a woman's body while the whole tribe chanted and danced in his honor—even with all that he did not feel lucky. He was a slave—well aware he should feel fortunate to be that and not just another dead man—but he did not.

Mark was taken into the jungle each time the Ninja Turtles left the village—forced to march alongside them down muddy trails on bare feet—brought along to carry loads for the hunters. They would point to something and look at him and he would have to scurry over and lift it off the ground—a log or lifeless body of some jungle animal they'd just killed.

Raphael was always the most eager to punish Mark—earning for himself the name of the Ninja Turtle with the worst attitude. Every day he carried a long, flexible stick so he could strike at Mark without restraint—swinging the flimsy weapon as hard as he pleased without incapacitating their beast of burden—rough fibers scraping and cutting into Mark's back at least once during each trip into the jungle—leaving his skin seldom free of fresh wounds. Raphael always walked behind Mark—staying close with his stick at the ready in case Mark slowed down or dropped something he was carrying—a bundle of fruit or dead snake or a load of wood destined for the tribe's cooking fires.

Mark tried to escape more often in the beginning—waiting

until it was dark before leaving the tiny hut he shared with Splinter—rushing into the jungle when he thought no one was looking. But somehow they always knew—the Ninja Turtles catching up to him only minutes after he left the village—closing in quickly with their nearly silent strides— the tiny thuds of their heels—quiet sounds of leaves and vines being shoved aside as they maneuvered through the nighttime maze of trails and trees.

They did not waste arrows on him anymore—not after the one they shot through his leg on the second day. Instead they made up all the distance they needed to on foot—using their knowledge of the forest—two pairs taking different routes so they could be sure to surround him eventually. Once the four young men had him trapped they would beat him with their spears and fists—striking him in turns while the other three watched and rested.

Thirteen full moons passed before Mark gave up on escaping—over one year but by how much, he did not know. There was never going to be a time when he wasn't being watched—even as most of the village slept—Splinter sitting there inside the tiny hut each night—never sleeping—barely ever moving—seeming never to even blink or look away. He was a nighttime fixture—planted on the bare ground and impossible to move—Mark's nocturnal guard and uncomprehending audience.

Mark considered killing the older man—the witch doctor with charcoal lines crisscrossing his weathered face— but he was unsure whether Splinter could die or not—if he was really alive or rather in some other state and therefore could not be killed. He wondered about this—wondered what he would do if he did get away—if he escaped into the night and found himself alone in the deep jungle—alone in the dark, dangerous night full of snakes and glowing jaguar eyes—without food or supplies or any idea which direction to go.

So with all hope lost—all anticipation of either being rescued or successfully escaping on his own now faded to nothing—Mark sat in the blue-black light and listened to the insects outside—the frogs and the distant silence of bats and owls and all the other nighttime hunters. Eventually the darkness and the quiet began to burrow deep into him—the solitude and the hopelessness—the cage of jungle and the barefoot masters—all day and all night.

Splinter sat there on the packed-earth floor across from him—inside the little hut they shared—his guard until the next day's hunt. Mark looked him over for a while—then let his eyes wander to the reed walls and out the open doorway. But Splinter's eyes did not move. They did not leave his captive's face.

After some time Mark began to speak—to shoot harmless sounds out the hole in his matted beard—to pray in his meek slave's voice—begging for a life other than his own.

STORY

"**I** don't know how you're keeping all these cuts on my back and feet from infecting, Splinter. That green paste must really work."

.

.

"Where'd you go to medical school?"

.

.

"Oh, really? I applied there—didn't get in, of course. I stayed in Denver and went to CU instead. Have you ever been to Colorado, Splinter?"

.

.

"Well, you should come and visit sometime—you and all the Ninja Turtles."

.

.

"We can start off in Denver but just for a day or two—see

the sights and then head to the mountains. You all don't really seem like city people."

.

.

"My hometown's an hour west—lots of cattle and hay-fields. On a clear day you can stand out in a pasture and spin in a circle—tilt your head back a little and all you see are mountain peaks—gray and white and jagged—scarred by ski runs and a few highways.

"There's a State Park just outside of town. We used to go deer hunting out there in the fall. Sometimes we'd go out there in high school and get drunk—set up a campsite and build a fire—invite some girls but nine times out of ten they wouldn't show. Does that ever happen around here? You go to all the trouble of building one of your big bonfires out there and all the ladies just stay in their huts—refuse to come out to dance and chant and let you blow that smoke in their faces?"

.

.

"Anyway, it usually ended up being just me, Geno and Steve. We'd get our tents up and a fire going. Then we'd sit around drinking cheap beer and telling bullshit stories."

.

.

"There was this one time I can remember we got rest-less—decided to paddle a canoe out into a little pond that was about a mile from our campsite. It was already dark and we'd probably made it through at least a twelve-pack by that point—probably more.

"We got Geno's canoe out of the back of the pickup and tipped it over our heads to carry it. Steve had his fishing pole and thought we might have some luck trolling at night. So we got everything we thought we needed and headed off through the dark—marching toward the pond.

"It must've been March or April. I remember we had our boots on and the snow had a crust of ice on top. That happens when there's some thawing during the day—then when the snow refreezes it gets coated in a thin layer of ice. I'm sure you know what I'm talking about—right, Splinter?"

.

.

"Anyway, the trail was wide and lined with Douglas fir and pine trees. We knew the way and the moon was out so we didn't even bother bringing a flashlight—just marched off with the canoe over our heads—paddles strapped onto my back.

"Geno and Steve gave each other a hard time the whole way. I was in the middle and just laughed. They were always going back and forth like that. Do you guys ever tell jokes around here? I think Michelangelo's the only one I've heard really laugh—besides some of the kids."

.

.

"So anyway, we got to the pond and it was frozen all along the edges. We used the paddles to slap at the ice and break enough of it to get the canoe in the water. Geno got in the front since he was the smallest and me and Steve slid the canoe down to where just the back was on dry ground. I got in and managed to plop down on the middle seat. Then Steve tried to jump in the back and at the same time shove us forward into the pond. I don't know if it was just because of the dark or the ice or us being a little drunk but we tipped right over—all three of us going into the water. The cold stabs at you when you fall into water that's just barely above freezing—hits you—worse than those sticks and spears you all use on me—makes your chest suck in on itself like your whole body's trying to turn inside out.

"The paddles were gone, of course—empty canoe floated off into the pond upside down—Steve's fishing pole disappeared. The water wasn't very deep and we were so close to shore that we stepped out and were standing together in the snow just a few seconds after tipping over—watching the canoe drift off. Our clothes were soaked—hats and pants and coats. Water pooled in our boots and I remember feeling my wet hair already starting to freeze.

"Once I got over the initial shock I realized how dangerous it was—us just standing there in the cold—soaked to the bone. So I grabbed Steve and Geno by the arms and started running through the snow. We had to get back to the fire and the pickup as fast as possible or we'd freeze to death in under an hour.

"Has anything like that ever happened to you, Splinter? I guess there's no way you could freeze to death around here. But maybe there's been a bad storm or a flood—something like that?"

.

.

"You know, one of these days you're going to answer me. This is all just a big joke—part of a social experiment or a reality TV show or something. You're going to bust out laughing and pointing at me and clapping your hands. Then the camera guy and the sound guy with that long Q-Tip microphone will pop out from somewhere. The Ninja Turtles will all come in here laughing and speaking English.

"This is all a big joke, Splinter. It has to be."

.

.

"But until that happens I guess I might as well get back to my story.

"So the three of us started running through the snow—hurrying back to our campsite—still able to see our footprints from when we walked out to the pond. We went in single file—Steve in front, then me, then Geno in the back.

The adrenaline and the running kept us warm for a few minutes. Pretty soon, though, we all slowed down. Our teeth started chattering and I can remember losing the feeling in my hands and forearms. My feet were just frozen nubs I was lifting and swinging and dropping down in front of me.

"Steve was doing about the same—maybe a little better. He started to pull away from me and I looked back to check on Geno—still moving forward through the snow as I turned my head. I didn't see him so I stopped and turned around—tried to yell his name but my mouth was shaking so much all I got out was some mumbled gibberish. I could see the dotted lines of our footprints in the white snow—the almost-black of the evergreen trees. But Geno wasn't there.

"I turned and looked toward Steve and could still see him making his way toward our campsite—too far away and I was too cold to try yelling again so I didn't even bother. Instead I turned back and went looking for Geno—tracing our footsteps through the snow—back toward the frozen pond and away from the warm fire.

"I remember it was so quiet I could hear every step I took—feet crunching in the snow. Frozen things made a cracking, echoing sound once in a while off in the distance— tree branches weighed down by the frozen snow—maybe water in the ponds and creeks. My heart was beating so hard I could feel it in my ears. I don't think it ever gets that quiet around here. Too many things are growing all the time for it to be that quiet."

.

.

"I finally found Geno huddled in a ball and shivering in the low branches of a cedar tree. He couldn't talk and I could barely get any sounds out of my own mouth. I grabbed him and tried to drag him away from the tree but he threw his arms up around my neck—falling toward me and sending us both down into the snow. My hat fell off and I remember that made me really mad for some reason. I struggled to my feet and looked down at Geno. He wasn't shivering as much—didn't even seem to be blinking. I was so mad I bent down and punched him right in the nose. He made a little noise and kind of woke up—looked at me with a shocked expression on his face. I smiled and tried to laugh but nothing came out.

"Eventually we made it back to our campsite where Steve already had the fire going—flames up as high as his head and he was completely naked standing there in the yellow light—steam coming off his head and arms—mixing with the smoke high up in the air. I got Geno over to the fire and started taking his clothes off—Steve soon coming to take over for me—my hands shaking so bad I couldn't work the zippers and buttons.

"After just a few minutes Geno was able to stand on his own and his hands stopped trembling so bad. I managed to get myself undressed and we stayed there in front of the fire for over an hour—naked as the day we were born. Eventually we got in the pickup and drove back to Steve's parents' house. It was early in the morning but I guess Steve's mother saw us all get out of the pickup in the driveway—naked still. We left all our frozen clothes in the back and just ran inside. I guess she sat Steve down a few days later and questioned him about the whole thing—tried to tell him it was okay if he was gay and that she still loved him.

"The funniest part is he almost went along with it—almost told his mother he was gay so he wouldn't have to tell her the truth. But he said he just couldn't do it. He ended up telling her everything and then his mother told my mother and Geno's parents and we all three were grounded for weeks—not allowed to go camping together for months after that."

SHOW

Mark walked toward the padded, embroidered chair—a man with a headset draped around his neck holding back the black curtain so he could enter the little square partition—bright lights overhead and the famous journalist with the white, wavy hair already seated—slim legs crossed and a stack of printouts in his hands.

Mark sat down in the empty chair and tried to find a comfortable position. He looked around at the cameras in each corner—the dark shadows in the curves of the curtains—thick, rubber-coated electrical cords snaking across the repeating pattern of the conference room carpet.

INTERVIEWER: Hi Mark we'll get started in just a moment did you need water or coffee or-or-or a snack or anything?

Mark shook his head—the older man smiling at him as he shuffled the printouts in his hands. The cameramen came in and out of the partition for a few minutes—black shirts and blue jeans and worn-down tennis shoes. The famous journalist spoke to a woman carrying a clipboard who'd peeked through the curtains—checked the cameras over his shoulders—the two stationed behind Mark—making sure everything was ready and everyone was in position. Then he looked around at everyone still inside the partition—soft pink thumb held up in the air—signaling it was time to start.

INTERVIEWER: First question I have for you, Mark, is why? Why did you walk off into the jungle three years ago?

MARK: I didn't. That's not—I didn't just walk off.

INTERVIEWER: Well that's what everyone thought at the time—the others in your tour group, the staff at the camp, your own family they all said the same thing that you—walked—away. You just stepped off the edge of the map and it was premeditated they all said the same thing at the time and-and-and the fact that there was a clear consensus among them is very convincing.

Mark sat there and looked down at his hands—slow to respond as the famous journalist waited—cameras trained on both their faces—Mark's back muscles tightening as he half-expected someone to strike him with a long, flexible stick or spear.

He looked up from his hands after a few seconds of silence—tried to relax as he reestablished eye contact with the older man—still holding his response—relishing the freedom he now had to stall.

MARK: I got lost.

INTERVIEWER: Yes that's what you've been telling everyone but I want to know if there's more if-if-if there's something more to the story that you haven't told anyone yet.

The famous journalist uncrossed his legs and leaned forward—elbows touching down onto his knees—hands held up near his powdered chin with fingers just beginning to interlock.

INTERVIEWER: Was there any part of you that *wanted* to get lost?

MARK: No. I mean, I was obviously going through a difficult time. I'd just gotten divorced—lost my job—went from married and trying to start a family to sleeping on my mother's couch—trying to find a one-bedroom apartment I could afford.

INTERVIEWER: So you wanted to go into the jungle to get over your divorce—all the difficulties you'd been going through?

Mark looked back down at his hands—ring finger where his wedding band had been—fingernails still chipped and brittle—tiny bits of jungle dirt still beneath them in places.

MARK: That's right.

CHAPTER
THREE

FACT

THE FULL MOON WAS JUST COMING UP OVER THE TALLEST trees when they arrived back at the village—Mark dragging a large branch the Ninja Turtles had broken off a fallen tree earlier that afternoon. It was still at least six feet long after they broke off all the thin, leafless sticks—thicker than one of Mark's legs at its base—too heavy for him to lift on his own. Raphael had to tie a braided rope around it—making a loop at the other end for Mark to pull against—to drag the branch backward over slick, narrow trails for hours. When he fell behind, they beat him. When he collapsed from exhaustion, they gave him a few minutes—then poked him with their spears until he got to his feet—thick blood trickling down his body from scratches and a few small puncture wounds.

Mark stopped now at the edge of the village—hands on his knees while he looked down at his bloodied, muddied feet. The Ninja Turtles walked off to their huts—leaving him alone where the bare, beaten earth met the wall of trees and vines—the constantly shifting shadows. After a few minutes he breathed deep and carefully started to stand up straight—letting the muscles and ligaments of his stiff back slowly unfurl.

"What am I doing here?" he said—looking around at all the huts—the village boundary of lush jungle. A few women were tending a small fire next to the stack of logs Mark had piled up over the past month. Children ran around chasing each other—screaming and laughing in the mix of light coming from the fading sunset and the rising full moon. "A slave—I'm a slave."

Soon Donatello walked out of the largest hut and came toward him—never breaking eye contact or changing his course as he marched through the swarming children—Mark staring back and trying not to look away. Donatello stopped suddenly just a few feet in front of him—turning to point toward the women and the stack of logs. Mark nodded—bent down and picked up the braided rope as quick as he could—turned and leaned and felt the rope coming taut as it pulled into the rubbed-raw grooves in his hands—blistered, dark pink skin burning against the weight of the wood.

By the time he got the branch over to the bonfire pit, flames were already shooting high above the heads of the women. The burning wood popped and shot embers into the air—ends of logs hissing and steaming as moisture bubbled out. Mark untied and coiled the rope—stood off to the side and watched the women—two of them beginning to chant as they piled more wood onto the fire.

He could feel the heat now—standing there facing the flames as he tried to ignore all the things that hurt—the sore parts of his body and the troubled corners of his mind.

Mark stayed with the women near the bonfire as they cooked dinner for the tribe—sitting quietly off to the side where they could easily see him—easily toss him scraps if they were in a generous mood. After the children had all been fed and after they had taken food to the men in the largest hut, the women gave Mark the bones of an animal he could not identify—gave him some leftover boiled tubers in one of the gourds—three or four spiders still wrapped in much of their own webs—more food than he was used to—a meal he only got when the moon was full.

It started to rain as an older woman handed Mark a gourd full of murky water—children screeching as every-one ran off toward the largest hut and left him there—alone in the almost-dark—sitting by the roaring, hissing bonfire.

He scooted closer to the flames and drank half the water. The rain came down in small, consistent drops and there was no wind. He stared into the fire and swallowed the spiders—drank more of the water and tried to ignore the taste—tried to see the raindrops hitting the flames and turning into steam.

Mark grabbed a handful of the bones and held them up to the fire—small and light with barely any tissue left attached. He wondered if they could be from a parrot as he peeled off what meat he could with his front teeth—then tossed them into the gourd with the leftover boiled tubers and mixed in the rest of the murky water—stirred the slur-ry with his finger and set the gourd on the ground next to a nearby pile of glowing embers—using two sticks to turn it as he waited—as he worried about the thin walls of the gourd cracking and breaking—losing his soup and breaking one of the tribe's treasured dishes.

The rain lightened to a mist just a few minutes later— Mark's back remaining wet while his face and arms dried quickly from the heat of the fire. He pulled the gourd toward him with the sticks after a while and sat there on the wet ground with it steaming between his legs—stuck his finger into the slurry of tubers and bones—feeling it warm in some spots and hot in others—stirring as he felt the temperature slowly becoming uniform.

A few members of the tribe eventually came out of the largest hut and began gathering around the fire—confident the rain had stopped for at least a while—full moon reappearing from behind the heavy clouds. Mark wandered off to one of the smaller huts and sat down on the bare ground—leaned back against the reed wall and chewed the bones still left in the gourd—little ribs the easiest to break apart—cracking and grinding them between his teeth until he felt comfortable to swallow.

Soon the Ninja Turtles emerged from the crowd that had gathered around the bonfire—walking toward Mark with their spears and their sticks. He knew what they wanted—what they were about to make him do—glancing at the bright moon as he stood up without the empty gourd—swallowing the last bits of bone in his mouth—trying hard not to yawn. He stared at the four men—strips of cloth tied around their waists and fresh ocher paint on their arms.

"Was that a bird or a baby monkey?" Mark said—glancing down and motioning toward the empty gourd—then looking back up at the Ninja Turtles with a smile on his face—Raphael seeming angry as always—hands clinched into fists and the knot of jaw muscle at his cheek flexing. "Whatever it was," Mark continued as the four men came forward and grabbed him by the arms. "It had good flavor but needed salt." They shoved him away from the hut and two of them held out spears—Mark looking back at them as he stumbled forward. "All your food needs salt, really—even the spiders."

The flames of the bonfire were reaching high above Mark's head as he walked past—light flickering off the huts and some of the closest trees above their thatched roofs. He could see inside the tiny hut as he approached—the one where he slept each night—where he told his stories to Splinter. A woman was there—on her back in the middle of the packed-earth floor—Splinter bent over her with a bundle in his hands. Mark could see him blowing into the collection of leaves and bark—smoke starting to float up toward the ceiling.

He stopped at the open doorway—bracing himself for the abuse that often came from the Ninja Turtles anytime they stood behind him—usually a slashing strike from Raphael's stick. But nothing happened as Splinter looked up at him—charcoal lines freshly painted over his creased face—sweating and breathing heavily just above the woman's body. They stared at each other in silence for a few seconds—then Splinter looked at the man just behind Mark and nodded. Michelangelo came forward and Mark turned his head—relieved when he saw it wasn't one of the others—smirking as he locked eyes with the small, jovial man—Michelangelo nearly smiling back before he resisted the urge and looked away.

Mark went willingly to the woman's feet—small, rough hands on his arm and back ready to guide him if he deviated. He looked down and saw the woman was younger than the others—slimmer in the hips and waist—skin brighter and softer. He saw the ocher paint covering her hands and breasts just like it'd been with the previous women—single line tracing down to her abdomen—arms stretched out— deep, nervous breaths filling her lungs.

Michelangelo moved his hands to Mark's shoulders—pulling him down to his knees. Mark watched as Splinter blew smoke over the woman's body—watched him whisper into the woman's ear—saw her chest start rising even higher now with each quickening breath—firelight flickering on the walls and over the woman's body. The Ninja Turtles began to spread out from where they'd been standing—moving toward each corner of the small hut.

"Not very romantic," Mark said—no one acknowledging his statement—Splinter now waving and shaking the smoking bundle over the woman—the Ninja Turtles settling into their separate corners—silent young woman lying obediently on the ground. "Never is."

After another minute or two Splinter raised up and looked at Mark—the two men staring at each other through heavy, fragrant smoke. Mark wondered how old he could be—to what age someone could survive in such a harsh place.

As Splinter started chanting Mark felt someone pushing him forward onto the woman—then heard the Ninja Turtles falling into the medicine man's rhythm—the five men beginning to dance around him inside the hut—rest of the tribe outside around the bonfire beginning to chant as well—Mark able to hear their shuffling footsteps as they started circling the flames together.

The young woman did not reach for Mark's waist—did not chant or raise her head out of the shadows like all the other women had done. Mark watched her swallow hard as she finally opened her eyes and directed them toward the ceiling—dead, unblinking stare showing she had no interest in seeing anything else. He raised himself up and looked down at her face—drops of sweat falling from his chin onto her pulsating neck. She made a small noise and began to move her mouth—nervous lips trembling as the firelight danced across the smooth skin of her cheek. Mark examined the long shadows made by the features of her face—leaned to one side so the drops of sweat from his chin would fall to the packed-earth floor.

The chanting grew louder—dancing intensified as Splinter carried the smoking bundle outside—casting his collection of burning leaves and bark into the wild, hungry fire.

The Ninja Turtles took the young woman away—leaving Mark alone inside the small hut with Splinter—bonfire still throwing light through the open doorway but the tribe had stopped dancing around it. Mark watched them all outside—eating and laughing together in the firelight—children chasing each other and everyone smiling.

For the next hour or so he could see the full moon arcing through the sky. After that it moved beyond the open doorway and behind the thatched roof—everyone outside slowly disappearing into their huts as the fire burned itself down to a bed of hot coals.

Splinter sat in his familiar spot and stared at Mark—not moving or speaking at all—seeming not even to blink or ever look away. He sat there on the bare ground—Mark's guard for that night and every other. Mark looked him over—let his eyes wander to the walls of the hut and out the open doorway. But Splinter's eyes did not move. They did not leave his captive's face.

Soon the darkness and the quiet began to burrow deep into Mark—the solitude and the helplessness—the reality of his place in the world as it then stood—a slave to a prehistoric tribe—all day and all night.

He began to talk—to dream out loud—to pray for all the things he'd lost and would never have again.

STORY

"I'd never been outside the U.S. before I came here—Puerto Rico once but that's still the same country—technically—even though they mostly speak Spanish. Have you ever been there, Splinter?"

.

.

"I bet you've never even been across the river—any river—gone anywhere."

.

.

"First time I swam in the ocean was on our honeymoon in Puerto Rico. The water was so blue—turquoise in some places. We spent each day at a different beach—just laying around—swimming when we wanted. We rented snorkeling equipment and went out and tried to look at all the fish and sea turtles where the water was clear and calm. Most of the hotels we stayed at were pretty shabby but it was our honeymoon—all we really needed was a bed with clean sheets. I'm sure you know how it is, Splinter—bet you haven't always just been the guy who chants and blows smoke all over the ladies."

.

.

"Anyway, the night before we flew home we stayed in the capital city, San Juan. We stayed in this big hotel near the airport and went out for dinner and drinks. There was this street somebody'd told us about that was lined with bars and restaurants. We didn't have much money left and they told us it was cheap—sort of a local's secret, I guess.

"So we got there and started walking around. There were some guys on street corners that looked like they were selling drugs—girls walking around looking like they were selling something else. We went into a couple bars and had a few beers. They were playing this Latin music we'd been hearing during our whole trip. My wife wanted to dance after her second beer—like she always did—so I got up and made a fool of myself for her. The bar we were in had this wall of mirrors with a horizontal brass pole—so everybody was just dancing in front of those mirrors—looking at each other and themselves—grabbing onto that pole every once in a while. Somebody even started passing around tequila shots—little napkins with lime wedges and a salt packet with each one.

"We were pretty drunk by the time we decided to leave—partly because we hadn't eaten dinner yet. So we started stumbling down the street looking for a restaurant. I remember there were lots of neon lights—lots of reds and some blues. That Latin music was blasting from most of the bars and it all mixed together out on the street. My wife would stop on the sidewalk and just start dancing if she heard a song she liked."

.

"And then all the sudden there was a gun in our faces—two kids standing there with ski masks over their heads. You could see the sweat around their eyes and dripping down the sides of their noses. It was about as hot and humid there as it is around here. I don't know how they were breathing with their mouths covered like that—but I guess you breathing through that bundle of smoking leaves and bark is probably worse."

"I started pulling my wife behind me and she put her hands on my shoulder and then on my back. I could see the two kids were nervous—kept looking around—didn't even say anything to us at first. They just stood there—one holding that gun in his shaky hand."

"It could've gone off, you know. That kid could've shot me—happens more than people think—somebody's in a tough spot—nervous and scared—feels like the most natural thing in the world to go around destroying things you think are getting in your way. And at that moment those two kids thought they had to get my wallet and my wife's purse to get themselves out of whatever trouble they'd gotten into—us still being alive was potentially going to complicate things for them.

"Anyway, they were getting more and more jumpy—still not saying a word. I was scared of going for my wallet in case they thought I was going for a gun of my own. So I just stood there with my wife behind me—the one with the gun an arm's length in front of me—his partner behind him and to the side. It was probably less than ten seconds but it felt like ten minutes—time slowing down like nothing else in the world was moving at that moment—just me and those two kids. Do you ever feel that way, Splinter?"

.

.

"So the two kids were standing there—my wife clinging to my back—maybe trying to say something or maybe just making some scared noises. I can remember hearing her but I don't think she was really saying anything. I don't know—guess that was always her main complaint about me—that I never really listened—just looked at her when I heard her making noise and nodded my head until she was finished.

"Anyway, I finally convinced myself that those two kids weren't capable of pulling off a successful robbery—either I was going to get shot or they were going to run off without saying a word. At that point I had to do something—so I almost reached out and tried to grab the gun but the kid was so jittery he might've been able to squeeze off a shot. Instead I backed up a few inches and shifted all my weight onto one foot. I could still feel my wife glued to my back and I felt her moving with me. Then I leaned back and brought my other foot up at the same time—kicked the gun out of the kid's hand and it went flipping through the air. We both looked up and then looked back down at each other. His partner was already running away. I took a step forward and the kid turned and ran after his friend. I think they were around the corner before the gun even hit the pavement."

.

.

"We found out later the gun wasn't even loaded. Can you believe that, Splinter?"

SHOW

The famous journalist sat back in his chair—picking up and shuffling through his stack of printouts—glancing down at them as he crossed one leg over the other. He wiped his index finger across his tongue and used it to flip a sticky page—passing the stubborn sheet of paper to the back of the stack.

Mark sat there and watched the older man—seeing frustration in his wrinkled face—probing as he was for some revelation or admission—some tears for the cameras that Mark was determined not to shed.

INTERVIEWER: Let's talk about your divorce—your ex-wife and how that situation triggered your trip to the rainforest in order to-to-to, as you've said, gain some sort of clarity about the whole thing. Why, exactly, did you and your wife split up in the first place?

MARK: You're better off asking her that question.

INTERVIEWER: But weren't you the one who filed the paperwork?

MARK: Well, I mean, just because I started the process doesn't mean I'm the one who ended it—who wanted the divorce.

INTERVIEWER: So you did not want to get divorced but you filed for a divorce and you did not want to get lost in the jungle but you walked off in a-a-a straight line away from camp without telling anyone and without knowing where you were going?

MARK: And I didn't want to come in here and get attacked—called a liar to my face—but here I am.

The famous journalist rested his hands in his lap—raising his eyebrows slightly. He stayed silent and stared at Mark—confident eyes of an old, rich man trying to wear an expression of shocked innocence—conscious as always of the cameras in each corner of the little temporary partition—the half-second or so during the one-hour special when the television audience would be shown his reaction.

Mark leaned forward—forcing himself not to break eye contact with the older man across from him—almost extending his counterattack but deciding not to at the last moment—looking away instead as he slowly nodded his head—teeth grinding against each other as deep breaths rushed in and out of his lungs through his nose.

INTERVIEWER: Cut the cameras cut the audio.

The famous journalist turned to the cameramen in each

corner and gestured with a pen in his hand as he spoke—loud and without any hesitation or pause. Then he turned back to Mark.

INTERVIEWER: I'm not attacking you, Mark, I just want to know the truth. That's all this is your story is so amazing so perplexing yet there's something so-so-so human about it that I just want to get to the bottom of what exactly happened.

It's something we all want to do at some point in our lives—run away and escape and just keep going and going and going until something changes and our old lives are gone and forgotten but-but-but no one really does it. No one has the balls except you and that's what makes this so important the-the-the true truth of it so vital for all of us to hear. We need to know how and why you did what we all secretly want to do but are too afraid to even try. We need your help, Mark—all of us—the whole world.

The famous journalist stood up and told everyone to be back in ten minutes—the four cameramen now huddled together in one corner of the crowded partition—producers and assistants and everyone else just outside the now-parted black curtains. Then he walked out and turned and was gone—Mark still sitting in his padded chair—bright lights still beating down on him from overhead.

CHAPTER
FOUR

Fact

THERE HAD BEEN THUNDER AND LIGHTNING SEVERAL HOURS before sunrise—during the darkest hours of deepest sleep—waking Mark and not allowing him to rest again until the flashes and the rumbles drifted off to another part of the jungle. Then as he woke for the second time—in the growing gray haze of early morning—there was only a slow, steady rain left over from the storm.

The raindrops came straight down out of a solid gray sky—smacking into the thatched roof and the bare, packed earth just outside the open doorway. Mark sat up and backed himself into a corner of the small hut—mostly dry but with the moisture in the air making everything slightly sticky— the four reed walls and the dirt beneath him—the animal skin he wore just below his waist.

"If I could get a hot shower," Mark said—closing his eyes and stretching his neck—pops emerging from the gaps between his bones. "A robe and some soft slippers—room service breakfast." He put his head down between his knees and felt the muscles in his back stretching—scabs cracking and opening fresh fissures in his healing wounds. "Hot coffee—hot, hot coffee."

Mark continued stretching as Splinter looked on—expressionless and without moving anything but his eyes. The rain kept falling and Mark watched the larger drops that collected and dripped down from over the doorway—the puddle that had formed hours earlier. There was no thunder or lightning now—no wind to blow and break apart the raindrops.

"It's still raining," Mark said—still seated in the corner of the hut with his back pressed against the two perpendicular walls—dirty, withered legs stretched out in front of him.

Splinter had suddenly stood up and stepped over to the doorway—stood there for a few minutes as midday approached—as the diffuse sunlight slowly brightened against the grayness—rain tapering off with smaller and smaller drops coming down in delicate, misty waves—still collecting on the roof and still dripping heavily into the puddle at the foot of the doorway.

Splinter stood there with the brightness behind him as he turned to stare down at Mark—the medicine man's eyes pulling him somehow up off the ground to venture out into the rain—communicating without words or noticeable gestures—a tick of the eyebrow, maybe—maybe an imperceptible nod of the older man's head or maybe nothing physical at all.

"Alright," Mark said—rolling to one side as he began the process of standing up—supporting himself first with one elbow and then using his hands to press his body upward until he could get his sore, dirt-covered feet underneath him—a string of pops from the bones in his back—then several more from his elbows and his knees.

Splinter led Mark into the jungle—a woman joining them at some point—Mark unsure whether she'd been with them since they'd left the village or if she had already been out amongst the trees—waiting for them.

The rain stopped soon after they began walking under the thick canopy of leaves and branches—sunlight trickling through and causing the drops still collecting above them to sparkle as they fell to the ground. Mark walked behind Splinter and no one spoke—the woman silently following them at a distance—eyes always meeting Mark's when he turned around. She was older than most of the women and maybe a little taller—or maybe just more confident—head always raised high—eyes always unafraid.

The trail was slick with mud as they wound their way through the jungle—brightly colored birds hurrying around—everything shiny and clean from the rain. Mark listened to the loud birdsongs—the breeze now rushing through the tops of the tallest trees. He smelled the earth and the post-rain fragrance of hungry growth and rapid decay—faint flower scents carried down by the leftover drops of rainwater still smacking heavily onto the sodden forest floor.

They walked at a slow pace—Mark not used to the absence of beatings—not used to traveling their network of trails with empty hands—no heavy logs or bundles of fruit or dead animals to carry. He felt the tension in his muscles as he repeatedly looked back at the woman—part of him expecting to see a threatening bow or spear in her hands. After a while, though—sun rising high and a thin coat of sweat now making his body shine—Mark was able to relax—to walk without the burdens of fear and pain.

Splinter stopped periodically—kneeling to examine some tiny plant just sprouting from the black, tropical soil—peeling back the bark of a tree or picking the leaves from a low-hanging branch. Mark would stop to watch him—turning first to check on the woman—her eyes always ready to meet his. Then he would turn back to Splinter and watch him carefully collect his specimen—testing samples on his tongue or the tender skin below his wrist.

After several hours—sun still high in a clear sky and a light breeze blowing through the trees—with the jungle quieter now than when they began their walk—Splinter's bundle of leaves and bark and plant stalks had grown too large to be carried in one hand. So he stopped and rolled the bundle tight—tied it off with a thin, flexible piece of vine—Mark watching the older man as he did his work—both crouched over a small patch of dirt with the woman standing several paces behind them.

They were back in the village by early evening—most members of the tribe either napping or relaxing inside the largest hut. Mark began looking around for something to eat—a group of women and children to beg scraps from—a gourd of boiled tubers abandoned but with enough white streaks left inside to coat at least one of his fingers.

He wandered from hut to hut—scanning the sunlit ground as he was never allowed inside except to deliver bundles of fruit—firewood or vines to make rope—the carcasses of unlucky birds, monkeys and snakes. But there were no gourds—no discarded fruit peels or animal bones. Eventually he found a puddle at the edge of the jungle and sat down next to it—idly scooping water into his mouth with one hand—murky brown liquid slipping down his chin and dribbling into his lap.

The sun was still up but dropping fast somewhere behind Mark—day's end hot and cloudless as he sat in the shade next to the puddle—watching the village and waiting for a chance to put something in his stomach—feeling his body slacken with hunger under the heavy, humid blanket of tropical air.

That night in the small hut where Mark slept—where they forced him onto all those full moon women—Splinter sat in his familiar spot—staring straight ahead. He did not move—did not seem to blink or to ever look away. He sat there on the bare ground—Mark's guard for that night and every other. Mark looked him over—then let his eyes wander to the reed walls of the hut and out the open doorway. But Splinter's eyes did not move. They did not leave his captive's face.

The darkness and the quiet began to burrow deep into Mark—the solitude and the helplessness—the sad truth of how much he'd enjoyed walking unburdened with the witch doctor and the confident woman—even a forced, barefoot march now considered a luxury—his masters perhaps taking pity on him in the smothering, primitive place he now lived—lived or at least survived.

He began to talk—to dream out loud—to pray for the pleasures of his past—relief from the pains of his present.

STORY

"I could kill you, you know—right now—if I wanted to I could. You know that, Splinter?"

.

.

"You're small and old. I'm twice your size and probably half your age."

.

.

"I could kill you and run away—wrap this stupid rope you gave me for a belt around your neck and strangle you—tip-toe out of here—back to the real world—back to civilization—back to shoes and pants and electricity—toothpaste and cheeseburgers and baseball."

.

.

"My wife."

.

.

"My son."

"You don't know how miserable this place is, Splinter. I can't keep living like this. People shouldn't have to live like this."

"You know I went to Africa once—long time ago. I was a photographer—a photojournalist, I guess—doing freelance work for newspapers and magazines—my dream job."

"I was in Africa working on a story about the coast of Somalia—stayed there six months—a walk in the park compared to this."

"I wound up focusing on the pirates causing trouble in the gulf. They'd take these fishing boats out with rope ladders and AK-47s slung over their shoulders—maybe a few rocket propelled grenades if they were lucky enough to have any. I hung around there and got to know this one captain well enough that he eventually promised to bring me along the next time he took his crew out. It's all wide-open ocean—flat and clear so you can stand on the beach and see for miles—not like here. I'm not sure what you'd do if you ever went somewhere like that, Splinter—place where you could see that far with nothing in your way."

"Anyway, one day the captain I'd become friendly with told me to grab my things and hurry down to his boat. They'd heard that a big oil tanker was coming down the coast. The captain knew enough English to tell me it was flying an American flag and he made some joke as we all crowded into the boat—maybe ten or twelve of us. Everyone except me had an AK—two or three even brought grenades in these little backpacks they carried.

"The ocean was calm that day. I remember cutting through the water and how it looked like the bottom of our boat was somehow melting a line across the surface of a mirror—blue sky reflecting up off the still water—no waves until our boat went slicing out to sea. It was beautiful."

.

.

"About an hour after we left we could just make out the tanker on the horizon. It must've seen us too because the captain said it wasn't in the normal shipping lane—maybe they knew we were coming somehow. I always worried about there being an American ship—pirates all turning on me if something went wrong—accusing me of tipping off the tanker's crew if they managed to get away. Some of them were already looking at me funny—making me nervous.

"But after another hour or so we managed to catch the tanker—coming up on its right side. It was enormous. I'd never been that close to a ship that big—not even a cruise ship. It must've been forty or fifty feet up to the deck and the whole thing was at least two hundred feet long. I knew the pirates had done it all before and I even knew roughly how they went about it, but coming up next to that tanker, I didn't think there was any way they were going to be able to get on board."

.

.

"Pretty soon they started unfurling this thin synthetic rope with knots every few feet. Two guys at the front of the boat were tying a rope ladder to the smallest pirate's back—two heavier ropes with wooden planks tied between them. The biggest guy stood by himself at the back of the boat and started whipping this homemade grappling hook around in a circle. He got it going pretty fast and then threw it up onto the outside railing of the ship—first try and then he stood there yanking on it to test its hold. Then the small guy with the heavy rope ladder on his back grabbed the knotted rope and started climbing as fast as he could. I was snapping pictures the whole time from the middle of the little fishing boat. With all the activity I was losing my footing so I just sat down and all the good photos came out from a really low angle.

"The little guy got up to the tanker and tied the rope ladder to the railing. He was looking all around the ship as he worked, but we hadn't seen anyone onboard yet. Then all the pirates started climbing up the rope ladder with their AKs slung over their backs. There was an old man near the back of the boat. He stayed sitting there next to the motor with his hand revving the throttle. I was the last one to step up onto the rope ladder and once I did, I looked back at him. He smiled up at me and yelled something in their language—then turned the little fishing boat away and I swung against the side of the ship. It was only a few feet but it scared me more than a little. I started climbing up the ladder so fast my head slammed into the bottom of the pirate's feet above me."

.

.

"Once I got onboard most of them had already gone off to other parts of the tanker—one or two staying back to pull up the rope ladder. I started following them as they went around with their AKs held out—sweeping around corners the way they'd probably seen it done in action movies. Nobody seemed to be on the ship, though. So I just went around a few steps behind them—snapping pictures every few seconds. Pretty soon another group of pirates turned a corner and saw me with my camera held up in front of my face. They started screaming at me and I thought I was going to get shot. But they realized who I was after a second or two and moved on—leaving me there covered in sweat—my hands shaking so bad I couldn't hold my camera and just let it dangle from my neck for a while. I stayed real close to the captain after that."

"We went all around the ship and didn't find anybody. Then we went up to the bridge and looked in all the rooms. Once my nerves settled I got a great picture of one of the pirates looking under a desk. Do you know what a desk is, Splinter?"

"There was one door that was locked. It was a thick, solid sheet of metal—several deadbolts above the heavy-duty doorknob. The captain knocked hard and put his ear against it. He yelled in his broken English. All the pirates congregated around the door and I snapped some pictures as I stood off to the side.

"Finally someone answered—an American. He sounded scared as he went through all the formal stuff—his name and his title and the name of the ship and country of origin and all that. He was the captain of the big oil tanker and said they weren't armed.

"I bet that's how I sounded when I first came across the Ninja Turtles out there in the jungle—or when they came across me—however it happened. They wouldn't have understood my words but they knew I wasn't a threat to them—just scared and lost—begging them to help me find my way back. They didn't have to feel sorry for me but they didn't have to take me either—drag me back here."

.

.

"Anyway, the pirates got to thinking about what to do. Some of them started examining the door and talking to each other in their own language. I just milled around—snapping pictures. Pretty soon it looked like they'd come up with a plan and the captain started yelling through the door again.

"He said he would blow up the door if they kept refusing to open it. The Americans inside said their company policy was to keep the door locked no matter what and that they wouldn't open it for any reason. I watched some of the pirates start pulling blocks of C-4 out of their little backpacks. They had rolls of wire and some electronics but none of them seemed to know how to rig them all together. The blocks were handed off from pirate to pirate and they were shouting at each other now. I kept backing up and backing up—scared one of them would drop some of the C-4 and the whole ship would explode. I didn't know how the hell any of that worked. You know what I mean, Splinter?"

.

.

"Yeah I'm sure you know all about it—pirates—C-4— great big oil tanker bobbing along in the ocean."

.

.

"So the captain calmed everybody down—went around and gathered all the explosives and the wires and everything. He came over to me and held it all out in his hands—asked if I knew how to rig up the C-4 and I told him I had no idea. But I got him talking and I asked him how they planned on getting the ransom money out of the oil company. He said usually once they took the crew captive they had them contact their employers and the process went from there. He said it was all about the crew. If they didn't have the crew they figured somebody's military would come along and they'd all wind up dead.

"Now that was all true but I also knew that if they started killing off the crew—either by blowing up that door without really knowing how to do it or just by shooting one or two of them—their chances of surviving—and mine along with them—were going to be a lot lower. So I managed to convince the captain it was all about time. They needed to cut a deal and get the hell out of there without being too greedy.

"Eventually he saw the logic and told me to go talk to the captain of the ship through the thick metal door. Being as they had the guns and all I had was a camera, it was pretty clear I was going to do what he said. It was similar to the situation I'm in here. You all have the bows and arrows and everything and I have literally nothing—nothing—this rope around my waist, I guess."

.

.

"So I went over and banged on the door—said I was American and the captain inside started asking me questions like he didn't believe me. Finally I convinced him— answering his trivia questions about the Super Bowl and state capitals for a few minutes. Then I started negotiating a ransom. The pirates had control of the tanker and a lot of C-4, I told him, and they were already in the process of rigging the entire ship to explode. That was a lie, of course, but I knew I had to get things moving or something bad was going to happen.

"I told the tanker captain the pirates wouldn't take less than one hundred thousand dollars. So he called somebody from inside that room and came back offering them fifty. The pirate captain was right next to me the whole time—nodding his head and whispering in my ear about what to say. Eventually we settled on eighty and I relayed the instructions to the tanker captain about how and where to wire the money. The pirate captain called the old man in the fishing boat and told him to come pick us up. Once we got the call that the money had gone through, we all scrambled down the rope ladder and back into the little boat—left the ladder attached to the oil tanker and took off back toward the Somali coast."

.

.

"The party they threw that night puts your little bonfires to shame. People came from all over to join in—so many people that vendors started selling cigarettes and chewing gum—fruits and vegetables and I even saw a woman with three or four pairs of high heels stacked on top of her head. She went around to all the young girls and the pirates who were flush with cash and looking for somewhere to spend it.

"I hung around that night and the next day and then figured it was time I got out of there. I never gave my name on the oil tanker and I hadn't seen any cameras on deck. Luckily I was able to slip out and get back to the capital city without anyone knowing I was there. The newspapers ended up dropping the story but eventually I was able to sell the photos under a fake name—couple of them showing up in a magazine a month or two after I got back to The States. Then a few months after that the U.S. military dropped bombs all along that coastline—destroying the little shacks and fishing boats—probably killing a lot of the pirates I'd been with on that ship."

.

.

"Maybe that'll happen here."

SHOW

Mark sat there and waited for the famous journalist to return—black curtain walls waving as groups of people passed by on the other side—rushed conversations and inside jokes as he waited alone. He kept his eyes on the empty chair in front of him—overhead lights buzzing—shining down bright on the white and gold parts of the chair's embroidery.

INTERVIEWER: It's one thing to make a terrible pot of coffee and it's another to let it get cold now go try again and add more grounds this time and-and-and have it ready next time we break. Hi, Mark, are we ready to pick up where we left off?

The older man marched in with a young woman behind him—headset wobbling loosely around her neck—her brown hair slinking over the puffy black ear pads. She took a paper cup from his hand and nodded with her eyes never leaving the conference room floor—turning back toward the parted curtains as the famous journalist sat down and adjusted the sleeves of his jacket.

MARK: Sure.

The famous journalist flipped through his collection of printouts—Mark wondering if he was actually reading anything or just buying time so he could collect his thoughts.

INTERVIEWER: Now let's move on to the other people visiting the camp the-the-the other tourists or perhaps we should call them your fellow pilgrims or solace-seekers or what have you. Why didn't you let one of them know where you were going? Why didn't you let an employee know a-a-a member of the outfitter's staff?

MARK: I didn't think I'd be out long—thought I'd just go for a quick walk by myself. But the trail didn't turn like I thought it was going to—didn't double back to camp like the map showed. I got lost.

INTERVIEWER: Yes that's what you say happened but you're not a novice when it comes to wilderness hikes we've spoken to your friends and family so-so-so you knew that you should have told someone or maybe even asked one of the other guests to go along with you, right? I mean, you wanted to come back to the camp, right? And you wanted to continue your-your-your therapeutic sojourn or whatever through the tropics and then come home? Right?

The famous journalist leaned forward—dark bags still visible under his eyes through a thick layer of makeup. Mark sat there and thought back to the day he entered the jungle alone—pushing his way through hot, smothering air—trails narrowing and winding and eventually disappearing—losing all sense of direction—sun disappearing behind gray clouds and thunder drowning out the sound of his voice—the shouted pleas for a helping hand.

MARK: I went on that trip to clear my head—to get some things figured out. But it's hard to think when you're around complete strangers—not sure whether you should talk or be quiet—try to be funny or serious—always having to be careful not to offend anybody. It's hard for me, anyway.

The famous journalist nodded—dropped his head and stared at the conference room floor—his shiny leather shoes and the clean carpet. Mark waited—glanced up at the cameras as the wavy white hair continued nodding—waited until the famous journalist finally started lifting his head—until they locked eyes again and he knew another question was coming.

INTERVIEWER: So you're in the middle of the rainforest and it's raining and you're lost and no matter how you got there, you're there now. You're all alone and it's getting dark now what do you do? What happens?

Mark watched the older man sit back and cross his legs— resting the handful of printouts on the inside part of his ankle. The white, wavy hair on his head seemed to be drying—gaining more height and volume—reaching up to the burning lights and out to the black curtains. He sat there and Mark watched his shoulders ease—watched a little smile form on his face—seemingly more accepting of the answers he was now getting—more satisfied or maybe just trying a new plan of attack.

Mark sat up straight and cleared his throat—arching his back and bringing a fist up to cover his mouth. Then he propped his elbows up on the arms of his chair and stared back at the famous journalist—pushing the pads of his thumbs back and forth over hangnails peeling away from each index finger.

CHAPTER
FIVE

Fact

THE MEN STOOD AROUND AND WATCHED—LAUGHING AND whispering jokes into each other's ears—spears held upright with the blunt ends resting on the ground—one or two with bows draped over their shoulders and a few arrows gathered in one hand. It was late evening and Mark had just handed off his load of fruit and one dead monkey to the women—ducking and dodging now as the children harassed him near the center of the village. He braced himself against their punches and slaps—held his genitals in his hands—wrapped in the filthy cloth he wore hanging down from a coarse rope belt—the only defense he was allowed. He knew that if he blocked the children's blows one of the Ninja Turtles would step forward and strike him with a spear. If he pushed them to the ground he'd then be beaten with fists and feet. If he retaliated against one of the older children—one of the boys on the verge of manhood—Raphael would slash at him and cut his skin with a metal-tipped arrow.

So Mark continued turning away from all the tiny fists—little hands balled into weapons and held up in front of skinny arms—bent at the elbows and ready to spring forward. The smallest children laughed as they struck his forearms and thighs—Mark dodging them and trying to make it a game. But then the older boys came running toward him and grabbed the rope wrapped around his waist—pulling him backward and spinning him in a circle. He tried to keep his footing but the boys tripped him and took him to the ground—piled on top of him and were soon followed by the younger children—anonymous hands ripping out patches of his beard and pulling at his long hair. Mark screamed and tried to shake his head loose—hands still covering his genitals as the collective weight of so many laughing children pressed down on his lungs.

The rains were heavier and storms more frequent for several months—jungle rivers swelling and sometimes spilling their murky brown water over the forest floor—burning sun spending longer stretches hidden behind heavy gray clouds—slightly cooler, wetter days lasting five or six full moons—extent of any seasonal changes Mark could discern.

Some days they stayed inside their huts and did not eat—rain coming down outside in a slow, steady patter— brief downpours and stray lightning bolts followed by sharp cracks of thunder. Mark would sleep as much as possible during the all-day rains. If he had any wounds Splinter would smear the green paste over them. If he wanted to tell a story Splinter would be his uncomprehending audience. And if he had no story Splinter would sit there with the same silent expression on his wrinkled face that he wore throughout each night—staring at him from the opposite end of the darkened, damp little shack.

Once the heaviest rains had stopped and there were more days of sunshine and only passing showers, Mark had more time to examine all the babies as their mothers carried them around the village—always strapped to either their backs or bellies. He looked for signs in the babies' skin—their eyes and hair—making rough calculations in his head about how long it'd been since the first woman— that first bonfire and the first time he smelled the smoking bundle—heard the chanting and saw the manic dancing. There was only a handful of babies in the village and only a couple who Mark thought could be young enough—examining them as best he could—walking as close to them as he dared—lingering an extra few seconds near the babies and their mothers inside the huts after unloading a stack of wood for the cooking fires.

On days when the men forced Mark to march into the jungle, he puzzled over the slivers of metal attached to the ends of some of their arrows—catching glimpses of them in Leonardo's hands—wondering to himself where they'd come from—wondering as he watched the tribe's best ar- cher sharpen their edges while all the other hunters rested by the river at midday—or as he stared at the shiny, hard surface while Leonardo pulled an arrow back against his bowstring—tilting and turning the deadly projectile toward something up in the trees.

Mark hadn't been able to examine any of the metal ar- rowheads up close since first seeing one sticking through his calf muscle a few days into his captivity. He kept his distance but always observed their sharpening techniques—how they shaped the small, jagged, rough-cut points—creeping closer to the hunters in the beginning and even trying to help—trying to tell them to wet the sharpening stones and to use a circular motion. But he was beaten and shooed away—left to watch silently and to wonder where the metal had come from—what the tribe could have possibly found in the jungle—maybe a dead prospector's shovel—an explorer's helmet or other piece of gear from centuries ago.

It hadn't taken long for Mark to learn that Leonardo was the best archer. Nearly all his arrows were tipped with metal that he'd carefully shaped to a skinny point not much wider than the wooden shafts they connected to—work he seemed much more skilled at than any of the other men. And during their hunts—if there was enough time and sufficient cover—the men would always stop and wave Leonardo to the front of the group to shoot up into the trees at the monkey or bird or snake they'd spotted. Mark would stand perfectly still—always behind and off to the side—watching as the arrow disappeared up into the jungle canopy—as it whistled up into the trees—the Ninja Turtles and the rest of the hunters watching for where the arrow and the animal would land.

After a successful shot they would chant and smile at each other—running to their quarry with spears raised—ready to strike if the animal wasn't quite dead yet. Leonardo would always get to the dead animal last—walking calmly as the rest of the hunters crowded around and waited. Then he'd crouch down and carefully pull out the arrow—seeming to pay little attention to the life he'd just taken—stepping away and standing off to the side by himself with the bloodied shaft—inspecting it closely from end to end—fretting over the wood and the metal—the feathers neatly attached to the back.

Raphael would usually be the one to shove Mark forward—making it clear when the time had come for him to lift the partially butchered animal off the ground. Depending on the size of the carcass and what else he was burdened with, Mark would either toss it over his shoulder or drape it around his neck—birds he'd simply tuck under his arm with the fruit and logs and the bundles of bark and leaves they always made him carry.

Toward the end of a long, hard day—a day much like any other—it had just stopped raining as the hunting party reached the village—late afternoon sun threatening to peek out from behind the low, fast-moving clouds—Mark not allowed to rest as Raphael pushed him toward one of the huts with a load of firewood. The logs were heavy and he'd slipped and fallen several times on the slick jungle trails— Raphael having beaten him back to his feet each time with the blunt end of his spear. So Mark was tired—more tired than usual as he entered the hut—his arms shaking as he tried not to stop—tried to keep from dropping even a loose piece of crumbling bark.

He bent forward and shuffled through the small doorway as the dipping sun finally shone through a break in the clouds. Raphael slapped Mark's back with his spear to direct him to one side of the hut. Once his eyes adjusted to the darkness Mark saw a smoking pile of ash and charred sticks on the ground in one corner—a woman and a small child sitting next to it. He set the logs down on the ground and examined the little boy—his curly head of hair—not long enough yet to need trimming—sitting there next to his mother—barely able to hold his own head steady—looking up at Mark with the same curious eyes he must've shown everyone except the woman who'd given birth to him. His eyes were dark but not black—skin a slightly different shade from all the other children.

Mark heard the whoosh of Raphael's spear—cruel, angry man behind him going through his windup. He braced himself and felt the wood come down across his back—felt the splitting of skin and the line of sting from shoulder blade to kidney.

He stood up slowly and looked away so the boy would not see the pain in his face—turned his body toward the door—his eyes squinted as they filled with watery tears. After a few seconds he looked down and saw the woman gripping a broken machete—black plastic handle in her hand. He traced the flat metal blade down toward the packed-earth floor—rusty surface stopping suddenly at a jagged break only halfway to its original length. Mark blinked hard to clear the moisture from his eyes—stepping toward the doorway as he saw deep grooves gouged into the visible parts of the handle.

The woman reached over and grabbed one of the logs Mark had just delivered to the dark, dingy hut. As he stumbled away with a spear jabbing into his side he saw the woman slowly raise the machete above the upright log— then heard the unmistakable sound of metal cutting into wood as Raphael shoved him through the open doorway— forcing him back out into the open expanse of the village.

He stood there and listened to the sound repeating itself over and over from inside the hut—listening carefully as he blinked against the relative brightness of the setting sun.

That night Mark sat across from Splinter in the small hut they shared and he told him about the machete—asked the older man where they'd found it—whether they'd traded for it or stolen it. He told him about the little boy he'd seen and about the boy's hair and eyes and skin—his approximate age and how long Mark thought it had been since that first bonfire and that first full moon woman. He did the math out loud—holding up fingers which Splinter would not look at.

He asked Splinter if he was a father but Splinter sat there on the bare ground and did not respond—did not move or seem to blink or even swallow. Mark looked him over and kept talking as though Splinter understood his words—his explanations of the outside world and his complaints about the life he was being forced to live. He let his eyes wander to the walls of the hut and out the open doorway—stars and trees and the huts that housed the rest of the tribe—his half-native son among them. But Splinter's eyes did not move. They did not leave his captive's face and they did not convey any emotion or understanding—any acknowledgement of Mark's troubles.

Soon the darkness and the quiet began to burrow deep into Mark—the solitude and the helplessness—the revelation of fatherhood without any expectation of a future with his son—the tropical death unwilling to take pity on him just yet.

So he continued to talk—to dream out loud—to pray for a tomorrow he knew he would never see.

STORY

"My wife and I always had our son's birthday parties at Chuck E. Cheese's. Have you ever been there, Splinter?"

.

.

"Well, you'd like it. I bet you could even get a job as their mascot. What do you think of that?"

.

.

"Anyway, all you do is call and reserve a table and tell them it's your kid's birthday and they basically do all the work. I guess my wife would go out and buy decorations and gifts and a cake but other than that, it was all taken care of.

"Our son would tell us who he wanted to invite and we'd send him to school with invitations to hand out. Then on the day of the party his little friends would come walking into the restaurant with their hair combed—all of them stiff in their nice clothes. They'd be carrying a gift or a card and our son would run up and greet them and then they'd run off somewhere together and play. They have arcade games there and jungle gym equipment.

"He was always so happy—my son. It was his favorite place in the world."

.

.

"I remember one of his birthday parties in particular—last one we ever had at Chuck E. Cheese's. A few hours into it—most of the pizza already gone and everybody getting ready for cake and ice cream—I heard these adults arguing so I looked over. They had to be screaming at each other for me to hear them over all those kids. There was a man and a woman off by themselves and he was yelling at the top of his lungs. She was looking around and about to start crying. I couldn't tell what they were arguing about but you can probably guess—always either money or one of them is cheating or they're splitting up and neither one can quite come up with a good reason why—one day one of them packs up and leaves and says it's because they just can't stay—can't take it anymore."

.

.

"So the man was already worked up. He was a country-club-looking guy—collared shirt and clean-cut. His face was bright red and you could almost see his hair getting wet from all the sweat. After a few seconds I saw him pull a ring out of his pocket and yank the woman's hand. She started pulling away but you could tell she didn't want to cause a scene. So at that point I started to stand up. I watched the guy as he tried to force the ring onto the woman's finger—shaking her whole arm while she continued trying to pull away—her hand clinched into a fist. Finally she started looking around with this pleading expression on her face—begging someone to help her—kids and parents all beginning to notice what was going on.

"I walked over and said something to them—a stupid dad joke, maybe, I don't know—just something to get their attention and maybe cool things down a bit."

.

.

"You know, you should maybe think about doing that sometime, Splinter—calming things down instead of making everybody crazy with your sick little full moon ceremonies."

.

.

"Anyway, they both looked at me and he still had ahold of her arm and her hand. I took another step toward them and I told him he should let her go. I could feel all the kids starting to gather around to see what was going to happen. Parents were mostly frozen where they sat or stood but there were a couple dads coming up behind me. Then the guy let go of one of the woman's arms and reached down into his pocket again. I saw the ring drop from his hand and bounce a couple times on the tile floor—big diamonds and shiny gold catching the light.

"When I looked back up I saw the country-club guy pull out a gun and point it right at me. I stopped and put my hands up—hearing all the parents behind me suddenly going for their kids and people running away. The woman tried to get away too but he grabbed her tight around the wrist and pulled her in close and then wrapped his arm around her neck. Then he started making his way toward the cash registers and I started talking—trying to reason with him—trying to tell him to let everybody go and trying to make him see that whatever problems he had weren't worth all the trouble he was getting himself into. But he just kept waving that gun around—pointing it at me and then the woman and then anybody that he noticed running by us toward the exits.

"Eventually it was just me and him and the woman left in the whole place. But by the time he made it around the counter and was standing in front of all the cash registers, I felt a tug on my arm. When I turned around and looked down my son was there—scared but I guess he felt better with me than outside with his mother and his friends and a bunch of strangers. Or maybe he just didn't want to leave me in there all alone with a crazy guy pointing a gun at me.

"He's a good boy—brave and tough—my little partner."

.

.

"So I kept him behind me and turned back around to try talking some sense into the crazy country-club guy. He was over there punching buttons on all the registers—talking to the woman about how they'll have plenty of money after he gets the cash drawers open and how she doesn't have to leave him anymore. Anyway, we all stood there for a few seconds and he kept getting more and more agitated as the cash registers refused to open. He was talking to the woman the whole time but she was looking at me—terrified. I kept talking and he kept the gun pointed at me and eventually he told me to shut the hell up. I turned and looked down at my son and thought about making a run for it but I knew he'd start shooting if we did. I didn't know what to do."

.

.

"Then my son walked out from behind me and made it around the counter before I could grab him. The country-club guy was startled—turned real fast and pointed the gun down at him. My son just stopped and calmly told him that he knew how to open the registers. His mother ran a little gift shop and he always spent a couple hours there right after school. I guess she'd shown him how to work the register because within a second or two he had all the cash drawers open.

"I stood there on the other side of the counter—ready to jump over at any moment—and the country-club guy kept waving that gun around between us. Pretty soon he waved my son away. I stepped over and yanked him by the shirt to get him behind me again—held onto him a little tighter this time as I started slowly shuffling backward.

"We stood there and watched the man make tall stacks of cash on the counter and it seemed like he'd forgotten about us—setting the gun down to free up his hand. So after a little while I grabbed my son and ran for the back of the restaurant—ran past the Skee-Ball machines and the arcade games and the jungle gym equipment. We ran out an emergency exit door and there was a SWAT team with those stubby machine guns and helmets and goggles over their eyes. They all wore bulletproof vests and were standing together in a straight line. Once they saw I wasn't armed they had someone escort us away from the building.

"It took them all night but eventually the country-club guy gave up and came out with the woman. He'd thrown the gun in the ball pit and we saw on the local news that the police dogs could smell it but weren't too sure about going in after it. It took the SWAT team a whole day to fish the gun out because they were worried about it accidentally going off—had to take the little plastic balls out one at a time until they could see it clearly."

.

.

"My son was a hero. We were in all the local papers and did a few interviews for local TV stations. His mother even made a scrapbook with all the newspaper clippings so we'd remember how brave he'd been."

"He's a good boy—my son."

SHOW

MARK: They'd probably been there for a long time—watching me—following me while I tried to find my way back.

INTERVIEWER: Back to the camp where you were staying?

MARK: Yeah.

Mark looked at the famous journalist—pausing as his heart pounded with the same panic he'd felt back then—those hours alone in the hot, suffocating jungle—endless maze of green and black—insects buzzing his ears and crawling up his legs.

MARK: It started raining pretty soon after I realized I was lost. I just kept walking—probably making big loops and ending up right back where I started. There was no way to tell where the sun was and I didn't have a compass.

INTERVIEWER: That must have been terrifying.

MARK: Yeah.

He paused again—eyes still focused on the older man across from him—wrinkled face nodding and frowning with interest and concern—whether authentic or not, Mark couldn't be sure.

INTERVIEWER: All the other guests who were staying at the camp at the time of your disappearance said the trails through the jungle were clearly marked and-and-and also we reached out to members of the outfitter's staff and they all said they had no knowledge of anyone else ever getting lost in that area. They said a person would either have to be carried off by a jaguar or drunk or on some sort of illicit substance or mentally unstable or-or-or just plain crazy to lose their way.

MARK: Well, I guess maybe I was crazy—maybe a little mentally unstable. Either way I got lost and then those people found me—ganged up on me and beat me and dragged me back to their village.

INTERVIEWER: Whatever state of mind you were in at the time I'm sure you didn't intend to place yourself in that sort of predicament.

Mark smiled with his mouth remaining closed—raised his eyebrows and nodded. The famous journalist smiled back and shifted in his seat—looked down and flipped through his stack of printouts. The two cameramen Mark could see in the opposite corners of the little curtained partition shifted their weight from foot to foot—keeping their eyes on tiny screens while their hands turned little plastic knobs.

INTERVIEWER: Let's move on to first contact because you're right, Mark, no matter what happened and why you walked off into the jungle, eventually you were taken into captivity by this-this-this primitive tribe—this group of people almost completely unaware of the outside world that's lived the same sort of subsistence lifestyle for millennia they-they-they found you wandering the jungle, took you back to their village their settlement, and they held you in bondage for nearly three years. I mean, what was that first moment like did you have any idea what was about to happen to you?

MARK: No. No I wasn't sure who they were or what they were going to do—thought maybe they'd been sent to search for me and we'd just make our way back to camp.

INTERVIEWER: What was your condition by that time your physical health and-and-and your first sighting of the tribesmen what was their behavior like what were they wearing? Can you set the scene a little?

MARK: I was tired—drained from all the walking and the lack of sleep—but otherwise I felt fine.

Mark watched the famous journalist nod his head—smile again as he lifted an index finger and started moving it in a circle—prodding Mark to continue—to give the cameras and the microphones what they wanted—the people in front of their TVs sometime in the future—the advertisers and the executives—the janitors who cleaned their offices and everyone in between.

MARK: I remember it had stopped raining—still cloudy and wet but at least the rain had stopped. For a while—since at least early that morning—I thought I could hear something out in the jungle not too far away—something moving—always about the same distance from me no matter how far I'd walked since the last time I heard it. At first I thought it was a jaguar—some hungry animal stalking me. But then one of them came out from wherever he'd been hiding— stood there with a spear pointed at me—five or six more surrounding me on all sides just a second or two later. It didn't take long for me to realize they weren't rescuing me—that they'd been following me for a while—studying me—watching me for who knows how long.

Mark tilted his head back and looked up at the conference room ceiling—high, smooth surface only visible between the puffy microphones and overhead lights. He felt the famous journalist shift around again in his chair—leaning forward into the empty space between them.

Mark looked down eventually and blinked as his eyes adjusted back to the relative darkness of the little partition—pupils shrunken from direct exposure to the overhead lights—tiny black circles now slowly returning to their previous diameter. He began to speak again before his eyes had completely adjusted—before the older man had a chance to say anything.

MARK: I tried talking to them—tried hand gestures— smiled and tried to give them some chewing gum.

INTERVIEWER: Were they threatening in any way?

MARK: Not at first—besides those spears, of course. They just stood there looking at me—naked except for a little loincloth in front and a rope belt around their waists—no shoes.

After a little while the closest one took a few steps toward me—lowered his spear and pointed it at my stomach—tightened his grip. I looked around and saw the others—the five or six men surrounding me on all sides—blocking any escape route I might've tried to take.

Mark cleared his throat and waited for the next question—scooting back deeper into his chair as the older man in front of him stared straight ahead—unmoving now except for the slight rise and fall of his chest with each deep breath—not checking his printouts as he'd done so intently before—not even seeming to blink.

INTERVIEWER: And that's when they took you when they began the process of stripping you of your humanity of making you into more of a-a-a beast of burden than a man.

MARK: Yeah. They had me surrounded and slowly closed in—young men—a hunting party, I guess.

INTERVIEWER: Did you fight? Did you try to escape?

MARK: Yeah. I had at least fifty pounds on each one of them and probably seven or eight inches. So I turned around and ran straight for the youngest-looking guy—grabbed his spear and threw him to the side. Then I started running but only took a few steps before they were on me—spears clubbing my shoulders and back—just missing my head. They're little but they're strong. Together they didn't have a problem taking me down—five or six of them with those heavy spears.

The famous journalist was still leaning forward—elbows on his knees with the stack of printouts curving over one thigh. Mark watched him and waited—tried not to look at the cameras over the older man's shoulders—to keep his mind from going too deep—from doing more than just skimming the surface of all the memories being summoned by his interrogator—the digging being done in order to feed a national audience yet another human-interest story.

INTERVIEWER: Then what happened?

MARK: They took me—forced me to march off with them through the jungle. Each time I refused or tried to fight back they all ganged up on me and beat me—took my shoes and passed them around before leaving them somewhere. I walked in my socks until they got too soaked and muddy— heavy and not really any use anymore. If I slowed down one of them would poke me with a spear. If I tried to run off they would surround me—close in on me and then all pounce at once—punch and kick me and rip out my hair.

INTERVIEWER: They took you back to their village their settlement how long did the journey take?

MARK: A night and a day—around twenty-four hours, I think—seemed like a lot longer, though. It rained off and on and I was barefoot most of the time. They ripped my shirt off at some point and I was bleeding all over from scratches and places where they'd hit and poked me with their spears.

Someone moved on the other side of the black curtains—a person walking fast just outside the little temporary room. Mark watched the ripples in the fabric—thin, loosely hanging wall pushing in with the force of a passing body. He listened to the hurried footsteps—turned his head to follow the wave of curling shadows as it crashed into one of the cameramen.

INTERVIEWER: How long did it take you to fully grasp what was going on what was happening?

Mark looked at the famous journalist—his soft, puffy skin and thick layer of makeup—whatever gel or mousse they'd put in his perfect hair—thin fingers and shiny, carefully filed nails. He sat up straight and met the older man's eyes—smiled and thought about what kind of person would ask such a stupid question.

MARK: Spears and fists and all the other stuff—the pain—stealing the shoes off your feet and the shirt off your back—it all makes things pretty clear pretty quick.

INTERVIEWER: I can imagine.

The famous journalist leaned back in his chair—knees bobbing up and down as he gathered the printouts into his hands.

MARK: Law of the jungle. You must know a lot about that.

CHAPTER
SIX

FACT

SOON AFTER MARK DISCOVERED HIS INFANT SON—SITTING quietly inside a dark, stuffy hut next to his mother—a mutilated machete in her small hand—he began to notice the Ninja Turtles were spending less time hunting and gathering in the jungle and more time in the village—making arrows and spears—repairing bows and sharpening metal arrowheads. They still made quick trips into the forest nearly every morning—forcing Mark to haul loads of wood for all the cooking fires—bundles of fruit and dirt-covered tubers—leaves and slabs of bark for Splinter's smoking bundles and medicinal concoctions—the green paste for wounds and a hot drink all the men sipped together at night. He was also still expected to haul the heavy logs they used for the full moon bonfires—stacking them up in a pile that would slowly grow over a month's time—sitting out in the rain and the sun next to the gray-ash crater at the center of the village.

The weather had changed as well—hotter, drier days Mark thought would be perfect for hunting—days the tribe instead spent mending the reed walls of their huts—tying bands of braided rope around their arms with ornaments sometimes attached—a piece of bone or tooth—small pebble from one of the nearby rivers. Mark felt things changing in the village—the Ninja Turtles more tense as he watched them work on their weapons—as he waited to see what they were preparing for—waited to see his son again.

One afternoon—Mark scavenging around the village after a morning spent dragging heavy, broken branches over the tribe's network of slick trails—he stopped to watch Raphael trying hard to break pieces of metal off the tip of the machete—smashing a rounded rock against the tarnished blade—crouching over his work near a small hut as the hot sun beat down on him. Mark stood back and watched—inching closer when he thought Raphael was most distracted.

Raphael was sweating as he crashed rock against metal. He held the machete against the bare ground and hit down on it with the rounded river stone. There was a depression now forming in the dirt and the end of the machete was covered with loose, chocolate-colored soil.

"You're not doing that right," Mark said—Raphael breathing hard as he rested back on his heels—hands on his thighs and eyes squinting up at Mark. "You want some help?"

Raphael stood up slowly and turned around—stepped over to the nearby hut and grabbed a long, flexible stick that had been leaning against the sun-bleached reed wall. Mark turned quickly and started walking away—trying not to look back as he felt footsteps following him—knowing it was pointless to flee—pointless as it always was to try to escape.

The stick slashed across his back—whipping through the air above his head in another windup just a split second later—coming down on his shoulder this time—bending and curling over his chest. Soon there were other men rushing toward him—forming a circle of scowls, bare teeth and clinched fists. They took turns with the stick as Mark went down to the ground and curled himself into a ball—hands over his face and knees tucked up near his chest. He tried to turn so the stick would hit only his back—the broadest part of his shriveled body—the part of him most capable of dealing with abuse—already lined with plenty of pink scars intersecting and overlapping each other in various states of repair.

When the beating was finally over—the men dispersing and leaving him there in the dirt—Mark wasn't sure if he'd be able to stand—at first—only raising his head to look around—seeing the men's smooth, muscled backs—children staring at him from open doorways—the tiny hut he shared with Splinter—dark clouds in the sky not close enough yet to block out the hot sun.

It rained the rest of the afternoon—Mark trying to sleep on the hard, bare ground of the tiny hut—no blanket or fire or other living bodies to keep him warm—aware of the bumps and bruises and possible broken bones from the midday beating. He tried to find a comfortable position—tried hard to drift off into a dream—Splinter sitting across from him in the angled block of dull light coming in through the open doorway—unmoving as always—staring at his captive as Mark opened and closed his eyes in vain.

As the rain began to taper off and the afternoon turned to evening, Mark watched Splinter reach behind his back and pull out the machete. He sat up and made sure he was out of reach in case the medicine man tried to slash at him with the jagged blade—clinched his tired, weak hands into fists—then leaned back and waited.

A few seconds later he watched as Splinter reached behind his back again—pulling out a small, rounded stone this time—then another and then a few smaller pebbles—laying everything out on the packed-earth floor between them—adjusting the stones until they were turned just right—placing them in a particular way for unknown, unknowable reasons. When he was finally finished the older man raised his head and looked at Mark.

"What am I supposed to do with all this?"

Splinter stared blankly at his captive—black charcoal lines tracing over his wrinkled face as always. Then he pulled out an arrow from behind his back and set it down in front of Mark. There were no feathers on the thin piece of wood—no decorative markings—no metal arrowhead fastened to either end.

"What?"

Splinter placed his hands back onto his knees and was once again the unmoving, unblinking guard—guardian—watcher of the slave and the only member of Mark's nightly audience.

"Do you want me to kill you with this?" Mark said as he picked up the machete.

Splinter did not move—did not blink and Mark knew he wasn't going to get an answer—wondering again whether Splinter was really alive or not—if it was possible he existed in some other state—somewhere between the living and the dead.

Mark looked down at the black plastic grip with his fingers wrapped around it—felt the uneven weight of the machete as he examined the jagged edge where the top half of the blade had been broken off—whittled down and formed into an unknown number of arrowheads.

He could hear the rain tapering off—rumbles of thunder becoming faint—raindrops still collecting and dripping from the thatched roof into a brown puddle just outside the doorway. The sun was setting and soon—once the storm clouds cleared as he knew they would—he'd have only moonlight to work by.

"I don't have any tools," Mark said—leaning forward as he looked out at the other huts—few women scurrying around in the rain—small children running and splashing through puddles—young girls carrying gourds full of water.

Mark reached and picked up one of the larger stones— slid it along the machete and listened to the metal sound— tapped the heel of the flat blade as he looked down at the other stones. They were mostly dark gray—some nearly black and others much lighter in color. He picked up the smallest pebble and balanced it on top of one of the larger stones—then used the one in his hand to smash it—dust and tiny fragments shooting off from the little pebble but it did not break. He hit it again and again and still it did not break.

He tried another pebble—a darker one that shattered into jagged fragments after just a few strikes. The largest piece had an almost straight, almost sharp edge. Mark picked it up and tested it with his fingertips—then laid the machete down on the large stone and held the chosen fragment where he wanted to break off a long, thin triangle of metal. He tapped it with one of the heavier stones and eventually made a visible scratch—then kept tapping and scraping with the pebble fragment until a crease formed— until he could almost bend the metal—working at it until finally the crease opened up and the long, thin triangle broke off the machete's blade.

Mark continued grinding and bending the tarnished blade until moonlight no longer shined through the open doorway. But Splinter never moved—never took his eyes away from Mark and his work. By the time the little hut was completely dark Mark had made three new arrowheads. He had little cuts all over his hands—forearms weak and sore from the constant scraping and pounding.

He laid his head down in the dark and folded his hands over his bare chest—packed-earth floor lumpy and cold beneath his tired body. He listened to the frogs who were always louder after it rained—listened to their mating calls as he stared at the thatched ceiling. Water still dripped over the doorway and he could feel the dampness in the ground—colder and softer than it was after hotter and drier days.

"Why do you need so many more arrows and spears?" Mark said—turning his head to look toward Splinter—seeing the medicine man's eyes there in the darkness—the outline of his head and body—but of course Splinter did not answer.

"Well, whatever's going to happen," Mark continued as he turned back to the ceiling. "I better get myself the hell out of here before it does—take my chances out there—alone—wander around lost until someone finds me—or I stumble across a little village or the camp where I was staying—or I die—alone."

He reached out into the darkness and ran his hand along the ground—searching with dirty, splayed fingers until he found the handle of the machete. Then he pulled it toward him and tucked the tarnished blade under his hip.

"I'll build a raft with this thing and float down the river."

He rolled onto his side—raising the machete and pressing the rusty metal to his chest. "You're a lifesaver, Splinter."

Mark stayed awake long into the night—asking Splinter again where they'd found the machete—whether they'd traded for it or stolen it. He asked about the river and whether there were any rapids or waterfalls he should look out for during his journey. Sitting back up to face his silent audience, Mark went through a list of supplies he would need—rope, a couple pebbles to sharpen the machete, rope, some food, some more rope and more food. He laughed and asked if there was a sporting goods store nearby and if they sold freeze-dried meals—that trail mix he used to love with the dehydrated strawberries and peanut butter cups—carbon fiber paddles and water purification tablets.

Mark stared across the few feet of darkness between him and Splinter and he spoke as though the older man could understand every word—explanations of the outside world—his increasingly complex escape plan—what he might do once he made it out—made it back home.

Eventually Mark let his eyes wander to the walls of the hut and out the open doorway—clouds and trees and the huts that housed the rest of the tribe—his half-native son still not mentioned during his late-night plotting. But Splinter's eyes did not move. They did not leave his captive's face—still not bothered by the absence of light or made drowsy by the lack of sleep.

The night, however, soon began to wear on Mark—the solitude and the helplessness—the darkness he felt all around him—sturdy walls of his jungle prison—dangers of escape beginning to overwhelm the hope he'd felt just moments earlier.

So he kept talking—kept scheming and dreaming out loud—praying for someone to wake him from the nightmare that had somehow become his life—the barefoot labor and the cold, wet, captive nights.

STORY

"You know, Splinter, I've gotten myself out of worse situations—I have—worse than this."

.

.

"I was in foster care when I was a kid—grew up that way. There was this one family I stayed with when I was a little older—maybe thirteen or fourteen. They were religious. I don't think they were Mormons or Baptists or anything else, really. I think they just made stuff up—had their own rules—own twisted way of interpreting the Bible. Have you ever heard of the Bible, Splinter?"

.

.

"Anyway, that family I stayed with was really strict about things—no TV, no movies, no radio. They wouldn't even let us read books—the Bible, of course, being the only exception."

.

.

"'Therefore I tell you, do not worry about your life, what you will eat or drink; or about your body, what you will wear. Is not life more than food, and the body more than clothes?'"

.

.

"That's from Matthew. He must've never been in a place like this—living like I'm living now. It does sound like something you might agree with, though."

.

.

"So this family didn't have heat or air-conditioning in their house. They had a wood-burning stove in the living room but hardly ever used it no matter how cold it got. In the summertime they never let us open any of the windows. When we misbehaved—or at least when they said we were misbehaving—they chained us to our beds—sometimes for days."

.

.

"They pretended to be homeschooling us but never taught us anything. Instead they made us work outside all day—gardening, mostly. And if they couldn't find something constructive for us to do they just had us carry cinder blocks back and forth across the yard while they sat in lawn chairs and watched.

"In the evenings we'd all sit down on the floor in the living room with our Bibles and read. Sometimes the father tried to do a little preaching—standing up in front of us— telling us all about Sodom and Gomorrah or some other story from the Old Testament. Mostly, though, we just read on our own."

.

.

"We are hard pressed on every side, but not crushed;

perplexed, but not in despair; persecuted, but not abandoned; struck down, but not destroyed.'

"I always liked that one."

.

.

"After a year or so the mother started taking a liking to me. Some days, when everybody else was going outside to work, she'd keep me inside and make me get in bed with her. I was too young and too scared to know what was going on at first—but she made it clear what she wanted soon enough."

.

.

"'To the pure all things are pure, but to those who are defiled and unbelieving nothing is pure; but even their mind and conscience are defiled.'"

.

.

"It went on like that for probably another year. Then one winter night—for some reason I'll never understand— something made me get out of bed and go to the living room. I'd been laying there awake and just felt this sudden urge—almost like something was pulling me out of bed and down the hallway—toward a specific window next to the couch. The house was quiet but I wasn't sure if everybody was asleep or not. I knew if they caught me I'd get a beating and be chained to my bed for at least a few days—at least.

"I think I'd rather take another arrow through the leg before getting chained to a bed again."

.

.

"I didn't even check to see if the window was un- locked—just somehow knew it would be. So I pushed up on the flaking paint around the wooden window frame and felt the cold air rush in from outside. It was wintertime and I remember the snow being crunchy like it'd thawed a little and frozen again overnight—stepping down from the window and feeling it under my bare feet—too late to look around for shoes. I was finally out of that house—no way there'd ever be any going back.

"So I started running and almost immediately I heard Samson, their German Shepherd—barking and coming after me. I knew there was no outrunning him so I stopped and turned around—got down on my knees in the snow and watched him galloping toward me. He was just a dark shape with white teeth and I could see his breath rising up out of his open mouth. I shouted his name and held my arms out like I was going to give him a hug. He was only a few gallops away when I saw a light turn on inside the house. Samson must've recognized me because he stopped running all the sudden and walked up to me with his head down. He always liked me best out of all the kids in the house. And he liked all us kids a lot more than his owners.

"You know, Splinter, I haven't seen any pets around here. Don't you think you should get the kids a little monkey or two? Something to play with?"

.

.

"I guess I'm basically a pet—some kind of animal, anyway."

.

.

"I could see the father through the window I'd just crawled out of. We actually made eye contact for a split second and then he ran toward the front door. He was big—too big to fit through the open window—had these buggy eyes he used to stare at us with.

"I didn't wait for him to get the door unlocked—just got

up and started running for the road. Samson ran with me and nosed my hip a couple times. I kept running and heard the front door swing open—looked back and saw the father barreling out into the snow with his boots slipped on and a shotgun in one hand. He held it out in front of him and I veered to the left and fell down just as I heard the buckshot whizzing over my head. Samson yelped and scurried over to me. He must've taken a pellet or two in his tail or a hind leg.

"The road was close but there still weren't any houses nearby. I got up and started running again and waited for another shot—cold bare feet crunching through the snow—everything so quiet except my heavy breathing—Samson's panting and his big paws galloping next to me. For some reason the shot never came—no shells left or maybe the shotgun jammed somehow—who knows. Whatever happened me and Samson eventually made it to the road—then turned downhill and kept running.

"The road was gravel but it'd been plowed so we ran mostly on the loose rocks and frozen dust. I looked back a couple times and could just barely see the house—living room light still on. My feet started hurting after a minute or two and I was out of breath. But then I saw the headlights of the father's pickup.

"Pretty soon the pickup was fish-tailing out onto the gravel road behind us. I took off through the woods and the snow was up over my ankles again—halfway up my shins in places. I heard a couple shots go off from the shotgun and the buckshot popped against the trees. Samson stayed right next to me the whole time—whining a little when he heard the gunshots.

"My feet were about frozen and the rest of me was getting cold too—sweating through my T-shirt and cotton pants. I kept running and could hear the pickup in a field next to the woods—looked over to see it bouncing along parallel to me and Samson. Then I saw a flash from the shotgun hanging out the driver's side window—heard the bang and heard the pellets hitting the trees.

"I turned away from the pickup and kept stumbling through the snow—kept going and going and Samson stayed with me the whole time. We came to a creek and I slogged through freezing water up to my waist. I came out soaked and shivering on the other side and looked back for Samson. He was whining and pacing back and forth—sticking his nose out over the water. I tried to call him for a few minutes but he wouldn't come. He was too scared to even try crossing.

"At that point I was getting light-headed and could hardly stand anymore. I knew I was going to have to leave him—get myself warm and dry or I was going to freeze to death. But I stood there for a couple more minutes—shaking as I begged him to follow me—waving and calling his name—telling him to cross the creek and keep going or he was as good as dead. Eventually I gave up—turned around and started climbing up the bank. I half-expected to hear him crashing through the freezing water behind me but I never did—just whimpering and those big paws crunching through the snow."

.

.

"A few hundred yards outside those woods I saw the backside of a house. I went up to the backdoor and started banging until somebody turned on a light and peaked out at me. It was an old man with a rifle and a stern look on his wrinkly face. But once he saw the state I was in he put the gun down and pulled me inside. An hour later I still couldn't hold the cup of cocoa his wife tried handing me—my whole body still shivering from the cold.

"I'm sure you've never been that cold, Splinter—never in your whole life."

.

.

"The cops found the father on a highway near the New Mexico border. I guess he made a run for it once he figured out I'd gotten away."

.

.

"I never told anybody what the mother did to me—never even told my wife."

SHOW

INTERVIEWER: Law of the jungle—only the strong survive and here you are you survived.

Mark touched his fingertips together—shrugged his shoulders as he sat up straight. He felt the chair's vertical cushion pull back from his arching spine as his chest filled with air.

MARK: Luck had a lot to do with me getting out of there.

INTERVIEWER: Yes-yes-yes of course but you have to be strong and smart to take advantage of the luck when and if it comes and-and-and you were able to do that and get yourself out of there.

Mark twisted one arm around behind his back and peeled his shirt away from the moist skin covering his ribs—snapshot memories running through his head from beginning to end—capture to escape. He cleared his throat and looked down at the printouts in the famous journalist's hands—silence as everyone waited for him to respond—the older man across from him and the black camera eyes in each corner.

INTERVIEWER: Let's take a step back and-and-and talk about how you adjusted to captivity how it affected you in those first days. Did you continue trying to escape?

MARK: I ran off into the jungle every chance I got but never made it far—ten or fifteen minutes at most before they caught up to me. Pretty soon they got tired of always chasing after me so they shot one of their metal-tipped arrows through my leg—had this older guy keep watch over me every night—their witch doctor or their chief—or maybe both.

INTERVIEWER: And we'll get to him in a moment but let's talk more about these arrows I-I-I read somewhere about a machete the tribe had procured somehow and that's how they fashioned these metal arrowheads is that correct?

MARK: They'd managed to make a few. But I didn't see the machete for a long time at first—maybe the whole first year. And not all their arrows had the metal arrowheads since they hadn't figured out a good way of making them yet.

INTERVIEWER: Why do you think they kept the machete hidden from you in the beginning?

MARK: I think they knew I was from the outside world— that the machete was also from the outside world. They were right to be afraid—to keep that distance between us. I mean if it wasn't for that broken, rusty machete I'd probably be dead right now—rotting away in the jungle somewhere.

INTERVIEWER: So you could be dangerous as someone from the outside world and they obviously knew that metal could do great harm so-so-so the two together you and the machete was something they had no reference of no idea what would happen or-or-or just how dangerous that combination could be.

MARK: And they had different prerogatives in the beginning—me as a slave and the machete to make arrowheads and to chop kindling for cooking fires. There was no need to make me aware of it so they didn't—better safe than sorry.

The famous journalist nodded—a pale, spotted hand cradling his chin—eyes cast down at his printouts. Mark watched him and waited—felt his mouth dry and his stomach beginning to twist with hunger. After a few seconds he glanced to his right and then his left—hoping in vain for a little wooden table with a bottle of water sitting on top—a plate of fancy cheeses and toasted crackers.

INTERVIEWER: As you've mentioned you were a slave to these-these-these people this tribe now what sorts of things did they make you do what duties were you expected to perform exactly?

MARK: Most days the men would take me with them into the jungle—hunting and gathering fruit and these tubers they always ate and whatever else—firewood.

If they were lucky they'd kill a monkey or two with their bows and arrows—sometimes snakes and birds. There was always wood to carry if nothing else—and bark and leaves for different things—vines for making rope.

INTERVIEWER: Was the wood you carried just for cooking fires?

The famous journalist sat back in his chair—casually flipping through his printouts as he crossed one leg over the other—feigning disinterest after finally coming to the topic Mark knew he'd been wanting to ask about since the beginning of the interview—the juicy details he was going to pile inside living rooms all across the country in a couple weeks—the story of Mark's full moon nights in the sweaty, crowded hut—the chanting and the dancing and the ocher-painted women—civilized audience members sitting transfixed in front of their TV screens—waiting patiently through at least one commercial break.

Mark leaned to one side—shifting his upper body toward the elbow he had propped up on an arm of his chair—flexing the muscles in his legs and wiggling his toes inside his shoes—molars clinched tightly together inside his mouth—breaths coming fuller and faster as he struggled to keep himself from digging his fingernails into the chair's upholstery.

MARK: No.

CHAPTER
SEVEN

FACT

A S THE DAYS PASSED—AS THE HEAVY RAINS BEGAN AGAIN—
Mark watched as the tribe continued preparing weapons. He watched them work every day through either downpours or burning hours of direct jungle sunlight—fortifying the thin reed walls of all the huts. Eventually the Ninja Turtles began taking him deeper into the jungle each morning—gathering logs and fruit—walking trails Mark had never been down before—stepping carefully as if entering enemy territory.

At the end of each day—as Mark entered the tiny hut around sunset—Splinter would pull out the machete and the stones and lay them out neatly on the ground between them—then lean back and stare blankly ahead at Mark—intent on keeping his slave hard at work making arrowheads for several dark hours at the start of each night.

Mark soon lost all hope in the escape plan he'd dreamed up weeks earlier—dwelling instead on the painful jungle death he'd almost certainly meet if he fled—out there in the wet maze of green and black—alone and forgotten—his body quickly blending back into the hot soil.

He came to the realization that he was keeping himself alive only by following orders—allowed to exist only so long as he made himself useful—obedient to sticks and spears and the mystical powers of a small old man with dark lines tracing across his wrinkled face. He finally accepted the fact that he would survive only by letting weeks and then months slip away—by allowing himself to be the slack-jawed brute with only dulled memories of his past—no hopes or desires for his future. He was nearly nothing but a draft animal now and he knew it—yoked and scared and almost thoroughly tamed—allowed to keep on living so long as he suppressed the urge to rebel.

"Can I ask what's going on around here?" Mark said one day—sitting outside near the place where they made the bonfires—sun on his tanned face as he ate out of a large gourd—small hands dipping into the same round container—women and children eating beside him—watching him as he made the strange sounds with his mouth—the words they did not recognize as words.

The men were having some sort of meeting in the largest hut and Mark could hear them talking loudly inside— the blended syllables of their language. Raising a hand to his mouth he chewed a clump of the boiled and mashed tubers they always ate—remembering the wooden raft he'd dreamed of building with the rusted machete—floating down the river for however long it took—fishing along the way and sleeping right on the rough-cut logs as he drifted gently through rainless nights—days without storms or biting insects or any other inconveniences.

"They're in there talking about me, aren't they?" Mark said—eyes never leaving the open doorway.

Eventually he looked down at the child sitting next to

him—his son—the boy with different hair and the curious eyes—probably not even a year old yet—definitely less than two.

"Hi," Mark said—waving and watching the boy examine his flapping hand. "It's been a while." They made eye contact and the boy almost smiled. "You miss me?"

Soon clouds began to build and to block out the midday sun—happening suddenly as it almost always did—thunder off in the distance as Mark looked up at the last bits of blue sky. The women and children stood up from the ground and began to walk off toward their huts—his son's mother lifting the smiling boy from the packed earth—carrying him around the gray crater where another bonfire would soon be built.

Mark sat there by himself and watched them go—pulled the large gourd toward him and started scraping the inside with his fingers—gathering one last handful of the mashed tubers and bringing it to his mouth. Raindrops began hitting the ground at the edge of the clearing as he stood up and licked the last streaks of food from his palm—a nearly naked man surrounded by lush green jungle—a father with a patchy beard and no shoes—bruises and cuts over much of his thin slave body.

The next morning—after another night of rain and storytelling—his uncomprehending audience of one sitting silently across from him through the dark, wet hours—Mark woke up just before dawn. Splinter was gone by then—had left the hut at some point during the early morning as he occasionally did—or maybe, Mark sometimes wondered, maybe he'd never even been there at all.

Water still dripped from above the doorway into a muddy puddle just outside the tiny hut—breeze just beginning to rustle the treetops at the edge of the village. He could hear someone out there—whispers and footsteps—several people or maybe more.

Mark sat up and tried to listen—peering out the open doorway at fog rolling through the jungle canopy—everything blue-gray and still asleep—coiled—still waiting for the day to start.

But the voices were real and the sneaking feet were close. Soon he saw a woman at the opposite end of the village—scurrying out of the jungle as her fearful head twisted around to glance behind her—back into the green darkness. She ran toward the largest hut—hair flying around her face and bouncing above her head—breasts waving with every pump of her arms.

Mark moved toward the doorway and began to stand up—his head twisting and his eyes searching the opposite end of the tiny hut—quickly finding the broken machete—tarnished metal lying flat on the bare ground with the sharpening stones placed neatly in a circle. He reached out and grabbed the worn plastic handle—brought it to his side as he raised himself up off the ground near the doorway—careful not to make a sound as he felt his cold muscles trying to stretch—his stiff joints wanting to pop.

The woman was gone when Mark turned back to look out the open doorway—village empty and quiet with high walls of jungle beyond. She must've entered the large, dark hut at the center of the village, he thought—the one she'd been desperately trying to reach—now not making a sound loud enough for him or anyone else to hear—staying silently hidden from whatever she'd been fleeing.

But the whispers and the footsteps soon began to grow louder and he realized they were coming from behind him—from outside the tiny hut somewhere. He took a small step forward and stuck his head out the doorway—drops of water slapping the top of his head and blending into his hair. He listened—turned slowly from side to side—watched the jungle breathing—exhaling as fog slowly rose and swirled from tangled branches and vines.

All the huts in the village stood empty and quiet. Mark looked around at the dark doorways and tried to listen—tried to hear and see everything at once—to catch the leading edge of whatever was coming next.

Distant screams suddenly broke the morning calm—startling Mark as he listened to the increased murmur of nearby whispers. The screams were from men somewhere out in the jungle and they sent birds flapping through the mist above the treetops. After a few seconds of quiet—of the whispered voices and shuffling feet—some of the men began to cry out in pain and others in rage. They shouted words that Mark did not understand—maybe names or instructions or curses or pleas for help—some of the voices getting closer as they called out—others seeming to have no choice but to stay where they were.

Mark stepped out of the hut and looked around—listened to the screaming men as he held the broken machete up in front of him—handle gripped tight with his knees slightly bent—keeping his back against the reed walls as he inched his way around the hut—searching for the whispering voices and pattering feet. It was cool compared to most mornings he'd experienced living with the tribe—so cool and wet that much of the fog refused to lift and melt away—clouds low and blending into the treetops—barely allowing any sunlight through.

Mark peeked around the back corner of the hut—machete ready to attack and feet ready to flee. He found what looked to be nearly all the women and children of the tribe—gathered together and shivering in the cold, wet morning. The women looked at him and held their children close—shuffling backward as they all took note of the machete.

The screaming continued from the distant men as Mark stepped around the corner—sounds of battle seeming closer after every silent pause. He looked back toward the center of the village—toward the desperate cries of pain and rage that echoed through the jungle—but all was empty and still.

"Come on," Mark said to the group of frightened women and confused children—looking down and seeing his son—pausing as he stared into the boy's bright eyes—bright and golden against the blue-gray darkness—small boy leaning quietly against his mother's leg.

Mark began motioning for the women to follow him—stepping backward around the corner of the hut. They hesitated for a few seconds—trading concerned glances among themselves but soon they were moving with him—nervous as they left their collective hiding spot. His son watched everything—watched his father most of all—his curious, contemplative eyes—his hair and the familiar features of his small face.

"In here," Mark said—waving them through the open doorway of the tiny hut—the women and children quickly crowding in against the four walls—jumping a little each time they heard another distant, echoing scream.

After the last woman had shuffled inside—pressing herself against the crowd of small bodies—Mark turned with the machete and scanned the other huts—listened for more sounds from the battle—watched the perimeter of the village for any movement.

It was quiet for what seemed like a long time as Mark stood out in the open—small sounds from the women and children behind him—but the distant screams from the men had stopped—last echoes of battle disappearing into the dense, wet vegetation—replaced by whispers at his back— the slow dripping of water from above the doorway of the little hut.

He stepped farther away from the hut and scanned the village from one side to the other—thinking about the woman he'd seen earlier fleeing the jungle—running into the largest hut that was now directly in front of him. He wondered what she had been escaping—the scenes of violence she'd witnessed or maybe even been a part of—why she'd been separated from the other women.

Mark walked over the flat, open ground of the village—approached the dark doorway of the largest hut and looked inside. He gave his eyes a moment to adjust and then stepped forward onto the dry, packed earth—broken machete still held up in front of him. The woman was nowhere near the entrance and there was no sound to give away her location. Mark went deeper inside—turning his head slowly from wall to wall.

He'd never been allowed inside this hut before—the reed walls more substantial than the others—ceiling higher with a small opening near the center directly above a fire pit. The opening let in some daylight and Mark's eyes were getting used to the darkness—allowing him to see dried herbs hung from the rafters—bundles of fruit, gourds, coils of rope and other supplies. He smelled it all blending together in the stagnant air—the jungle natives that were his masters now—the foods they ate—paints they spread over their bodies.

Mark was standing near the middle of the large hut when someone grabbed him around the neck—a woman's voice straining with effort behind him. He turned quickly and ripped a pair of small hands away from his throat—held the woman by one wrist and bent down to look at her face. She tried to fight—tried with all her strength to get away—forcing Mark to pull her close and wrap an arm around both her shoulders in order to stop her flailing.

"What the hell's going on?" he yelled—knowing there would be no answer.

He turned and marched the woman out into the gray morning—struggling with her as she fought to escape—machete loosely held in his opposite hand—pushing and pulling the woman over to the small hut—then releasing her as she started squeezing herself through the crowd of bodies inside—the other women grabbing her and moving her away from the open doorway. She spoke to them in a low voice with fear still showing on her face—Mark pausing as he wondered what came next—his mind racing as he looked down at all the children but was unable to find his son—standing there scanning all the tiny faces he could see—giving up after a minute or two—turning around and starting back toward the largest hut as the women continued whispering—scanning the jungle as he went—waiting for another round of screams to echo through the village.

A spear whistled over Mark's head just after he passed the gray crater where they built the bonfires. He bent down and instinctively raised his hands to his head—turned to see where the projectile had landed—hearing the women screaming now inside the hut as he saw the spear sticking down through the thatched roof. He thought about his son— worried about where the next spear would land—whether or not arrows would start falling from the sky soon.

Turning back around Mark saw two men running toward him—both decorated in a style he hadn't seen before—one with yellow feathers hanging from his elbows and hair down nearly to his shoulders. The other had shorter hair with objects tied around the collected strands—ornaments hanging down and swinging over his ears. Neither had ocher paint on their bodies or hands—covered instead with sweat and dirt. Only the one with the yellow feathers held a spear.

Mark watched the two men as they continued running toward him—the one with shorter hair screaming as he pulled ahead of his partner—spit flying from his mouth as Mark realized this man would not stop—would keep running and fighting until one of them was dead.

Mark stood there as the two men approached—out in the open so they couldn't pin him down against one of the huts—knees bent so he could dodge if the trailing man threw his spear. The ground was slick with mud so he crouched and shifted his weight to the balls of his feet—clouds just beginning to burn away—the sun suddenly peeking out from behind the two men—shining brightly over Mark's face and blinding him briefly. He blinked and lowered his eyes—squinted and leaned to one side but still could not see the two men or the spear.

Behind him the women and children were screaming—some running from the little hut and scattering into the jungle—children in their mother's arms or latched onto their backs. Mark did not hear them, though—did not turn when his son began to cry—his mother cowering over him against the back wall of the emptying hut.

Mark jumped to the side as he caught a glimpse of the man with the yellow feathers raising his spear—holding it high but not throwing it yet. The other man was still running and screaming in front of his partner—within ten feet now. Mark braised himself in the slick mud—stabbing his curling toes down into the slime—raising the broken machete—then lunging forward at the last moment as the man with the short hair reached out—angry fingers close enough to touch—wild screams and saliva flinging freely from his mouth.

The machete slid along the inside of the man's arm—Mark turning it as he felt the contact—pressing it into flesh. The man screamed and pulled away—momentum taking him past Mark and toward the tiny hut. Mark turned from him and looked for the spear—seeing it held high in the other man's hands—seeing the fire-hardened tip as he waited for it to be hurled at him from just a few yards away.

But the man with the yellow feathers gripped the spear with both hands and extended it forward as he ran toward Mark—colorful strips of cloth tied tightly around the shaft—Mark looking down at the man's rough, dirty fingers wrapped tightly around the polished piece of wood.

The man kept coming—running until the spear was nearly touching Mark's stomach—Mark lunging to the side at the last moment—grabbing hold of the smooth wooden shaft with one hand—swinging the machete with the other toward the man's neck and feeling it stick—then seeing the blood and the man's teeth—hearing the scream and somehow understanding instantly the look in the man's eyes.

Mark yanked the spear from the man's hands—pulled the machete away from his neck and let him slowly collapse down to the muddy ground—something forcing him to keep eye contact with the man as he died—his yellow feathers clumping together with mud and splattered blood. Mark stood there breathing hard with a weapon held tightly in each hand—witness to the man's last few seconds of life.

Mark heard a loud scream and looked up—seeing the

man with shorter hair and now blood coating one arm—watching him as he climbed up the tiny hut toward the spear stuck in the thatched roof. Mark raised the spear he now held—feeling its weight as he put a foot forward and prepared to throw it—but then hesitating as he noticed movement from within the hut—looking down and seeing his son screaming in his mother's arms—surrounded by several other women with small children—some cowering in dark corners while others fled out the open doorway.

Mark started to run but slipped—fell near the man he'd just killed—dropped the spear and hurried to gain his feet again—running more carefully toward the hut this time—watching as the man pulled his spear free from the wet thatched roof—then jumped down to the muddy ground without losing his balance. Mark kept running as the nearly naked man—the enemy with strange objects decorating his hair and blood gushing from his arm—as he turned and hurled his spear in one quick, violent motion.

Mark was too close to stop—to try dodging the heavy projectile by twisting or lunging to his right or left—wet, packed earth too slick for him to change direction. So he dove forward and closed his eyes—head bent down as he left his feet—thin slave body in midair as the spear flew just over his back.

Mark's chest and stomach hit the mud first—body sliding forward with his back arching—skin sticking as he went—legs bending and feet curling up over his head. Then he came to a stop—machete somehow still in his hand—the women and children still screaming and crying as Mark opened his eyes and raised his head. The man's feet were there in front of him—small and calloused. One foot raised while the other pivoted—Mark seeing the toes in the air above his head—dripping and caked around the edges with mud—sunlight reflecting off the drops of water—making them sparkle as they fell to the ground in front of his face.

Mark rolled to one side and felt the man's foot come down hard next to his head—then swung the machete and hit the man's shin—feeling the rusty metal blade cut deep into bone. The man screamed and yanked his leg away—Mark losing his grip on the plastic handle as the machete stayed with the man's shin—stiffly wobbling up and down as the man hopped away on one leg.

Mark got to his feet and chased after the man—only a few yards away—hopping and screaming with an unknown weapon somehow lodged in his lower leg. Mark ran with his upper body bent forward—knees bent and ready to tackle the man with all the ornaments in his hair. But just as he was about to make contact—to overpower the smaller man and take him to the ground—the man spun around with the machete pulled free from his shin. Mark tried to lean back—tried to stop his momentum. But the man spun with a slashing motion and ran the machete across Mark's chest—scraping and pulling at his skin with the rusty, blunt tip of the blade.

Mark slipped and fell to the ground—wondering for a brief moment if he was dying—feeling a burning line running diagonally across his chest—knowing there was already a lot of blood without even looking down.

The man stepped forward and swung the machete down at Mark—Mark somehow able to roll away before the blade made contact—retreating and somehow getting to his feet—fleeing backward as he avoided the wild swings and thrusts the man was making. The man was still scream-ing and shooting saliva from his mouth—unsure how to use the strange new weapon—Mark still retreating—staying just out of reach—letting the man thrash away at the air—watching as the man quickly tired—blood coating his arm and now the bottom half of his leg. Mark was also tired but thought he might only have a few more minutes to live—a couple hundred heartbeats to use and he refused to spend them in fear or exhaustion or any other condition that had always held him back.

Finally the man lunged too far—bent his body too far past its center of gravity—paused too long with the machete stuck out in front of him. Mark grabbed the man's wrist and pulled him in—punching the man's nose at the same time—then shaking his arm to get the machete free. He saw the man's eyes watering—a line of blood trickling down out of one nostril.

The machete soon wobbled out of the man's hand and dropped to the muddy ground. Mark grabbed the man by the neck and threw him down a few feet away—picked up the machete and stood over the exhausted, bloodied body of the enemy who nearly killed him—barely alive now as he labored to breathe—Mark examining the objects adorning his hair—the wooden crescents piercing his small ears— then looking down at the bloody arm and the blood mixing with the mud around his legs—the man's chest—expanding and contracting with more difficulty each time.

Mark never looked at the man's eyes—never saw the helpless, pleading expression—having learned that lesson just moments before and only feet away.

He swung the machete as hard as he could—doing his best to make it quick—the man making a wheezing sound and then a gurgling—Mark staring at the mud and the bloody, swirling water and the ornaments in the man's hair—waiting until the hair stopped moving—head stopped shaking and the sounds stopped coming from the man's open throat. Then he pulled out the machete—plying it back and forth until it came loose from the bone.

That night he was back in the little hut—resting on a bed of fresh leaves and bark with a thick layer of green paste covering his chest wound—across from Splinter as always. He told the older man about the two men he'd killed—asked about the battle that had taken place out in the jungle—about Michelangelo and Leonardo—whether they were alive or dead since he hadn't seen them all afternoon—neither of them having entered the small hut to check on the slave who'd saved their women and children.

Mark looked down at the blood-stained machete and talked about what he'd done—saying over and over again that he had no choice—that he had to protect them—the little boy with the bright eyes most of all.

He asked Splinter again if he was a father but Splinter sat there on the bare ground and did not respond—did not move or seem to blink or even swallow. Mark looked him over and kept talking as though Splinter understood his words—his reasons for taking two lives and how it made him feel. He asked Splinter if he'd ever killed a man but he did not wait for a response—never having received one in the past, after all—never sure if the older man even heard him talking—but sure he knew the answer anyway.

Mark cried off and on throughout the night but he never stopped talking—letting his eyes wander to the walls of the hut and out the open doorway—stars and trees and the huts that housed the rest of the tribe—his half-native son. But Splinter's eyes did not move. They did not leave his captive's face and he made no attempt to comfort the weeping man—to thank him for the killing of enemies or to assure him that his wounds would not infect.

As the night passed into early morning, the stream of

words and tears began to wear on Mark—the solitude and the helplessness—the awareness that he must now call himself a life-taker—his victims lying dead in the hot mud with the jungle already digesting their bodies.

While he waited for sleep to pause his grief, he continued talking—dreaming out loud of lives he could have lived—praying for places and people he knew in more innocent times—as a much gentler sort of beast.

STORY

"The only thing I ever killed before today was a deer—from a safe distance and with a rifle—at least fifty yards away when I pulled the trigger—half awake at seven or eight in the morning. That's what we did every weekend during hunting season—me and Steve and Geno."

.

.

"Steve owned some land where we planted a few rows of corn every year right at the edge of the trees for the deer and turkeys. We'd even put out an automatic feeder or two and go around spreading this artificial deer scent we bought at Walmart. You'd love Walmart, Splinter."

.

.

"Maybe you'd hate it. I don't know. Anyway, we'd get out there before the sun came up and climb the ladder to our deer stand. It was just a little shack ten or fifteen feet in the air with windows to shoot out of."

.

.

"Once we got everything situated we'd usually just leave the shutters down over the windows for a while—sit in a circle on the ground and lay out our breakfasts—almost always from McDonald's or some other fast-food place and almost always way too much food. We'd sit there and eat and drink coffee and give each other a hard time. Steve's wife ran a health food store and we always teased him about that. She must've weighed around a hundred pounds, maybe, and here he was almost three times that—eating a greasy breakfast sandwich and hash browns.

"Geno had the opposite situation—skinny, wiry-framed guy and his wife just kept getting bigger and bigger. And he could eat—always ate more than me and Steve—not sure where it all went but he did. His wife, according to him, hardly ate anything and just kept gaining weight.

"You've probably never even seen a fat person—have you, Splinter?"

.

.

"Wonder if I'll ever see a fat person again—get out of here before I forget what they look like."

.

.

"So, anyway, the day I shot the deer was cold—past see-your-breath cold and right into rattle-your-bones cold. It wasn't quite at the stage where any moisture in the air freezes and drifts on the wind almost like it's snowing—but it was close, I'm sure.

"The sky was clear and blue and we'd put out feed for the deer before the sun came up. After we ate our breakfasts and talked a little, we wrapped ourselves up in our sleeping bags and huddled around the space heater for a quick nap.

"It's basically a little girl's slumber party, now that I think about it. We'd get together to eat and talk and laugh and we'd sleep on the floor. The only difference is we needed an excuse to hide behind—hunting—whereas little girls are just honest about it.

"What do you think about that, Splinter?"

.

.

"So this particular morning I was the first to wake up. It was so cold, though, I'm not sure I ever really fell asleep. I got out of my sleeping bag and poured myself another cup of coffee—pushed the shutters up on one of the windows and there he was—biggest buck I'd ever seen. He was down by the feeders—eating away at the feed we'd sprinkled all over the ground before sunrise. His antlers looked like one of those chandeliers you see in ski lodges—swooping up and around on each side of his head. He ended up being a twelve pointer but he was better than that. That doesn't really say much about how nice he looked—how big and powerful he'd gotten over the years."

.

.

"I didn't waste any time reaching for my rifle. It was in its case on the ground below the window. I bent down slowly without taking my eyes off him—watching him as he kept eating—straining my neck so my eyes never went below the window frame. He looked up a couple times like he'd heard something but never turned toward the deer stand. I remember wondering what it felt like to lift a heavy set of antlers every time you wanted to look around—how it must've felt to run with those things attached to the top of your head."

.

.

"So I got my rifle out and lifted it up to the windowsill. Luckily I had a couple rounds tucked into a little side pocket of my case. I fished one out and while I was bringing it up to the chamber, my hand caught the new strap I'd attached to my rifle just a few days before. It had this big puffy shoulder pad. Steve and Geno loved to make fun of me about it.

"Anyway, the round flipped up out of my hand and sort of flew in an arc over my rifle. It came up about eye-level to me and I watched it like it was in slow motion. I knew that if it hit the ground and made too much noise, that buck would be long gone.

"I guess it's just like when we go out hunting for those birds and monkeys and snakes you all love to eat so much—any little sound can scare them away."

.

.

"So the round was up around my face—flipping through the fog of freezing breath I'd just exhaled. It was getting closer to me and I was worried if I jerked my hand up to grab it, I'd knock something else and make a bunch of noise. So instead I leaned into it and let it drop down into the little pocket on the front of my coat. It all happened in slow motion and, somehow, I managed not to make a sound—didn't panic and the buck still had no idea what was about to happen to him—or how close he'd just come to escaping. Steve and Geno, of course, refused to believe me when I told them—wouldn't shut up about how big a liar I was on our way home."

.

.

"So I took a couple breaths—fished the round out of my pocket and loaded it into the chamber. I looked through my scope and the buck was still there—still eating that feed out there in the cold—weak morning sun shining on his light brown coat and those massive antlers.

"There wasn't any wind and we'd already calculated the distance and the elevation so there wasn't much to the shot—such a big target—body turned broadside almost like he wanted me to take him down.

"He dropped right there where he was standing—probably never even knew what happened."

.

.

"The funny part is, Steve and Geno were asleep until I pulled the trigger. I wish you knew how loud a rifle is, Splinter—especially inside a small shack with most of the shutters still closed.

"They both started scrambling to get out of their sleeping bags—screaming and looking around wide-eyed like we were under attack or something. Steve even rolled against the space heater and burned his hand a little.

"I think I must've laughed for at least fifteen minutes."

.

.

"I miss those guys. I wonder what they'd say if they could see me now."

SHOW

The hotel conference room was silent—unlit except for the bright overhead lights positioned around its center—reaching over temporary walls of black curtains—tangled cables snaking underneath the loose fabric.

Mark sat there and focused on maintaining eye contact with the famous journalist—both of them clean-shaven and wearing clean clothes with freshly vacuumed carpet beneath their polished leather shoes—breathing filtered and mechanically cooled air. He waited for the next question—the next attempt by the older man to extract something quotable—a sound-bite for the commercials.

INTERVIEWER: What were these other fires for were they ceremonial in nature did they only have them at specific times or-or-or specific nights?

MARK: Every full moon they built a big bonfire out in the middle of the village—even if it was raining.

INTERVIEWER: And what was your role what did they expect of you other than to carry the wood, of course.

Mark sat back in his chair—shoving his toes forward in his stiff new shoes—grabbing the armrests and feeling his knuckles tighten. He glanced at the two cameras he could see in the corners of the little black-curtained partition—black circles behind clear, shining glass. The famous journalist raised a finger to get Mark's attention and shook his head—pulling his subject's eyes back to where they needed to be—back to the soft, puffy bags sitting on the older man's cheeks.

MARK: They made me have sex with some of the women—some sort of ritual—fertility ritual, I guess.

INTERVIEWER: How many women?

MARK: I'm not sure—different one every night the moon was full. After a while I made sure to close my eyes or look away—just zoned out until it was over.

INTERVIEWER: Until it was over meaning—that—that you—that it was over after you had—

The famous journalist sat up straight and motioned with his hands—printouts in one and pen in the other. Mark refused to give in to the prodding—to finish the older man's sentence with the graphic details he desired. He looked down at the floor instead—stared at the repeating patterns in the carpet as the famous journalist's cadence slowed—mouth open as he begged for more—pleading with Mark to give him what he wanted.

After the older man had stopped talking and a few seconds of silence had passed, Mark felt the famous journalist sliding forward out of his chair—cameras moving to follow him as he carefully kneeled less than an arm's length away—soft, wrinkled hand pressing into the carpet where Mark's eyes had been focusing.

INTERVIEWER: I know it's hard to talk about, Mark, but the world needs to know what you went through what incredible obstacles you overcame and-and-and the impossible odds you had to beat in order to escape.

Mark watched the carpet with the famous journalist's fingers digging down into it—the delicate white hand supporting a portion of the older man's weight—pulsating patches of red near the flexing joints—pockets of blood waiting for the pressure to ease.

MARK: After a while I started faking it—went through the motions for a few minutes and then faked it. I didn't want to leave any of my kids behind when I left—when we made our escape.

Tears pooled in the lower lids of Mark's eyes—enough to notice but not enough to overflow and send drops sliding down his cheeks—white knuckles and stiff jaw muscles holding most of them back—eyes and mind racing to find something else to focus on.

INTERVIEWER: What was the old man the witch doctor doing during these-these-these rituals these full moon nights?

Mark breathed deep—shoulders rising and then dipping—chest filling and deflating—neck stretching and twisting as he cleared his throat.

MARK: He was in charge of everything. He'd put together a bundle of bark and leaves and whatever else and get it smoking—blow the smoke all over the woman and wave the bundle around inside the hut—the tiny hut where everything happened. Then he'd start the chanting—the dancing.

INTERVIEWER: Why didn't you resist? Why didn't you struggle when they tried forcing you into this-this-this nonconsensual sexual encounter this forced copulation?

Mark finally looked up to meet the famous journalist's eyes—still down on one feeble knee in front of him—soft, wrinkly hands now loosely clasped with an elbow resting on his thigh—close enough for Mark to smell the coffee on his breath and the cologne he was wearing.

It had been at least an hour since Mark first sat down—at least an hour with no water and no break to stretch his legs or to use the bathroom. He looked at the glare coming off the shiny skin near the older man's hairline—the perfect hair with a gleam from some product—some gel or cream Mark never bothered with anymore.

MARK: I'd been fighting since the moment they found me in the jungle. At a certain point you just give up and do what they want—whatever they tell you to do, you do it. I'm sure you would have done the same thing—climbed on top of whatever woman they put in front of you—if you still can.

With the famous journalist already responding—words and stuttered syllables pouring out of his mouth—Mark stood up and walked toward the place where the black curtains came together. He grabbed an edge of the fabric and swung it to the side—revealing the rest of the dark hotel confer-ence room—stacks of chairs pushed back against the walls and the glowing red exit signs above multiple sets of double doors.

CHAPTER
EIGHT

FACT

Soon after the battle—after Mark had killed the two men—the one with the yellow feathers and his partner with the strange ornaments dangling over his ears—six women and girls that Mark had never seen before showed up in the village. Some had strands of rope wrapped around their arms—pieces of bone and pottery tied into their hair. Within a day or two, though, their hair had been cut short and everything was taken from them—strips of cloth cut away from their bodies—empty gourds ripped from their hands—paint washed from their skin.

Mark rested inside the tiny hut and watched the village through the open doorway—slowly recovering from his chest wound on a thick, springy layer of leaves and bark—only moving when the Ninja Turtles came in to change his bedding. He could see the six women and girls inside their hut when the sun was low in the evenings—huddled together as they were all too afraid to venture out—knees up to their mouths and short, choppy strands of hair standing up from their heads.

Every morning Mark woke up to Splinter leaning over him—spreading more of the green paste onto the gouge that went across his chest—the jagged, swollen line where the machete had ripped into his skin. It only hurt when he moved, though—scabs breaking—puss dripping down his stomach and over his ribs. But there wasn't much blood after the first day and night—never any sting from an infection. Day after day Mark carefully monitored his symptoms—examined his wound and watched the village—resting inside the tiny hut—waiting to heal or die.

"That's my son," Mark said one afternoon—his first shaky venture outside the hut since the battle.

He was standing over a circle of women and children near the place where they built the full moon bonfires—gray crater sloping down into the packed brown earth—chunks of charred wood scattered within the ashes. They were playing a game Mark had never seen before—laughing and joking with each other as they took turns tossing sticks into the middle of the circle. Mark watched the little boy more than the game—watched him smile and his clumsy laugh and the way he grabbed at his mother's shoulders as she knelt beside him.

"I'm taking him," Mark continued—talking to no one in particular—none of the women or children paying any attention to him—engrossed in their game—accustomed to hearing the strange sounds from the strange man who had saved their lives less than a month earlier.

"When he's old enough. When he stops needing so much milk. I'm taking him home."

After a while Mark reached down and touched the top of the boy's head. His son looked up and studied Mark's face—curious eyes tracing down his beard and neck to the green stripe running diagonally across his chest. The boy studied the wound for a long time—then looked back up and met Mark's eyes.

It was another two or three weeks before they forced Mark back into the jungle—back to the long hours of slave labor he'd grown accustomed to before the battle—forcing him out of the tiny hut one morning after Splinter applied the green paste—Raphael stepping inside and motioning for Mark to follow him—no thrust of a spear—no sweeping strike with one of the long, flexible sticks.

A group of men was waiting at the edge of the village. Mark still had the machete and carried it now in his right hand—feeling his chest as he walked—new, papery skin crinkling with every breath—feeling the unbalanced weight of the broken machete—bouncing the blade up and down as he reached the group—suddenly worried he might have to fight again.

But after an hour or so of walking—after his heart slowed and steadied—he understood there would be no battle. The men were relaxed and took their time—trying to home in on the sounds of monkeys and birds up in the jungle canopy. They did not talk and none of them, not even Raphael, made any effort to beat or bully Mark.

He felt less like a slave since the battle—beds of fresh leaves and bark to rest on—healing green paste each morning and now with the lack of beatings. But when they found a fallen tree—broken, decaying branches deemed good enough to be used for firewood—it was assumed by all that Mark would carry the load. So he was soon scurrying around lifting the designated pieces of wood—straining and struggling with them cradled in his arms—his masters marching in front and behind him just as before.

On another trip into the jungle—just a week or so later—the men stopped at the river for their midday break. Donatello and Raphael were the only Ninja Turtles left after the battle. Two older boys had replaced the dead men in the hunting party—one of them now carrying Leonardo's bow and metal-tipped arrows as he passed by Mark at the edge of the water—Mark wondering why he hadn't seen the bodies— why he hadn't seen the bodies of the two men he'd killed either—noticing how all that was left of the battle were the cuts and bruises still visible on some of the survivors—addition of the six women and girls to their tribe.

The men rested along the bank of the river as Mark sat alone near the flowing water—not swimming for fear of infecting the wound on his chest—fear of what might happen if he let go of the machete he now carried everywhere. His scar was mostly healed by now—shiny pink skin stretched and creased in hairless patches. But there were still scabs where the deepest gouges had been and Splinter was still applying the green paste each morning.

Mark stood up and stretched—then walked over and sat on the ground beside the boy with Leonardo's bow and arrows—watching him as he inspected the wooden shafts. They had splintered in places and, over time, would warp and bend.

"Those were Leonardo's," Mark said—the boy glancing up at him with a smile on his young face. "I guess I could start calling you Leonardo—cut a couple eyeholes in a blue piece of cloth—maybe tie a turtle shell to your back. How does that sound?"

The boy looked up again with the same smile—lifting one of the arrows and holding it out to Mark. Mark looked down at it and then looked around at the other men—some sleeping—some trying to spear fish at the edge of the river. He turned back to the boy and grabbed the arrow's wooden shaft. The boy let go and Mark examined the metal tip—the little black feathers attached to the other end. He held the arrow out in front of him and closed one eye—checking the straightness of the shaft.

Once Mark had finished inspecting the arrow he looked up and saw the boy reaching for the bow—two hands dragging the heavy, curved wood as thick as the boy's arm. It was dark and polished smooth by an unknown number of hands—string black and pulled taut by the tension in the bow. Mark flicked the string hard with his middle finger and watched it vibrate—a low hum that slowly disappeared.

He took the bow and held it together with the arrow and the machete in his lap—watching the boy—waiting for what came next. They were both in the shade—beneath the thick jungle canopy of interlaced branches, leaves and vines—both able to see the river just feet away—sun sparkling over the flowing water—no wind and somehow no sweat on any of the tribesmen—Mark wiping his forehead with the back of his hand as he wondered what he should do—the other hunters taking notice of him now—Raphael and Donatello and all the rest—all on their feet and quickly walking toward him.

Soon he was surrounded by the entire hunting party—gesturing and whispering jokes to each other. One of them came close and pointed toward a tree—twenty yards or so from where Mark was sitting. Then the men between Mark and the tree parted as he stood and turned to face it—Raphael saying something that caused all the men to laugh and back away suddenly—giving Mark an exaggerated amount of room in case he missed the target.

Another man called out to the group and they all retreated even farther—scattering among the trees and underbrush. Mark could still see their faces, though—amused eyes watching him between wide, low-hanging leaves—peeking around the trunks of trees. He felt sweat beading and dripping down his face as he spun around in a circle—watching them all giggling as they scurried to their hiding places. He tried to laugh along but his heart was pounding and his hand kept clinching the machete—clinging to the only connection he had to the outside world.

Mark tried to focus on his breathing—chest filling past full as he turned again toward the tree they had assigned him as a target—exhaling as he tossed the machete a few feet away and watched it hit the ground—metal sound mixing with the laughter and the shifting feet of all the men. Then he raised the bow and tried to figure out how to load the arrow—no groove on the blunt end of the thin shaft to hold the string steady—no notch above the handle of the bow in which to rest the slender projectile. Mark was unsure as he adjusted the arrow and the bow many times—causing more laughter and more exaggerated retreats—more sweat from his pores as the men yelled and screamed and scrambled through the jungle all around him.

Eventually he got the blunt end of the arrow against the string—rested the shaft along the top of his hand—then began pulling the arrow back as he looked toward the target. He'd seen the much smaller men easily stretch the string back and shoot arrows so far they lost sight of them—sometimes spending hours tracking them down—so high up into the tangled branches that some of them never landed. But Mark found the string was so tight—wood of the bow so strong—he barely moved the arrow—trying again and again as his arm began to shake—teeth showing as he struggled with the primitive weapon—the tribesmen howling even louder—even farther away.

Mark finally moved the string as his arm continued trembling with effort—finally pulled the arrow back as he worried about it slipping from the string—then released it and felt his body lunge forward. He heard the whoosh of the arrow and the small hum of the black string—watched the sad wobbling of the arrow as it rose in an arc slightly higher than his head—then fell to the ground at least five feet short of the tree—bow and string still vibrating in his hands.

The men came running—screaming through the jungle as Mark dropped the bow and quickly picked up the broken machete. Some of the men went to the arrow—pointing and laughing and looking at Mark—turning toward the tree and then looking down at the arrow. Some came to inspect the bow and quickly had him surrounded—pointing and laughing just the same—their eyes alternating between Mark and the missed target.

That evening Mark sat outside the tiny hut he shared with Splinter and watched a full moon rising over the treetops—orange, tropical sun slipping away behind him—behind the rough reed walls and leaky thatched roof. He looked up at the dark gray craters and the pale yellow brightness of the moonscape—thought about the Apollo missions—the men that blasted off into outer space to go walk on the moon—to float around and laugh together in zero gravity—watched by millions back on Earth from their cozy living rooms with their black-and-white TVs—things that had taken place years before he was even born.

He leaned back against the outer wall of the hut—watched the women carefully stacking sticks over a tiny flame—beginnings of another bonfire. It seemed to Mark like it'd been a long time since the last full moon. They must have skipped one or two of their twisted little ceremonies, he thought—letting him recover from his chest wound. But now the ritual would begin again and he wondered who it would be—which woman's body would be painted and laid out for him on the floor of the tiny hut—how long it would take him to do what was always demanded and if it would ever stop—if he'd ever be free to sleep unwatched when tired—eat when hungry or love a woman in private.

Mark stood up and strolled around the perimeter of the village—went from hut to hut and peeked through each dark doorway. Most were empty as a crowd had begun to form around the young bonfire—thick, ground-hugging smoke giving them all a reprieve from the blood-sucking insects out for their evening meals.

But Mark didn't mind giving up a little blood. He was looking for food—pieces of meat left clinging to little bones—scraps of fruit still attached to torn and oxidizing peels—streaks of boiled and mashed tubers left painted onto the insides of gourds.

Inside the largest hut—the one with bundles of herbs hanging from the ceiling—Mark saw several gourds around a smoldering cooking fire. He walked inside and sat down next to the still-warm coals—facing the jagged rectangle of the open doorway—the fading light and the black jungle under the first few stars.

He let go of the machete's handle and felt its weight dangling from the rope he'd recently tied around his wrist—coarse fibers rubbing his skin raw.

The first gourd—the largest—held a few handfuls of the white, mashed tubers the tribe always ate. As Mark raised the first handful to his mouth he sensed movement somewhere close to him—a shifting body near the edge of his field of vision—subtle vibrations of another living thing—or maybe just that unmistakable feeling that something is there in the dark—watching.

Mark reached for the machete as he twisted his head to see who was there—felt the handful of boiled tubers squeeze and ooze between his palm and the machete's hard plastic handle. He saw the shape of a woman standing there—inching toward him along the wall. As he relaxed his grip on the machete he looked more closely and saw a small child clinging to her chest—covered with a dark cloth or skin—a blanket over most of the tiny body—chubby legs and feet sticking out the bottom. As the woman came closer Mark recognized her as his son's mother.

She came closer and closer through the smoky darkness of the hut—eyes locked on Mark and limp little legs dangling across her abdomen. Mark shifted his body and wondered if he should stand—turning in a crouched position to watch the woman as she walked up beside him.

She stood there within a foot or two—reaching down after a moment to turn over one of the empty gourds—taking a seat next to Mark on its rounded surface—all done in one smooth motion so as not to wake their sleeping child.

They looked at each other through the dark, stuffy air—Mark noticing her odor blending with the varied smells of the hut—body and smoke and the drying jungle herbs—sour milk of his son's breath. The cloth was covering his son's head and Mark watched as he shifted beneath it—still asleep but awake enough to search for a more comfortable position. Mark moved slowly to touch the boy's hand. It had come reaching out of the cloth and was now resting on his mother's shoulder. Mark touched it with one finger—soft, delicate skin with tiny bones beneath. Soon the little fingers stretched and then curled into a fist—his son's head turning once more under the cloth.

A peaceful baby sound rose to Mark's ears. He smiled as he watched the boy—touching the tiny fist again with his filthy, calloused finger—trying to see the cloth push out as his son took in a breath.

That night—full moon rising to the top of the sky—Mark was escorted to the hut he shared with Splinter. He was not poked or shoved or beaten and Raphael didn't even try to take the machete from his hand—placing his open palms gently onto Mark's back and applying a light amount of guiding pressure—other men walking beside and in front of him.

As they passed the bonfire all the women and children stopped dancing—stood in a tightly packed group on the opposite side of the flames—then resumed their practiced moves as Mark approached the doorway to the hut—the men leaving him to walk inside alone.

Splinter was there—ever-present old man with the charcoal tracings curving around his weathered face— leaning over a woman with a smoking bundle of leaves and bark in his cupped hands—wafting smoke over the naked, painted body as burning flecks of ash floated down to the woman's skin. Mark watched her flinch and struggle—protest unlike any of the others that had come before.

He saw Raphael enter the hut and quickly walk past him—kneeling down to pin the woman's arms to the ground above her head. Mark lowered his eyes to look at her—hair cut short and her terrified face covered in ocher paint—one of the women who'd arrived after the battle—spoils of war, maybe—refugees maybe or maybe completely unrelated to the violence that had taken place.

Two more men entered the hut and struggled to control the woman's legs—Splinter ignoring the commotion as he leaned forward and started chanting near her ear—the woman still kicking and flailing her body—grunting through clinched teeth. She's afraid, Mark thought—angered by her helplessness—desperate for the simple dignity of keeping her legs closed.

Splinter soon stood up and began marching around the woman's body—chanting and dancing and waving the smoking bundle—voices and stomping feet growing louder and louder from the bonfire outside. He stopped in front of Mark and they stood there looking at each other—little man with black lines painted on his face—tall, hairy slave with a shiny pink scar crossing his chest—filtered firelight hitting their bodies and smoke rising between them.

Mark waited—watched Splinter as he began to dance again—shuffling in a tight circle around Mark's shriveled body—waving the bundle over his shoulders and in front of the cloth he used to cover himself. Then he felt Splinter grab his forearm and start to pull him toward the woman's feet. He looked down at the still-struggling woman's face as he stepped toward her—watched her try to scream as Raphael covered her mouth with his hand.

The two men at the woman's feet had her legs spread and her knees bent. Mark knew there was no sense in protesting—knew it would only make things worse to look again at the woman's face—wet, pleading eyes and the uneven clumps of hair.

He dropped to his knees without any prompting—lifted his cloth as the chanting grew louder—shadows on the walls of the hut leaping higher as dancing bodies moved wildly in front of the tall flames outside. He placed his palms beside the woman's shoulders and lowered himself down until he was on top of her—staring at the packed-earth floor beside her head.

After the dancing and the chanting had stopped—after the woman was taken away and the bonfire had finally died down—Mark sat in the dark, tiny hut—across from Splinter as always. He told him about seeing his son and his son's mother earlier that evening while scavenging for food—told him about the boy's chubby little legs and his sleepy head—turning from side to side beneath his blanket—the tiny hand that reached out and the fingers that curled themselves into a fist.

He looked down at the machete and the rope wrapped around his wrist. Splinter sat in silence without even blinking—there but not there—charcoal lines still curling around his face. Mark thought again about killing him—hacking him to death with the broken, rusty blade he held in his hand. He thought about the scared woman with her face covered in ocher paint—arms and legs pinned down—firelight bouncing off her naked body—fragrant, smoke-filled air inside the crowded hut.

He confessed to Splinter his deceit—how he'd taken no pleasure in the act—the sudden plunge toward the center of the woman's body—how he'd made them all think another full moon ritual had been consummated. But Splinter did not respond—did not move or swallow or even seem to take a breath. Mark looked him over and kept talking as though Splinter understood his words—his admission of guilt—his refusal to contribute anymore of his DNA to the medicine man and his tribe.

Mark smiled and laughed as he talked about escaping and leaving behind no bastards—no pregnant women whose babies would never know their father. He let his eyes wander to the walls of the hut and out the open doorway—stars and trees and huts that housed the rest of the tribe—his half-native son now growing so fast. But Splinter's eyes did not move. They did not leave his captive's face and he made no attempt to discourage the tall, bearded man—to assure him there would be no escape—no triumphant return to whatever strange world he came from.

As the night passed into early morning, the darkness and the quiet began to wear on Mark—the solitude and the helplessness—the realization of how small his victory had actually been—his refusal to procreate bringing into focus just how dire his situation was. So he kept talking—dreaming out loud of a resurrection from his jungle tomb—praying for the strength to carry himself back to life—emerging one day from the untamed wild to begin again—his son held high—riding on his father's broad shoulders.

STORY

"I'll have to introduce him to things little by little. He'll probably be scared of just about everything at first—don't you think, Splinter?"

.

.

"We'll probably come across some fishermen or poachers or miners or maybe a little farming village. Their clothes are going to be strange to him—their hats and boats and dirt bikes and plates and forks and strange new foods and everything else about them. I'll have to keep him close and figure out how to calm him down."

.

.

"Ice cream. I can't wait to see his face the first time I give him ice cream. The cold is going to be the biggest shock. What's the coldest thing around here, Splinter?"

.

.

"Anyway, it's going to be fun introducing him to all that stuff. We'll have to get to the nearest big town as soon as possible—probably in some fisherman's boat—sure the motor will terrify him at first. Then, once I get in contact with the U.S. Embassy, we'll get a big fancy pickup or SUV to come pick us up and take us to the capital—maybe even a helicopter—who knows. They'll put us up in a fancy hotel downtown and he'll stare out the windows at all the tall buildings. I'll have wrestled him into some clothes by this point and he'll probably be tugging at his shirt and pants as he stares outside with his nose touching the glass.

"It'll probably be hard for me to get used to clothes too—at first, anyway—wearing shoes again."

.

.

"It'll be nice to get him into a hotel room—close all the curtains once he gets tired of looking out the windows—shut off all the lights—get him to relax and go to sleep beside me—cover him up and turn on the TV with the volume down low.

"And then, maybe the next day, they'll come pick us up and bring us to the embassy. I'll probably have to go through some questioning—let them do whatever they have to do to verify that I am who I say I am. I'll insist on having a doctor take a look at my son and make sure he's alright. Then I'll insist on them issuing him a U.S. passport. Have you ever seen one of those, Splinter? A passport? I had mine in my pack when the Ninja Turtles found me—long gone by now, I'm sure."

.

.

"After we jump through all their hoops at the embassy, we'll get in a car and head back to the hotel—our story probably already leaked to the press—probably be some photographers out on the street as we leave—maybe even some TV cameras."

.

.

"We'll probably just hide out in our hotel room until our passports come through and we can get plane tickets back to Denver. Every day will bring something new for him—ice cream, TV, the tall buildings, cars—then the plane ride and looking out the window at the ocean and the cities and the trees. We might even fly right over this terrible place."

.

.

"My mother and sister will meet us at the airport. There'll probably be some cameras and reporters crowding around to ask us questions—maybe even some directors interested in making a movie about me. I'll tell them about you, Splinter—your twisted little full moon game—the battle and about being a slave—this machete and the raft I'll build with it and how I managed to escape with my toddler son down the river—how I somehow did it all by myself.

"Do you think people would want to see something like that?"

.

.

"I guess it's time I gave him a name—my son."

.

.

"We should probably stick with the Ninja Turtles theme—a character I like, of course—that's strong but not too rebellious or mean or lazy or too connected to all the rest of you."

.

.

"Mondo. I'll call him Mondo."

.

.

"What do you think, Splinter?"

SHOW

The conference room carpet felt soft and springy under Mark's feet—burgundy with neat rows of vacuum lines barely visible—fibers gripping the soles of his shoes as he walked toward the double doors that led out to the hotel lobby.

Mark pushed through the doors and stepped onto the polished, white tile floor—sudden rush of noise and moving bodies—sun-filled windows and lazy background music as he looked around for a bathroom. In front of him was a busy front desk with new arrivals pulling wheeled suitcases—children bouncing off hard couches as their parents checked in.

INTERVIEWER: It's just over there. I came out and did the same thing earlier.

The famous journalist had walked up beside Mark and placed a hand on his back—extending his other arm to point toward a space at the far end of the long front desk.

MARK: Thanks.

Mark walked off without turning to look at the older man—navigating the uneven lines of tired travelers—suitcases and sturdy hotel furniture and loud, restless children. He appreciated the obstacles—the distraction they provided—focusing on how to make it through as quickly and politely as possible—sunshine hitting his face through tall windows adding to the difficulty of his task.

The bathroom was clean and empty—a speaker somewhere playing the same bland music he'd heard in the lobby. He took his time in the stall—checking his new cellphone and flipping through pictures he'd recently taken—baseball scores and breaking news headlines.

Eventually he washed his hands in the sink farthest from the door—checked his hair and teeth in the mirror—adjusted his shirt and his belt—then stood there looking at himself—staring with a crumpled paper towel in one hand—moving to leave the bathroom only when two men pushed open the door—breaking the stillness as they talked and laughed and marched past him toward the wall of urinals.

INTERVIEWER: Ready?

Mark nodded—meeting the famous journalist's eyes as he sat down again inside the conference room's little partition—black curtains boxing them in—bright lights and puffy microphones hovering over their heads.

The older man turned and nodded at the cameras in the corners behind him—causing nobs to be turned and buttons to be pushed. Then the big black eyes of glass and plastic lifted and swung around to focus on Mark's face.

INTERVIEWER: Let's talk about your children for a moment how are they doing?

MARK: They're fine—good.

INTERVIEWER: Are they adjusting well how are they assimilating to all the new things the-the-the food and the weather and the language and so on?

MARK: Fine. My mother watches them when I'm not around. She's a better cook than I am—better at teaching them things.

INTERVIEWER: When you're not around where do you go what do you do?

MARK: Well, I'm around most of the time. I take them to the park a lot. I'm not great at being indoors for too long yet—they're even worse.

The two men looked at each other and smiled—Mark wondering how friendly he should be—how bad he should feel for what he'd said earlier—how much he should let his guard down. He glanced up at the cameras in the corners— then down at the printouts in the pale, soft hands across from him—all the talking points and biographical details the older man was trying to use to get what he wanted. He thought about the millions of critics that would be watching him—listening and judging from their couches in a few weeks—threatening every second to turn the channel if the famous journalist couldn't deliver.

INTERVIEWER: My grandchildren are about the same age.

I can't imagine them being any more excited about going to the park than they already are.

Mark stayed silent—nodded and smiled and looked down at the older man's shoes—shiny black leather with thin laces and no creases.

INTERVIEWER: How is their health? I'm sure they endured a lot of hardship as you made your way out of the jungle.

MARK: They're fine—great—gaining weight fast and bouncing off the walls like any other kids.

INTERVIEWER: Were they dehydrated at first or malnourished? What did the doctors say that examined them immediately following your-your-your emergence from the wild?

MARK: It's a rainforest so there's plenty of water.

INTERVIEWER: Well yes, I suppose that's true but what about food wasn't food a problem and-and-and what about disease or infection?

MARK: We managed. I was able to find some fruit along the way.

INTERVIEWER: You know we tracked down the man who found you and he said that you weren't alone that there was someone else with you.

Mark tried to maintain eye contact with the famous journalist—tried to think of something to say—the best way to explain what had happened—how he'd managed to save himself and his children.

INTERVIEWER: A woman a native woman. I mean I just don't understand why that little detail hasn't been part of your story thus far so-so-so can you tell us who she is who she was?

CHAPTER
NINE

FACT

Months went by with little change to Mark's day-to-day existence within the tribe. The men took him hunting—their pack animal as always—loaded down with logs and bundles of fruit and the lifeless bodies of any animals they were lucky enough to kill—less now since Leonardo's death. They never went so far into the jungle that they could not return to the village before nightfall—did not beat Mark anymore or try to take the machete which he carried with him always—dangling from his wrist when his hands were busy with the things he was forced to carry.

The rains grew heavier and more frequent as time passed—regular bursts of lightning and thunder and strong gusts of wind—the weather eventually returning to its gentler state—light showers or an indecisive mist—sometimes only fog rolling through the tall jungle trees.

The full moons rose at sundown every month or so and Mark always walked voluntarily into the tiny hut—Splinter always there with another smoking bundle—bonfire roaring just outside the open doorway—repetitive chanting and fevered dancing.

Mark would lift his cloth and lay himself down on top of

another naked woman—smooth skin covered in sweat and ocher paint—some of them screaming and fighting—others resigned to their fate—always faceless as Mark stared at the ground—playing the part of an obedient slave performing the task his masters had given him—without protest—without complaint.

There were no more battles during these months and Mark could feel himself growing stronger. The wound across his chest slowly healed—shiny pink scar stretching from his collarbone over to the bottom of his rib cage.

He sat with the women and children during every meal and ate whatever they left him—fruit peels and little bones—unwanted organs and bitter, unripened tubers. He would sit off to the side and watch Mondo, his son—stumbling around the adults with the other toddlers as everyone ate—never too far from his mother.

Mark began carving wooden toys for him with the machete and they played together after some of their meals—walking little elephants and jaguars through the dirt—roaring and showing their teeth. Mondo grew stronger every day—Mark chasing him around the village as they played—testing him—holding his toys above his head to make him jump—wrestling with him near the bonfire crater—waiting for him to gain the strength he'd need for their escape.

In the meantime Mark was soon hard at work carving wooden toys for all the children—wooden spoons and combs for the women—arrows and spears for the men. He even made a few wooden balls and a bat and tried to teach the tribe how to play baseball—scratching out base paths in the dirt and marking two trees at the edge of the jungle as foul poles. But no one had the patience or the interest to learn the strange game—the balls soon lost in the underbrush—one of the tribesmen walking off with the bat.

Everyone kept coming to him with new requests—new things they wanted carved or old things repaired or altered. He was rarely taken into the jungle once his carvings became popular—kept busy in the village nearly all day—the Ninja Turtles only taking him to see animals they wanted him to carve or to carry the logs they burned in the full moon bonfires.

"I need rope," Mark said one day to the group of women standing over him—his back against a tree at the edge of the village—one of the women holding his son's newest wooden jaguar in her hands—intimating that they each wanted their own. "If all of you want one, I'm going to need a lot of rope."

Mark stood up from the ground and walked toward the largest hut—fingers tapping against the machete's scarred plastic handle as it dangled from the rope tied around his wrist. He walked inside and let his eyes adjust to the darkness—waiting alone near the doorway for the group of women to follow—then walking over and finding a coiled rope hanging against the wall. He came back and held the rope out to the women—grabbed the little jaguar from the one who'd approached him outside—then took the rope back and gave her the jaguar—doing this several times with a smile on his face—telling them in English what each jaguar would cost—holding the rope up next to the little figurine and telling them why he needed it—his plan to escape—to build a raft and float away downriver with Mondo—back to civilization where his half-native son could have a life worth living.

For several more months Mark watched his son grow bigger and stronger and less attached to his mother—watched the boy eat solid food and drink more water and less of his mother's milk—walk and run without stumbling. He waited patiently for Mondo to be ready—capable of a journey of unknown length but guaranteed to include hardships.

There was now a collection of coiled ropes and empty gourds and a small pile of sweet-smelling bark in the corner of the hut he shared with Splinter—payments for his popular jaguar figurines. Recently, though, the men had been demanding more arrows and more metal tips from the broken machete—shrinking little by little the only thing that gave him hope—only reason he thought escape might be possible—in his hand or dangling from his wrist at all times. It worried him—the growing cache of arrows—the growing disquiet of the village—the prospect of another battle.

But Mondo was healthy and could eat anything put in front of him now—could run over the uneven packed earth of the village and never fall—play with the toys Mark had given him and be away from his mother for hours at a time.

They were almost ready to leave—to make the hard, dangerous journey—return home and live in a place a million times better and a million times safer and with a million more opportunities for Mondo to lead a fulfilling life of his own someday—to be happy and to be a part of the world.

One evening as Mark sat outside and thought about their escape, he smiled as he watched Mondo—running and laughing with another child around his age—consoling the other little boy when he fell and hurt himself. Mark watched until two women came and took the children away—then leaned back against the outer wall of the tiny hut he shared with Splinter—looked up from time to time at the sky—softening to blended sunset colors of orange and pink and purple. The women were moving around the village with gourds full of water, stacks of firewood and bundles of fruit. The men sat around in small groups—some outside in the open air and some inside the largest hut. Mark could smell the bark they sometimes burned to repel mosquitoes—sweet with something familiar to him that he could not place—a perfume or lotion or soap he'd known at one time.

Soon he watched as a woman came out of a hut and began walking toward him—taller than most and older than some—the one Mark always heard laughing the loudest during their meals. She was carrying a sleeping baby—at least a few months old but probably less than a year—Mark could not say for sure. The woman cradled the baby's head in the crook of one arm and supported its body with the other—never taking her eyes off Mark as she approached.

"Hi," Mark said—the woman standing there in front of him—silent—swaying from side to side as her baby slept.

Mark looked around but no one was taking any notice of them—women still hurrying from hut to hut and the men were still sitting together—talking and eating and gesturing with their hands when they wanted to emphasize something. Mark watched a man point toward the jungle and shout at the others he was sitting with—raising up slightly from his crouched position—imploring his audience to heed his words.

"Do you want another jaguar?" Mark asked the woman.

The woman stood in the same place—did not respond and did not move her eyes from Mark's face—stepping closer to him eventually—still swaying from side to side. There was a cloth covering much of the baby's body and she turned and pulled it down—showing Mark the baby's face—lifting the baby's limp arm as Mark watched the infant shift and slowly start to flex the muscles of its cheeks and forehead. The woman motioned with the tiny arm—motioned with her head and her whole body and somehow seemed to tell Mark something through her eyes.

"No," Mark said. "No. It's not. It can't be." He stood up and stepped away from the woman but she followed him. "I can't wait. I can't stay here even if it—"

The woman said something as Mark took another hurried step—moving with him and managing to block his path—still talking and looking up into his eyes. The baby was awake now and on the verge of crying—squinting and grimacing with toothless gums. Mark stopped and looked down at the infant—tried to find some resemblance—some sign like Mondo's bright, curious eyes. But the baby's eyes were closed and the hair was just beginning to grow—features of the tiny body too small and delicate to tell him anything.

He shook his head and walked away—going around the woman and not stopping until he'd reached the opposite end of the village—tall trees with their wide trunks and the darkness of the jungle in front of him. He turned around and looked for the woman—the tall one with the big voice and the newborn baby she thought was his—but she hadn't followed him so he stood there alone—watching life in the prehistoric village proceed just as it had for thousands of years.

That night Mark sat across from Splinter in the small hut they shared—talking to him about the baby—about the woman who presented it to him and how she must have thought he was the father. He asked Splinter about the woman—describing her as the one who laughs the loudest and is taller than most and older than some—asked him whether the baby was really his. He told him about the infant's thin hair and closed eyes—wondered how long it would take for him to be sure.

He asked Splinter if he was a father but Splinter sat there on the bare ground and did not answer—did not move or even seem to blink his eyes. Mark looked him over and kept talking as though Splinter understood his words—his nervous prognostications—the unraveling of his escape plan. He let his eyes wander to the walls of the hut and out the open doorway—stars and trees and huts that housed the rest of the tribe—his half-native son and possible second child—Mondo's half-sibling—not even knowing yet whether the baby was a boy or girl.

But Splinter's eyes did not move. They did not leave his captive's face and they did not show any concern for Mark's troubles—his fate as a father or the doubts he had about ever breaking free of the lush jungle—the living prison of leaves and bark and wet, hot dirt.

The darkness and the quiet began to wear on Mark— the solitude and the helplessness—the fear of another battle—death at the end of one savage tool or another—death or enslavement for his child—his children.

So he began to talk—to dream out loud—to pray for safety and calm—the boring, comfortable life he knew and left and now obsessed over day and night.

STORY

"My son—the one back home in Denver—he's probably the most good-hearted person I've ever known. I never really believed people could be that nice—that good—until he was born and started growing up. But maybe that's just how all kids are—who knows."

.

.

"Once when he was maybe two or three—one of the first times his mother let me take him out by myself—just the two of us. See, my wife didn't think I could handle him if he started crying or got tired or whatever. But I packed his bag—got all his toys and snacks and extra clothes and made sure I had all the emergency numbers saved in my phone. She didn't think I could do it but it wasn't a big deal.

"Anyway, I took him to this kid's fair downtown—one of those events where they block off a couple city streets and put up bouncy houses and have food vendors and music and performers dressed up like cartoon characters—easy way to rip off parents and get some extra tax dollars for the city. It'd be like you charging people for the right to dance around the bonfire every time there was a full moon. I guess you'd have to charge them in fruit or dead monkeys or something like that—rope."

.

.

"So we went to this kid's fair and my son was a little scared at first. He was still pretty young and there was a lot of noise and most of the kids were older than him. But I took him over to this girl who was painting faces and had her draw a baseball on his cheek. It had all these flames coming off it and the girl showed him with a mirror. The mirror thing was a great trick because then I had to buy a little plastic one from the girl for probably ten times what she paid for it. My son loved it, though—kept staring at that baseball on his cheek and moving it around with his tongue."

.

.

"Pretty soon we came across another little boy. He was all by himself—around my son's age—crying and looking all around—just standing there on the sidewalk. My son saw him and right away you could tell he was worried—handed me his new mirror and just stared at that little boy. We walked over to him and I went down on one knee—tried to ask him where his parents were. But the kid couldn't say a word—he was so terrified.

"My son was better with him, though—more patient—just stood there by his side—put his hand on the kid's shoulder and said 'it OK, it OK' until he finally looked up. Then my son showed him the baseball on his cheek and showed him how he could make it move with his tongue—how he watched it in his new mirror. The kid laughed a little—tears and snot smeared all over his face."

.

.

"Pretty soon his parents walked up—both huffing and puffing like they'd just run a marathon. They grabbed him and hugged him and kissed him and said they'd been looking all over for him. My son looked up at me and smiled.

"As we walked away the parents said thank you and we waved at each other—both of them barely able to take their eyes off their little boy."

.

.

"I don't know what I would've done if I'd lost my son in all that mess—all the people and food trucks and performances going on—the whole rest of the city just past a line of orange traffic cones."

.

.

"Scares me even more to think about what his mother would've done to me."

SHOW

MARK: We were alone—me, my son and my daughter. It was just the three of us.

INTERVIEWER: You're telling me that you were able to escape and spend several days and nights in the rainforest with a baby and a toddler and-and-and no food to speak of except for the fruit you say you found along the way and you did all this by yourself? Why would the man that found you lie about there being another person with you a-a-a woman a native woman?

MARK: You should ask him. I'm sure it was a shock when he first saw us—me screaming at him in English with a beard and loin cloth and two kids in my arms. Maybe he just saw something that wasn't there.

INTERVIEWER: He also seemed to think there was something strange about the whole situation something almost nefarious or-or-or artificial in some way. He told us you seemed like you were acting the whole time and-and-and that the woman the native woman seemed to pretend to not understand him when he spoke to her.

MARK: He's just—that's not how it happened—how anything happened. He's just confused, I guess.

The famous journalist looked down at his printouts—shuffling sheets of paper too fast to read anything—heel of one foot bouncing up and down. Mark relaxed a little in his chair—still feeling his heart as its tempo slowed—coolness of sweat evaporating off the exposed skin around the collar of his shirt.

INTERVIEWER: Let's go back to your time with the tribe.

The wrinkled face of the older man crumpled itself into a closed-mouth smile. He stared at Mark through squinted eyes—Mark watching the muscles along his clean-shaven, powdered jawline—flexing and twisting as he thought through his next plan of attack.

INTERVIEWER: Was there ever any kindness shown toward you by any member of the tribe or-or-or was it all spears in your back and forced insemination of their women?

MARK: I was their slave. The witch doctor treated any open wounds I had with a green paste he made from different plants. But he was just keeping me alive so I'd continue being their slave—carrying their firewood and doing whatever else they told me to do.

INTERVIEWER: But you were there for years are you saying there was no one you formed a bond with or joked with or-or-or fell in love with during all that time?

MARK: One guy would joke around with me a little bit—one of the four who seemed to be more responsible for me than the others—the ones who first found me. He'd laugh if I did something stupid—instead of getting mad and hitting me like everybody else—and sometimes he'd pretend he was going to whack me with something—fake me out and then just laugh and walk away. I didn't like that game too much.

INTERVIEWER: What happened to him?

MARK: He died. There was a battle and he never came back. Their best archer died too.

INTERVIEWER: Did he have a name? Did any of them have names?

MARK: No.

INTERVIEWER: You never figured out their names in almost three years of living with them I-I-I mean what did you call them how did you address them?

MARK: I didn't. I didn't call them anything.

The famous journalist raised a finger and scratched the side of his head above his ear—ruffling a few short hairs as the bright overhead lights reflected off his fingernail.

Mark turned his head away from the older man when he heard footsteps on the other side of the black curtains—someone trying to be quiet as they carried something—stumbling a little and then freezing where they stood.

INTERVIEWER: So the battle you mentioned can you tell us anything about that?

MARK: Sure. I guess I should start with the machete. I don't know how they got it but eventually it became my job to break off pieces of the blade and grind them down—shape them and sharpen them into arrowheads. They forced me to work on that during the night so they could still take me hunting with them during the day.

INTERVIEWER: And this was in the lead-up to the battle?

The older man lowered his hands and leaned forward—printouts dangling between his legs. He looked Mark in the eye and waited for him to continue.

MARK: I knew something was going to happen. Everybody was on edge and they kept wanting more and more arrowheads. Then one morning I woke up and everything was quiet—calm and overcast with no breeze or rain. You could tell something was going on, though. Pretty soon I started hearing whispers and shuffling feet. Then a woman came running out of the jungle—sprinting—running away from something.

INTERVIEWER: Was there a battle of some kind taking place was there another tribe attacking or-or-or was it something internal an internal conflict?

MARK: We were attacked. They were attacked—all the men—somewhere out in the jungle away from the village.

I gathered all the women and children together and guarded them. We waited and could hear the fighting going on out there—men screaming and barking orders at each other—dying.

The famous journalist sat there with his bony elbows stabbing down into his thighs—leaning forward with hands held up to his mouth in his signature pose—the one Mark had seen on countless televised interviews—leaning forward toward presidents, dictators, celebrities and regular people with strange stories like his.

MARK: We listened to the battle for a while—screams echoing through the jungle—then silence. I could hear the women and children behind me—huddled together and whispering to each other.

It wasn't long before I saw a group of warriors—four of them—running toward us from the opposite end of the village. They weren't from our tribe—their tribe, I mean. They were bigger than anyone I'd seen up to that point—bigger and stronger and with longer hair—colorful feathers and knick-knacks dangling from armbands and necklaces. Their bodies were covered in red paint and they started yelling once they saw us—high-pitched and in sync with each other—their tribe's war cry, I guess. The women and children behind me started screaming and I could feel them starting to scatter—running off to hide in one of the huts or in the jungle somewhere.

I knelt down and picked up a handful of dirt—looking back to check on my son at the same time. He was calm—just standing there next to his mother—staring right back at me like he knew everything would turn out alright.

Anyway, I crunched the dry dirt in my hand and stood up to face the four warriors. I raised the machete in my other hand and started running at them. They each had a spear—longer and thicker than the ones I'd seen before—the ones they'd been hitting and poking me with. I knew I had to dodge them—get in close where I could use the machete.

The famous journalist stayed in his signature pose—engrossed in his subject's story and well aware of the cameras peeking over Mark's shoulders—framing his pale, weathered face—furrowed brow and perfect hair.

MARK: So I juked to one side—then veered off to the other and ducked under the spears they were swinging toward me. I raised the machete as they passed and I sliced open one of their stomachs. He was already on the ground when I turned around and now I was down to three.

One of them threw his spear at me—missed and then bent down to take the dying man's spear. The three that were left started charging me again and I could see some of the women and children over their heads—still scattering but unsure where to go—screaming and some of them crying.

The men didn't lunge at me this time and I stayed where I was. We danced around each other for a little bit—trying to fake each other out—them with their spears and me with my handful of dirt and broken machete. We looked at each other and I could see how confused they were by me—my eyes and beard and different-colored skin from theirs. It must've been like coming across an alien—living your whole life with only a certain kind of person—certain kind of hair and then all the sudden you see something totally different but still familiar—still human.

They started talking to each other—trying to figure out what I was, probably. Then one of them rushed toward me—swung his spear at me and the point of it cut across my chest. I backpedaled and nearly lost my balance—then threw my handful of dirt in his eyes—got my feet under me again and lunged forward and slit his throat.

The last guy didn't look so confident after that. We stood there across from each other—panting and sweating—him with his spear held up like he wasn't sure whether he should throw it or not—feet shuffling like he wanted to run away.

One-on-one it was easier—even without a handful of dirt to throw in his face.

INTERVIEWER: What about the fourth man?

MARK: What?

INTERVIEWER: You said in the beginning there were four warriors but you've only told us how three of them died.

MARK: The last one ran back into the jungle—back the way they'd come.

The famous journalist smiled—raised his eyebrows and nodded his head—leaned back in his chair as Mark felt the sweat again on his neck—felt his hands squeezing the arms of his chair—his toes curling inside his stiff shoes as memories flashed across his mind's eye.

CHAPTER
TEN

FACT

MARK WOKE UP TO CALM AND QUIET IN THE VILLAGE—ONLY able to hear birds squawking and bouncing on thin branches high up in the trees. Splinter was gone and Mark was almost cold—still curled into a ball on the packed-earth floor—no blanket—no bed or mosquito net or pillow.

There'd been a dream playing out in his head and he fought hard to fall back asleep—kept his eyes closed and pushed the cold away—ignored the damp morning smells and his aching body.

The memory of the dream stayed with him for a minute or two—tastes and laughs and the boring scenes of boring people he once knew doing boring things he once hated. But then he was opening his eyes—stretching his thin legs and arms—looking over to Splinter's side of the hut—knowing already the older man was not there—drab reed walls and empty, uneven floor—nothing clean or smooth or safe or permanent.

Mark scratched the line of pink skin running across his chest—puffy, permanent reminder of how close he'd come to dying—how near his adventure had been to its merciful completion.

"Another day," he whispered—eyes staring up toward the ceiling. "Another day another day another day."

There was still no sound from the rest of the village outside the tiny hut—chattering birds that didn't really count as noise—as much a part of the jungle as the trees and the rain. Mornings were always slow—everyone but Mark sleeping late—slowly coming to life a few hours after sunrise—men sitting around in small groups—women and children fetching water—tossing wood onto smoldering fires.

"Another day. Today. Come what may," Mark said—still on his back with his arms and legs stretched out—staring up at the fraying strands of the thatched ceiling. "A slave I'll die if I stay. If I stay." Mark rolled over and slowly began to stand up. "But I'll probably die even if I run away."

He walked to the open doorway—stretching his limbs and blinking his eyes—joints and vertebrae popping as he breathed deep—bending and twisting his body.

The blue-gray morning light bounced off the low, heavy clouds—fog lifting slowly through the trees. The sun hadn't made it above the treetops yet and he knew no one would be out of their huts for at least another hour or so. Mark enjoyed the early mornings he spent alone—when he could do as he pleased and could pretend he was there out of choice—a vacation he chose to extend indefinitely. He enjoyed the coolness and the quiet and the chance to relax, however briefly, without Splinter or anyone else watching over him—pretend cup of coffee in one hand and a newspaper in the other.

Mark was standing there in the doorway—watching the fog

floating up to join the clouds overhead—when he saw all the men of the tribe silently file out of the largest hut—bodies painted in ocher and black—weapons held at their sides as they jogged together. They made no noise and were gone in just a few seconds—leaving Mark to wonder if he'd really seen them or not—if he was crazy or maybe still asleep.

But then the women and children came out of all the other huts—coalescing near the center of the village—around the gray, sunken place where they made their full moon bonfires. Mark watched them from the doorway—heads whipping around as they scanned the edges of the jungle—younger children already starting to cry—two or three babies still asleep against their mother's chests.

The sun was beginning to peek through the tops of the trees behind Mark's tiny hut—clouds just starting to break apart. He watched as the women shaded their eyes—weak morning light hitting their faces and bodies—wet, muddy ground and the sloping circle of ash where no one stepped or stood. They kept scanning the jungle and whispering to each other—Mark watching them from the doorway—everyone listening for sounds of battle to begin echoing through the village.

Mark turned his head and looked down at the stash of supplies he'd slowly accumulated—payments for wooden spoons and little figurines he'd carved over the previous months—piled in the corner of the hut that had somehow become his home. He studied the coiled ropes and empty gourds for what seemed like a long time—then turned back toward the women and children when he heard the first sounds coming from the jungle—first angry, guttural screams of men—attacking or about to attack—killing or dying. He gripped the machete and felt his body tense— deep breaths filling his lungs—ribcage pushing out and stretching the shiny pink scar on his chest.

"Screw it," Mark said—moving quickly to the pile of supplies—bending down to tie all the coils of rope together—leaning over to look out the doorway every few seconds—listening to the whispering women and the crying children—the battle sounds now coming more frequently from the jungle.

Once he finished with the ropes Mark threw them over his head—draping the coils over one shoulder and under the opposite arm—fibers scratching at his back—intersecting with the scar near the middle of his chest. Then he grabbed two of the gourds and placed his collection of strong-smelling bark inside the largest one—tied them to his belt and left the hut with the machete held up in front of him—barefoot and nearly naked with the rough rope chafing his skin—two gourds bouncing against his hip.

"Come on," Mark said to the group of women and children—standing a few steps away as he tried to direct their eyes to the doorway of his former home—the tiny hut where he'd spent so many nights.

Some of the women broke from the group and began walking toward him—still watching the jungle and twitching with every angry scream that echoed through the village. Soon the rest followed and Mark herded them all back toward the tiny hut—scanning the children's faces as they passed—his son, Mondo, mixed in among them somewhere—held in his mother's arms or scurrying beside her with their hands clasped together.

But the first child Mark recognized was the infant he'd seen asleep just the day before—carried by the tall woman with the loudest laugh—the mother who'd accused him of fathering her helpless child. She walked up and stood in front of him with the baby in her arms—awake now and crying—both of them staring at him just a few feet away.

He looked down at the baby as the rest of the women

and children ran past them—a girl with the beginnings of a curly head of hair—bright, curious eyes with two parallel trails of tears sparkling down her cheeks.

Mark turned and looked above the small hut—treetops swaying in the sun—shaded, silent jungle beneath. The women and children were all inside now—pressing against each other as they pushed away from the open doorway. Mark looked inside and saw Mondo—tiny and confused—clinging to his mother's leg. He started walking toward the hut and felt the woman with the baby close behind him—bare ground slick still from rain and dew.

"Give him to me," Mark said—stepping through the doorway—then bending down in front of his scared, half-native son—looking into the boy's eyes and grabbing him by the arm. "You're coming with me, OK?"

They looked at each other and Mondo began to cry. The women mumbled amongst themselves as Mark hurriedly tried to coax his son out of the hut—more shouts and screams coming from the battle with each passing moment—more frequent and some sounding much closer than before.

Without acknowledging the boy's mother, Mark lifted his son and stood up with Mondo in the crook of his flexed arm—tiny legs kicking against the two gourds—surprisingly strong toddler arms pounding against his chest and shoulder.

The mother said something—tried to grab her son but Mark turned away and stepped out the open doorway for the last time. She managed to get a hand around the ropes he'd draped over his back—holding tight as she pleaded with him. But Mark dragged her and twisted his body—shaking her off as he left the hut.

The sounds of battle were even closer now as Mark looked around the perimeter of the village—waiting to see the men he'd watched sneak away that morning with their weapons and war paint—or invaders coming for plunder, retribution or some combination of the two. But the fighting hadn't reached the village yet—Mondo's weeping mother and the nervous, chattering women behind him still louder than the echoing voices of violence not far away.

Mark turned to the woman walking beside him—the one with the loud laugh who was now marching in dutiful silence—swaying back and forth with her infant daughter— Mark's second child somehow having gone from crying to now sound asleep.

"I'm not sure what to name her," Mark said as he looked down at the sleeping baby—Mondo struggling and screaming against his chest—head twisted over Mark's shoulder— little toddler arms reaching out for the tiny hut.

The woman was calm at Mark's side as they turned and made their way to the edge of the village. She said something to him as if he could understand her words—kept close against his arm as their daughter slept.

"Come on," Mark said to her. "This way." He stepped into the jungle and began hacking his way through the vines and leaves—the fallen branches and the thin stalks of new trees all competing for specks of sunlight—the woman moving behind him now—staying a few feet away so he could swing the machete.

It rained all day as they marched away from the village—night eventually turning the dark jungle black—Mark stopping at some point during the nocturnal downpour—twisting his head around to check on the woman and her baby—his nameless daughter. He didn't see them so he turned his body and began scanning the blurred landscape—squinting through dark drops of falling water at the outlines of tree trunks and tangled vines—swollen, rushing river just a few steps away. The hard rain made it pointless to shout—to scream through the darkness—to listen for the woman's loud laugh or the piercing cries of his daughter.

He held Mondo in his arms and felt the boy's head resting over his shoulder—sticky heat of his son's belly against his chest. The coiled ropes were still chafing Mark's skin—carrying only one of the gourds now—aromatic bark still stuffed inside with rainwater pooling at the bottom.

His feet were in good shape—toughened by all the trips into the jungle—the forced labor—loaded down with logs and provisions—trudging over the same ground he now walked as a free man—as an escaped slave with only a broken machete to keep them all safe.

His body still felt strong—coping with the journey well even after the initial adrenaline rush had worn off. But he began to worry about the tall woman and the baby they'd made together—still not far enough away from the village—still wet and still trying to protect his son—now searching through the darkness and the unrelenting rain for his lost infant daughter.

Mark picked his way back through the vegetation—river rushing past him in splashes of silt and foam—its banks crumbling into the fast-moving current—every few minutes an uprooted tree gliding by. He backtracked as best he could in the dark—fresh cuts in leaves and branches from his machete letting him know he was still on the right track. He called out for the woman—words in English she would not understand—sounds she would not be able to hear over the rain and the roaring river. He stopped to listen—searching in vain for the blended syllables of the woman's strange language.

It took Mark at least an hour to find the woman and his unnamed daughter—stumbling with Mondo asleep in his arms over fallen trees and other obstacles he could not see. The woman had reached out and grabbed his arm as he passed—silent and strong—startling Mark and waking Mondo. Mark had swung out blindly with the machete after feeling her touch—the woman backing away just in time— retreating to a safe distance until he recognized her. Then she came to him and grabbed his arm again—holding on this time and leading him through the dark rain—over slick mud and slimy dead leaves—heavy jungle plants pressing against them—full of water and heat and the nutrients held within the restless soil.

They soon came to a makeshift shelter at the base of a large tree—thin saplings bent over and somehow fastened to the sloping edges of the tree's star-shaped trunk. Large green leaves had been layered over the saplings to form a roof that would mostly shield them from the rain. Mark crawled inside with Mondo—now crying and shivering against his chest. He scooted back into the divot of the trunk and felt the solid, smooth bark cradling him on three sides. In front of him he watched the woman crawl inside with their sleeping baby—covered by a cloth and resting firmly against her breasts.

Raindrops still hit Mark's ankles and feet—slid down between his back and the tree in a thin, flowing sheet. But Mondo was sheltered completely—curled into a ball on his lap—the woman and their unnamed daughter scooting up between his legs.

Soon they were all asleep—all except for Mark, of course—their heavy, rhythmic breathing pressing against his tired, desperate skin.

Mark sat there—awake in the dark while his children and the woman slept—trying not to move too much—to endure the tingling feet and hands and the rainwater running down his back—insects crisscrossing his arms and legs.

He felt them all breathing as the rain began to soften—his baby's short, quick breaths—Mondo's chest contracting with regular blasts of hot air against his scarred ribs—the woman inhaling slow, giant gulps of air—pressing against his knees as she huddled on the ground.

He whispered to them as the rain slackened and the insects and frogs came out to begin their songs—first thanking the woman for finding him in the dark and for building the shelter—asking how she could do such a thing with a baby strapped to her chest. He apologized for swinging the machete at her—admitting how scared he was—disoriented in the dark jungle when she suddenly touched his arm.

He told his infant daughter that his name was Mark and that he was her father—bright, curious eyes and burgeoning curls quickly erasing any doubt. He introduced her to her brother, Mondo—explaining how he'd come up with the name. Then he discussed girl names with her as the rain lightened to just a few heavy drops—intermittently smacking into the green leaves over their heads—not clear whether they'd fallen from a cloud or had collected and dripped down off the wet jungle canopy.

Soon the darkness and the quiet began to wear on Mark—the dangers they faced and the helplessness he felt—the fear of being tracked down by the tribe—torture of watching one or both of his two young children die.

For hours that night Mark continued to whisper—to push away the dark thoughts—to dream out loud—to pray for the detachment from death he once enjoyed and took for granted. He whispered to his children—hopes and dreams for their futures—warm beds and locked doors—clean clothes and a house with hardwood floors—refrigerator full of food—fireplace in every room.

STORY

"I'll have to wake you two up every morning once you're old enough to go to school—teachers always pushing to start classes too early. I think it's just because they want to get home early in the afternoon. So I'll have to drag you out from under your warm blankets and sit you down at the kitchen table. It's cold during most of the school year in Denver so you'll probably be in your warm pajamas—hair going all over the place—especially yours, little girl, once it grows out."

.

.

"I'll have to brush it and work the tangles out—me or your mother—if she comes with us, that is. Maybe she'll be so terrified once she sees her first car or motorcycle or TV that she'll turn around and run straight back into the jungle.

"We'll see, I guess—once we make it out of here—we'll see what happens."

.

"You'll probably be used to American food by the time you're both in school—sugary cereal and buttered toast and fried eggs. I'll make your lunches while you're both sitting there eating breakfast at the kitchen table—make sure your backpacks are zipped up and your clothes are ironed—shoes are tied tight before you walk out the door."

"You'll have to help your little sister, Mondo. She'll be slower than you as you guys walk down the sidewalk to school—backpack might drop off her little shoulders—bigger kids might pick on her. You'll have to protect her when I'm not around."

"Maybe I'll marry your mother. She's a foot shorter than me and we don't speak the same language—could work, though—maybe. She'd take good care of you two once she got used to everything—the people, the language, the food, the cold, the noise.

"We'll see."

"There's an elementary school near my mother's house—your grandmother. We could live next door and I'll walk you two to school at first—then come pick you up each afternoon. When it's warm we'll go by the park on our way home. Maybe we'll get a dog."

"Your cousins probably still live close by with your aunt—my sister. In the summertime we can get together and barbeque every weekend. Maybe you'll have some new cousins by the time we get back—born around the same time as you two. All you kids can run around the backyard like little wild animals while I work the grill—drink beer and flip burger patties. I'll check the steaks and move the charcoal around—try to look like I know what I'm doing—everybody else either in the kitchen or sitting around a picnic table—playing cards or something. Potato salad, sweet corn, some hot bread with butter—and the beer—cold beer. I might let you take a drink, Mondo—just a sip and it'll be our secret."

.

.

"Cold, cold beer. Cooler full of ice."

SHOW

INTERVIEWER: So you killed the three men the-the-the enemy combatants and one ran away so you saved the women and children now how badly were you injured you-you-you said one of them cut your chest is that right?

MARK: With the tip of a spear—not bad—broke the skin but just barely.

Mark focused on a space next to the famous journalist's ear—curves in the black curtain behind his head of white hair—pushing in and flowing back out as someone passed by on the other side. Mark watched the lazy motion of the fabric—slow, shadowy wave—harsh overhead lights accentuating the movement.

INTERVIEWER: And they took care of you? I would assume after saving so many lives that your days as a slave were over that-that-that you were subsequently elevated to being a sort of guardian or protector or even an equal member of the tribe.

The curtain behind the famous journalist slowly stilled—soft footsteps on the other side fading into the distance. Mark moved his eyes to the older man sitting across from him—focusing on his fancy tie—his seeming comfort in such stiff clothing—such a carefully selected costume.

INTERVIEWER: Did the sexual rituals continue?

MARK: They never stopped.
     The old man—the witch doctor—he took care of the little wound I had across my chest—slapped green paste over it for a few days until it healed—not long.

INTERVIEWER: What about your status within the tribe were you still a slave?

MARK: Yeah.

The famous journalist nodded and narrowed his eyes—both men leaning back in their chairs now. Mark extended one leg and felt his muscles stretching—toes wiggling inside his new socks—still not used to sitting in chairs or wearing shoes—feet claustrophobic inside the thick, stiff leather.

INTERVIEWER: You were still brought along on foraging trips into the jungle and-and-and still forced to have relations with their women every time there was a full moon?

MARK: Things still needed to be carried—firewood, fruit, tubers, bark and plants for the medicine man, dead animals. I was still their donkey.

INTERVIEWER: Except during the forced intercourse I think we'd be wise to drop the-the-the zoomorphism when we delve into that topic.

The famous journalist laughed as he adjusted in his seat—pinching his pleated pant legs and pulling them down toward his bent knees. Mark watched him but did not laugh or even smile. The older man was still amused, however—sitting there looking down at his thighs for what seemed like a long time—sweeping away tiny pieces of lint with the back of his hand.

INTERVIEWER: Now when exactly did you decide to start faking your climaxes and-and-and withholding your ejaculate?

MARK: I don't remember—sometime after the battle, I guess.

INTERVIEWER: And they never found out never suspected anything never checked or-or-or somehow had, I mean, some sort of verification process whereby they could make sure you had inseminated the assigned woman?

MARK: No.

Mark stood up suddenly from his chair and asked if they could take a break—could stretch his legs and get some water—use the bathroom again and then call his mother to check on his children. He looked down at the famous journalist and watched the older man nod his head—mouth a little open—eyebrows raised and hands perched on the armrests of his chair.

Mark left the conference room and walked through the hotel lobby—marching past the now-vacant front desk and angling away from the bathrooms. The automatic glass doors began opening as the sensors detected his approach—so slowly he had to stop and wait—watching the gap widen until he was able to squeeze himself through—out into the sunlight and the dry summer heat—the concrete and the river of people flowing along the sidewalk.

He stood in front of the hotel and stared at the park across the street—trees and manicured patches of grass—benches and brave dogs—swing sets and monkey bars. He breathed slowly and listened for the birds he could see in the sky. The traffic was too loud, though—the engines and a few blaring radios—mechanical noise of the automatic doors opening and closing behind him.

Soon a young woman nearly ran into him as she walked past—jabbering into a cellphone—carrying a nice-looking purse and a small plastic shopping bag—strong fruit smell hitting Mark's nose as they looked at each other. The woman glared at him and kept walking—turning away and leaving him wondering why he'd smiled—why he'd been in her way—why he was just standing there in the middle of a busy sidewalk like a crazy person.

CHAPTER
eleven

FACT

I**T HAD STOPPED RAINING SOMETIME DURING THE NIGHT—**
during the dark, early morning hours as the four of them
slept—warm but still wet in a huddled ball of tired bodies—
on their own but still too near the village—still too close to
the battle that had broken out less than twenty-four hours
earlier.

Mark blinked himself awake as daylight began piercing
through the jungle. He looked up and saw the sun shining
through openings in the makeshift roof—the shelter built
over their heads by the woman—wide green leaves and the
interlocking sticks and saplings.

He heard water dripping throughout the forest—near
and also far away—rainwater collecting into fat drops too
heavy for the thirstless plants—slowly sliding off the edges
of plump leaves—plummeting down to the ground.

Birds flew from branch to branch—making shadows
that passed over his sleeping children and the native woman—quick flashes of black darting over their skin. Mark
looked down at them—still sleeping as though there could
be no more comfortable place in the world—no dryer, softer or safer place to rest. This is their home, after all, Mark

thought—only home they've ever known—balancing so precariously between life and death. This is no way to live but it's the only option they've got—only way they think is possible.

"Let's go," Mark whispered. "Come on." He was shifting slowly as he spoke—waking the woman and trying not to disturb Mondo or his daughter too much.

The woman raised her head and looked at him—eyes open and focused with no sign of recent sleep—unblinking as if she'd been awake a long time. She rolled backward and held their baby against her chest—sunlight streaking across her face and body—shadows waving lazily across the bare ground.

"We need to build a raft," Mark said—gripping the machete as he started to scoot with Mondo in one arm toward the opening of the little shelter—the woman refusing to move, however—causing Mark to look down and see his daughter now suckling at the woman's breast—eyes still closed and little fingers flexing—testing whatever they touched.

Mark stopped—carefully retreated and leaned back against the tree. Mondo shifted in his arms but continued to sleep—hair still wet in places—skin smudged with dirt.

He watched the woman feed their baby—his daughter still with no name—her bright eyes slowly opening and gazing up at her mother.

The sun kept rising and eventually placed them in complete, unbroken shade—lines of sunlight climbing and shrinking over their bodies until they all disappeared. Mark watched the woman and his daughter through the dim, humid air—listened to the woman as she hummed and rocked back and forth. He rested his head back against the tree—listened to the birds—the dripping of the heavy drops that were still collecting up in the jungle canopy. He felt the warm body of his sleeping son and felt his own eyes closing—heavy breaths slowly filling and then leaving his lungs.

It was midday by the time Mark found a suitable place to build and launch a raft—young, flexible trees nearby and a gentle slope down to the water. He stood at the river's edge and watched the current—cloudy brown ripples moving more slowly since the rain had stopped. He lifted the coiled ropes from his shoulder—inspected the red lines across his chest and side where the rough fibers had irritated his skin—scratched his back with dirty, broken fingernails. Then he raised his head to look across the expanse of muddy water in front of him—width of the swollen river—deep jungle beyond—his children and his daughter's mother standing behind him.

"It's alright, Mondo," Mark said—turning around and kneeling down in front of his crying son—gently raising the boy's chin. "Are you hungry?"

Mark felt his own stomach grumble as he placed his hands on the boy's shoulders—trying to pull Mondo toward him—to hug his son—assure him the suffering would soon end—sooner or later, anyway. But Mondo resisted—wiggled away from his father and stood sniffling next to the woman—his curly hair greasy and matted—smudges of dirt on each of his wet cheeks.

"I'll find us some food," Mark said. "I'll figure something out."

The woman looked down and said something to Mondo. Mark saw him smile for a brief moment as he wiped away some of his tears—his skinny body still strong but too young and growing too fast to go without food for too long.

Mark watched the woman as she continued speaking to his son—still watching her as she began to sing. She was taller than most of the other native women—as tall as the men almost—enough flesh on her body still to keep her ribs from showing. She was strong and relaxed—standing there with her baby in her arms—being shepherded through the jungle farther from her village than she'd probably ever been—ever would have wished to go.

"Stay here. I'll try to find some fruit," Mark said—the woman continuing with her song—closing her eyes with her hand on Mondo's back. "Those red and yellow things should be ripe this time of year—I think." He gripped the machete and turned away from his children—away from the woman and the swollen brown river. "Maybe a snake or two," he said over his shoulder—marching off now into the tangled underbrush—fat, wet leaves and spiny, wooden stalks—vines and young trees—all fighting for tiny scraps of sunlight.

Mark cut notches into tree trunks and low-hanging branches as he walked through the jungle—moving slowly—careful to mark his route so he could find his way back. He looked for fruit as he went along—mostly for the red and yellow bundles he'd collected with the men of the tribe just days before their escape—days before the second battle and the distant screams—women whispering inside the tiny hut as their anxious children cried.

He looked for snakes in piles of dead leaves lining the forest floor—walking for hours in search of food—walking away from the quiet, constant sounds of the flowing river—the woman's strong voice as she sang to his children—now only able to hear noisy insects and nervous birds—his own footsteps and the ping of the machete's blade.

After giving up on his search for fruit and snakes—not even finding a tuber or edible spider—Mark began navigating his way back toward the river—picking his way carefully between marked trees, scarred branches and his own fresh footprints.

Eventually he heard the woman singing just as she'd been when he left. He followed her voice until he saw the clearing where the river had to be—holding the machete up in front of him as he ran to the water's edge—the woman's song still ringing through the jungle behind him—echoing off the trees that lined the other side of the river. Mark recognized the song as one the tribe chanted together during their full moon rituals—Splinter kneeling over the chosen woman or girl—whispering into her ear as the rest of the tribe—the women and men and all the children—sang and danced wildly around the bonfire.

When Mark turned away from the muddy brown water—still breathing hard as the afternoon sun burned his naked back—he saw that the woman was not there—his children not where he'd last seen them as he ran back into the jungle—following the woman's soothing voice as fast as his legs could go—same lines of the song being repeated— the two or three that Mark could almost recite himself.

He ran between the trees—tripping over exposed roots and fallen branches—trying to pinpoint the woman's location. A few minutes into his search he found her leaning back against a tree—Mondo on her lap and suckling at her breast—unnamed daughter asleep in her opposite arm—little mouth open and a shiny line of drool curving down her cheek. The woman's eyes were closed but Mark knew she was aware of his presence. She kept singing as he inched closer—stopping where he stood when he noticed Mondo closing his eyes—pale white milk at the corner of his mouth—chin relaxing as his head slid back—nipple stretching as it emerged from his lips.

Mark sat down as quietly as he could and leaned back against a nearby tree. He watched his children sleep and he listened to the woman's singing—pace slowing as she tired—syllables blending to a hum as she started drifting off—then only breathing as she slept—arms wrapped around their infant daughter and Mark's toddler son.

For the rest of that afternoon Mark stayed busy building the raft he'd already assembled so many times in his mind—had dreamed about and prayed out loud for so many nights with Splinter sitting across from him inside the tiny hut they shared. He chopped down saplings as thick as his thighs and dragged them to the river—pulling them into the water to make sure each one would float. Then he began tying them together with the coarse rope he'd carried from the village—taking breaks to stretch his back and drink from the river—to watch his son play with sticks and dead leaves—his daughter smiling at her mother and suckling as she pleased.

It was difficult cutting down the young trees with what was left of the machete. Mark had to stop often to sharpen the blade and to rest his arms. But he kept working at it and by the time the sun was setting he had five logs laid out on the sandy, narrow stretch of shoreline—rope at one end wrapping and weaving them together. He stood over the rough-cut saplings and tried to imagine a completed raft—seeing another five or six logs and more rope tightly wound around them all—gourds full of fruit and two carved paddles resting in the middle where his children and the woman would sit.

The woman hadn't watched him at all as he worked—talking and smiling at Mondo and their daughter as the sun sank below the treetops along the opposite riverbank. She sang the same song over and over and Mondo always tried to join in—watching her lips and mumbling along when he felt he knew the words—sounds that still meant nothing to his father.

Once Mark had finished his day's work he walked toward the tree the woman had been leaning against all afternoon—sat down ten feet away in the almost-dark and looked up at the sky—the few stars between the leaves and branches he could see overhead.

"Do you think it'll rain later?" he said—dropping his head suddenly to look at the woman—Mondo and his daughter with the bright, curious eyes resting in her arms. "I'm sure it'll rain soon—early tomorrow morning if not tonight. I don't remember ever going twenty-four hours without it raining around here."

The woman looked at him and said something—eyes seeming to glow in the dark—insects and amphibians calling to each other in the background—stolid river flowing beside them.

"I already took out the garbage, honey." Mark smiled at her and was surprised when she did not look away—expression on her face not changing—eyes still glowing against the black, rough surface of the tree trunk.

The woman repeated the same phrase as they stared at each other. Mark looked away first—trying not to feel defeated—trying also to ignore all the dangers they faced—ignore his stomach—the sinking, contracting abdominal muscles trying to close in around something to digest.

After a few more minutes—as the darkness settled in—Mark stood up and walked over to the uncompleted raft. He dragged it back to where the woman sat—staring up at him with his children now asleep in her arms—pressed against her skin. He lifted the end of the raft where the logs were all tied together—leaning it against the tree over the woman's head. The rough-cut saplings were at least six feet long and heavy—forcing Mark to slip and strain as he positioned the makeshift shelter—the ribs of a lean-to teepee.

The woman whispered something to him—peering up through the spread-apart logs. Mark looked down at her but could barely see her face. He could see that she was moving, though—scooting toward him and leaning forward as if to stand—still with the two sleeping children in her arms. Mark bent down to help her and to support the weight of his son—the woman leaning on him and raising herself up—standing with her head barely reaching Mark's chest—sliding between two of the leaning logs. She handed Mondo to him—then adjusted his other arm and placed their infant daughter in the cradle she'd made—the little girl's head resting in the crook of his bent elbow—curly head of hair barely visible as he stared down at her in the dark.

Mark felt the woman step back but he had no idea she'd left—eventually looking up from his daughter to nothing but the upright, unfinished raft leaning against the tree—black jungle beyond with all its night sounds—soft burbling of the river behind him. He turned slowly—careful to keep his children asleep—looking for the woman but finding only darkness—waxy leaves reflecting tiny bits of starlight.

There was nothing to do but enter the skeleton of a shelter he'd made—sit down and lean back against the tree.

Mark sat there—awake in the dark while his children slept—trying not to move or make a sound—withholding sneezes and enduring tingling feet and hands—insects crisscrossing his arms and legs. He felt Mondo and his unnamed daughter—breathing as the young night wore on and the woman stayed away—the girl's short, quick breaths—the boy's chest filling more slowly and then contracting with blasts of hot air blowing over Mark's chest.

He whispered to them as the insects and the frogs continued their songs—the river's relentless flow. He told them they would never remember this—their desperate scramble through the jungle—rafting down an unknown river—the moment they were introduced to the outside world—the civilized world. They would never remember living with the tribe—the strange language Mondo was just beginning to learn—barefoot hunting trips and the full moon rituals—prehistoric battles.

He told his daughter he would come up with a name for her soon—told her again that he was her father—bright, curious eyes and burgeoning curls leaving no doubt.

As Mark spoke to her, Mondo squirmed in his other arm but stayed asleep—skin appearing almost blue in the night. Mark turned to him and told him about his own father and how he wasn't going to make the same mistakes—days and nights away from home—callous words and rough hands.

Soon the darkness and the quiet began to wear on Mark—the danger of their journey and the helplessness he felt—fear of snakes and jaguars—of infected wounds and river rapids—starvation—the torture of watching one or both of his two young children die.

Mark continued to whisper—growing more tired with

every word. He tried to push away the dark thoughts—to dream out loud instead—to pray for his children's lives—deliverance from the strange, evil place he'd found himself in. He told them about the things they could have—could experience if they somehow managed to escape—the ice cream cones and amusement parks—movies and music and baseball games.

He talked about the life he'd known and had abandoned—family members left in the dark—the tears they surely shed—empty coffin they must have buried as the last bit of hope faded—his headstone covered in snow somewhere in Colorado—engraved with the wrong date of death.

STORY

"We'll take a ski trip every winter—maybe January or February—miss the holiday rush. My sister's birthday is at the beginning of February—maybe we can use that as an excuse to get everybody together. Or maybe I'll say you two were born around that time—beginning of February—Groundhog Day.

"Would you mind sharing a birthday with your little sister, Mondo?"

.

.

"So we'll start planning around Thanksgiving every year—probably stay in Colorado mostly but maybe we'll go to Park City or California once or twice. We could go up to Idaho or Montana or some other place none of us have ever been. Maybe we'll even go to Canada."

.

.

"We'll have to make packing lists—clothes and gear and

snacks. I'll help you two decide which toys to bring. Maybe you'll get along with your cousins and you can all pile into one car together. My sister and mother can drive you and I'll follow in another car with all the luggage—skis tied down to the roof.

"And we'll have to keep an eye on the weather, of course—leave before the roads get bad. We'll bring chains and extra blankets just in case. I'm sure they've gotten better at predicting the weather since I've been gone. They're always coming up with something new."

.

.

"It's usually cheaper if you rent a condo at one of the ski resorts and bring your own food—cook instead of eating out for every meal. Somebody will be in charge of the groceries—my sister, probably. We'll either go shopping before we leave or once we get there—might depend on the weather and how close the stores are, I guess.

"I'll be in charge of checking the weather and deciding when we should get on the road and everything like that— get us checked in wherever we're staying—make sure the TV works and everybody gets their own bed and there's enough towels and blankets and toilet paper. I'll spread a map out on the kitchen table and we'll all decide what we want to do—which runs we want to start with and where to meet up and when.

"You two will be running around with your cousins like wild animals when we first get there—screaming at each other and bouncing off the walls—probably get yourselves in trouble doing something you're not supposed to be doing."

.

.

"Your little sister—headful of wild curls trying to keep

up with you, Mondo—chasing after her big brother from room to room."

SHOW

Mark turned around and walked back into the hotel—sliding glass doors opening automatically as he approached. He felt a cool blast of air-conditioning as he left the hot, chaotic sidewalk and began crossing the lobby once again—felt his skin still cooling as he marched through the dark conference room to the little square partition set up in its center—brightly lit from overhead lights and surrounded by walls of black curtains.

INTERVIEWER: We'll start back up in a few minutes. I let the crew take a little break.

The famous journalist was still sitting in his chair—flipping through his printouts with a yellow highlighter in his hand—not bothering to look up as Mark entered.

MARK: That's fine.

Mark put his hands inside the pockets of his new pants and paced back and forth behind his empty chair—looking at the folds in the curtains and taking slow, small strides—testing his balance before each footfall.

INTERVIEWER: You can sit down it might be a little while. The fellas that work the cameras said they needed a lunch break. I don't know if you noticed but they're not terribly concerned about keeping a slim figure.

Mark nodded—continued pacing until he reached one of the curtains—black fabric swaying away from him as he pivoted toward the older man. He went around his empty chair and scanned the little partition—hands still in his pockets—lights shining down on the famous journalist's pleated pants and polished shoes—unattended cameras in each corner—pattern of the conference room carpet repeating in all directions.

    Mark sat down and pressed his back against the length of the padded chair—adjusting his shirtsleeves as the older man stared intently at his printouts—crisp white sheets of paper fanned out in both hands.

INTERVIEWER: It's just so astounding I mean the whole story your story it's just amazing every part of it but I'm-I'm-I'm struggling to find the right thing to focus on the best questions to ask.

MARK: People like violence. I think they'll like the story about the battle.

INTERVIEWER: People do like violence that's true but they also like sex and money and power and-and-and exceptional intelligence and determination and sex and sex and, oh yes, more sex.

The famous journalist looked up from his printouts and laughed—top edges of the fanned sheets blocking his chin and part of one cheek from Mark's view. Mark smiled and nodded—patting his thighs as he avoided the older man's eyes.

INTERVIEWER: Now that's certainly not a comprehensive list but I think we've shown your extraordinary determination and quick-thinking and your selflessness. We've got the battle—the violence people always want.

There was a pause as the famous journalist went back to his printouts—mumbling to himself with a highlighter held up near his chin.

Mark watched him—chewed the inside part of his cheek—then allowed his eyes to wander to the rest of the little partition after a few seconds of silence—knees dancing up and down while his fingers clawed and picked at each other in his lap.

MARK: A love story.

INTERVIEWER: What?

The famous journalist slowly lowered the printouts to his lap—staring at Mark and leaning forward. Mark was looking down at the carpet now—tracing the snaking lines of gold and white with the toe of his shoe.

MARK: I fell in love with one of the women—my daughter's mother.

INTERVIEWER: Go on.

MARK: Shouldn't we wait for the cameras?

INTERVIEWER: They're on I had the fellas leave everything focused and running before they went to lunch. Go on keep talking.

The cameras peered at Mark over the famous journalist's shoulders—glass panels framed by black plastic—bright overhead lights shining down on the vacant stools where the cameramen had been perched.

Mark cleared his throat—rubbed his eyes and straightened his back. He ran a calloused hand down the back of his head—recently cut hair not trained to stay down just yet.

MARK: She had more of an independent streak than the other women. I liked that about her.

INTERVIEWER: And how did this independent streak manifest itself specifically when you were forced to have sex with her was she a-a-a willing participant or did she fight more than the others?

MARK: She dealt with it the best she could—body being painted against her will—all that smoke being blown in her face while some of the men pinned her down. She made the best of a bad situation, I guess.

I couldn't help but look at her—her eyes. Like I said before, I never looked at the women. She was different, though.

INTERVIEWER: So how did it happen did you have a chance to get to know one another before all the-the-the pomp and circumstance with the medicine man and his smoking bundle of herbs and the chanting and the wild dancing around a bonfire that you've described?

MARK: No. No it was just another time—another full moon—another woman I didn't know. But then her voice caught my attention. I was brought into the hut and the medicine man started chanting and going through his rituals. She was talking to the other men off and on—the ones holding her down—telling them off, probably.

Then she joined in when everyone started chanting—mouthing the words and barely making any noise at first. But then she fell into a rhythm—getting louder than everyone else pretty soon—like it was her way of distracting herself or protesting what was going on. But she had such a good voice it just sounded like she was singing—belting out a song better than anyone else could.

The famous journalist was in his signature pose again—elbows on his knees with his hands up around his mouth. Mark sat erect in his chair—hands on his thighs and toes dancing inside his shoes.

INTERVIEWER: And she was there on the ground like all the other women had been with-with-with the paint and everything?

MARK: I was trying not to look at her—waiting for the medicine man to finish his rituals and then for somebody to pull me down to my knees—push me over on top of her.

But I kept listening to her voice—couldn't help myself so I looked at her legs first—then the rest of her. She was bigger than most of the other women—taller and a little more filled-out. I looked at her face and she didn't seem nervous at all—didn't look like she was mad at the men pinning her arms and legs to the packed-earth floor of the little hut where everything happened—singing with that beautiful voice while everyone else just yelled in unison. She was actually smiling at me.

And she was looking at me the whole time—not scared or resentful or anything—made me feel almost comfortable for the first time since becoming their hostage—their slave—first time I felt connected to someone else—loved even.

She even put her hands on me once they let go of her arms—held onto my shoulders and ran her fingers over my back—my shoulder blades. It would've been nice to have had some privacy—but it wasn't long before we both forgot about the medicine man and all the others—dancing around us and chanting—whole rest of the tribe just outside the hut around the bonfire.

INTERVIEWER: And so that was it from then on you were in love with a woman you couldn't even talk to but could communicate with by way of-of-of something deeper through some connection you two had and your daughter would soon be the manifestation of that love?

MARK: That's right.

CHAPTER
TWELVE

FACT

MARK OPENED HIS EYES SLOWLY—BLINKING INTO FOCUS slanting walls of green leaves—son and daughter still sleeping in his arms—daylight just beginning to make things visible. He looked down and saw the woman—his daughter's mother and the nighttime builder of their makeshift shelter—huddled on the ground by herself—curving spine pressed against his leg.

He looked up at the leaves and sticks all around them—the wide slabs of bark covering the leaning logs of the unfinished raft—birdsong and the persistent, soft sounds of the river.

"Wow," he whispered—yellow-green glowing sunlight just starting to push through the paper-thin walls—shadows of birds and insects crisscrossing the spotlit leaves.

Mark shifted his body carefully so not to wake his sleeping children—twisting and bending his neck until he felt the vertebrae pop. Then he sat there and waited for everyone to start waking up—watching the morning light getting brighter as the sun moved higher through the sky—birds louder and more varied as the minutes passed. He tried to ignore the emptiness of his stomach but thoughts of food would not leave his mind—smell of eggs and bacon on the stove—sound of the toaster snapping off—familiar feel of a cup of hot coffee in his hand.

The woman had found some fruit the night before and gave it to Mark and Mondo later that morning—retrieving the bundle of rough-skinned, dark purple balls from where it hung suspended in the air next to their shelter. Mark tried hard not to eat them all—to leave at least half for Mondo—to offer a few to the woman, which she refused—sitting there on the bare ground as Mark watched her—nursing their daughter—humming as she rocked gently back and forth with her eyes closed.

After all the fruit was gone and their baby had filled her tiny stomach with the woman's milk, Mark tore down the broad green leaves and slabs of bark from the upturned raft—pushed the logs together and then tipped them over and set them flat on the ground. The ropes were loose now at the end he'd tied together so he took them off and wound the coarse strands around the logs again—using his foot and the tree to press them tightly together—trying to remember the knots his father had taught him on fishing trips as a boy—the coiling and looping back through—the blood knot and the one they used for trotline. He fumbled through a few tries and then went back to the simple crossover knot everyone uses to tie their shoes—crossing the ropes again and again until knots on knots clumped into a sort of braid between the last two logs.

Mark eventually dragged the half-finished raft back to the edge of the river—Mondo and the woman trailing close behind—infant daughter asleep now with a belly full of milk. He found the same flat spot away from the trees and vines and saplings—the dry patch of sand that sloped gently down into the muddy water—dropped the collection of logs there and stood up straight—breathing hard now and stretching his back.

The woman looked upriver and studied the flowing water—looked up at the sky and then turned her head toward Mark—slightest bit of concern now showing on her face.

"It's alright," he said to her. "We'll be OK." Mark nodded—continued stretching and massaging the long muscles that ran along his spine—still looking at the woman with their sleeping baby held tightly to her chest—his son leaning against her hip.

Mark worked all day on the raft—using the broken machete to chop down three more small trees—tying them to the logs already fastened together—fashioning two paddles from driftwood found along the riverbank—using several long, thin sticks as crosspieces to sturdy the raft—testing its construction after each improvement.

Sometime that afternoon—as Mark chopped and carved with the broken machete—the woman went off into the jungle with Mondo and their unnamed daughter—returning several hours later with more fruit—some of the same dark purple bundles and a few larger, light green pieces that were fibrous and not quite ripe—hard on Mark's teeth and jaw muscles as he paused his work to eat—sitting there on the sand next to the river in the late afternoon heat—the woman chewing the green fruit into a mash before giving it to Mondo—Mark watching them as he swallowed large chunks he could not break down.

"I don't know how long we'll be on the river," Mark said as they ate and rested—looking down at his stomach—pulling on the thin layer of flesh around his belly button—short, curly hairs and dirty skin. "Maybe we'll see a boat tomorrow—a fisherman's boat. Maybe we'll make it to a farm in two or three days—a cattle farm and we'll have steaks that night—baked potatoes with butter and sour cream—cheese and bacon."

He looked up at the cloudy gray sky—clear view above the width of the flowing brown water—fingertips eventually releasing their pinches of belly—arms raising and extending to dangle over his bent knees.

The rain started early that evening—coming straight down in big, heavy drops that made divots in the sand—filling their footprints and the little parallel ditches where Mark had dragged the rough-cut logs.

The four of them were soaked before Mark could even get the raft propped up on its side—driftwood paddles stabbed into the sand at each end supporting its weight—making a short, long shelter they could huddle underneath. The woman looked down at him through the heavy rain and seemed worried—eyes serious as she bent to peer under the slanting roof of logs—Mark motioning for her to crawl inside next to him but she stayed where she was—said something to him as she tried in vain to keep their daughter dry—yelled at him through the fat raindrops and pointed upriver.

"What?" Mark shouted—looking past the woman at the flowing brown water—ripples and tiny white splashes as the current carried itself past them—the steady force of so much liquid moving in the same direction.

The woman did not respond—standing there looking down at him—baby crying against her skin—Mondo tugging at her arm. The rain had soaked her hair—collected strands now matted against her forehead and her cheeks—drips dropping from her nose, lips and chin. Mark watched her and tried to understand—tried to decipher the concerns of the native woman who knew the jungle so well—much better than he ever could. He tried to decide whether her worries were valid—based on something real that presented real danger—or if she was trying to communicate irrational fears based on superstitions—beliefs borne of the primitive, terrible place they were trying to escape.

"We're too high here for it to flood this time of year," Mark shouted up at the woman—motioning toward the river not twenty yards away. "I'm not dragging this damn thing back into the trees. We'll be fine."

He began again trying to coax the woman inside the makeshift shelter—steadying the driftwood paddles that supported the lean-to structure he'd made—showing her that it was large enough for all four of them. When she did not move he motioned for Mondo to come join him—rain beating down on the boy's wet head. Any trace of daylight was quickly fading as Mark glanced around at the surrounding jungle—bright tropical colors muted by the dark clouds, black soil and the brown, murky river.

The woman finally guided Mondo toward his father—knelt and whispered something in his ear—causing Mondo to step toward Mark—to stand obediently under the shelter of the slanted raft. He kept his eyes on his father and stood there in front of him—waiting—wanting to cry but holding it back—behaving himself just like the woman must've told him to.

Mark grabbed his son and set him down on his

lap—shifting the dangling machete so it stayed safely out of the way. He reached up and the woman handed him their infant daughter—wet and crying with her eyes clinched shut—damp and dirty cloth covering her belly and her legs. Mark held her close to his chest—bouncing her lightly as he'd seen the woman do—rubbing the wet, soft curls that coated her small head.

When he looked up again he saw the woman still standing there in the rain—watching him with that concerned look on her face.

"We need a roof," Mark yelled through the downpour—pointing up at the raft with his free hand—streams of water falling to the sandy ground all around them from the gaps between the logs.

The woman tried saying something to him again—something he could not understand but which sounded familiar—the syllable count and the rhythm. He thought she was repeating whatever she'd tried to tell him earlier but he did not care anymore. Whatever she said would not change anything—stop the rain or bring back the sun or make a warm fire suddenly appear in front of them—juicy steaks in a cast iron skillet with butter and onions and whole cloves of garlic. Whatever she said, all they could hope for tonight was a roof over their heads—a relatively dry place for the children to sleep.

Mark watched the woman turn and walk away—stepping from sand to mud and then entering the jungle—disappearing between the tree trunks and the wide green leaves—behind the rain and hidden in the almost-dark.

Mark sat there under a makeshift raft in the middle of the

jungle—two half-native children in his arms—wet sand coating his skin and rainwater dripping down his back. He felt himself breathe—his body pressing out against Mondo and his unnamed daughter—their tiny, shivering bodies—observant eyes and shoeless feet.

He talked to them and pulled them close—trying to be heard over the rain—trying to warm them without a fire—without a blanket or a dry towel. He told them they would never remember this—their desperate scramble through the jungle—teeth chattering under an upturned raft of rough-cut logs. They would never remember the tribe they'd lived with—the lack of food, clean water, schooling and decent clothes—the strange language still spoken to them by the woman.

He went over the narrowed list of names for his daughter—still rubbing her head and clutching her to his chest—his knee pulled up around her back. April was the obvious choice—well meaning, strong-willed ally of the Ninja Turtles—independent and loyal at the same time. Then there was his mother's name, June. She had many of the same qualities and the benefit of being family—the one who raised Mark largely by herself after his father left.

"Let's just split the difference. What do you say, little girl?" Mark said—looking down into his daughter's sleepy eyes. "May. How do you like that for a name? May?"

Mondo began to cry as Mark spoke—pressing himself against his father's side—soaking wet still and unlikely to dry anytime soon. Mark told him it would be alright—that they'd be warm every single night once they escaped this horrible place. He put his arm around his son and told him about different heaters and how they worked—woodstoves, propane furnaces, space heaters and electric blankets.

Soon the darkness, the cold and the constant hunger began to wear on Mark—the dangers they faced—ever-present threats of sickness and starvation—hypothermia if his children stayed wet for too long. He felt weak and began to obsess over food—steaks in a cast iron skillet—cooking over and over again in his mind.

He continued to talk as the young night wore on—growing more tired with each word he shouted over the sound of the rain. He tried to push away the dark thoughts—to dream out loud—to pray for his children's lives—deliverance from this evil place. He told them about his own childhood—the troubles between his parents—Little League games and going to the movies—his friends and the awful, boring routines of a comfortable life in a safe place—hated so much then but yearned for now.

He talked about the life he'd known and how hard he'd worked to escape it—family members so familiar they could hold no surprises—quiet, insular suburb where he'd grown up—tedious, insufferable days filled with food, warmth and more laughing than crying—more smiles than tears.

STORY

"Every Sunday when I was a kid we'd have to get up early and go to church. I hated it. My sister liked it because she always got up early anyway and was always dying to get out of the house—also because she loved getting dressed up—bracelets and necklaces—earrings and makeup when she was older. She'd be in the bathroom for hours—getting ready along with our mother. I could hear them talking and laughing as I tried to keep sleeping—one of them yelling through the door at me every few minutes—saying I'd better be out of bed—better be getting myself ready before it got too late. 'Get up and comb your hair!' they'd shout at me between giggles. 'Iron your clothes and eat something for breakfast!'"

.

.

"But I won't make you two do any of that. Kids should sleep in as much as they want. Adults should too, I guess."

.

.

"So every Sunday we'd get up and put on our best clothes and our mother would drive us to church. We were always late but we always seemed to find room in the last few pews. Most of the time we were able to miss the awkward handshakes at the start of the service—people turning this way and that—smiling and saying 'hello' and shaking hands with people they didn't know—turning to the next stranger and saying 'good morning'—pretending to be in a good mood—not tired—not counting the seconds until they could sit down again."

.

.

"The old lady up on the stage would play a song on the piano and people would smile and wave and shake hands until the last note. It was awful. I think my mother and sister hated it just as much as I did. So we were late every week and none of us ever complained."

.

.

"The church we went to had high ceilings and stained-glass windows. The preacher had a deep voice and wore a tiny microphone on his lapel. When he got excited and a little too loud, the speakers would blare and make a funny noise and he'd have to pause and apologize—make some joke and then go on with whatever he was saying—drenched in sweat and just as excited but without all the yelling."

.

.

"I remember our mother would try to keep up with all the Bible verses the preacher referenced—but at first she wasn't very familiar with how the different books were arranged—the order they were in—whether they were in the New Testament or the Old Testament. The preacher would shout out a verse and you'd hear those thin pages start flipping all around you. I'd look over at our mother and she'd be glancing at her neighbors—flipping in the same general direction as them. She got better, though—going every Sunday after my father left—reading along every time the preacher wanted to highlight a particular passage—got to where she didn't need any help."

"But I never liked going—the dressing up—the interrupted sleep and the way it was like going to school. I told the preacher that one time when I was really little. He was standing there by the door—shaking everybody's hand as they left. I told him they should do church on Friday nights so we could still have two days to sleep in before going back to school on Monday. He laughed and slapped me on the shoulder—leaned down in front of my face with his big, purple-red nose and bushy eyebrows. My mother apologized and laughed along with him—obviously embarrassed by what her son had just said. Then she hurried me out the door—kept smiling until we got to the car and away from all the people."

"But I won't put you two through all that—won't put myself through all that either. I'm sure your grandmother will want to take you every once in a while, though."

"She's probably been going more and more since I left—praying for me—for my soul once she gave up on me ever coming back."

"It'll be a nice surprise for her—seeing me again—seeing me alive—bringing her two new grandkids to spoil."

SHOW

INTERVIEWER: And how did things progress after that first encounter with your daughter's mother that-that-that night of forced copulation during one of the tribe's full moon rituals?

There was a pause as Mark leaned back and scratched the skin under his chin—silence as he looked over the famous journalist's head—focusing on the ripples and shadows in the temporary wall of loose black curtains. He was still getting used to not having a beard—touching his face even when there was no itch to scratch.

MARK: We spent a lot of time together—as much time as we could, anyway. I was out in the jungle during the day with the men and she stayed around the village. At night I was stuck in my little hut with the medicine man watching over me—making sure I didn't sneak off—never seeming to sleep or even take his eyes off me.

INTERVIEWER: He didn't sleep?

MARK: Not at night—maybe during the day he did. I mean he had to sleep at some point—just like everybody else. I'm sure he slept during the day and I just never saw him.

The famous journalist laughed and nodded his head—showing his teeth and looking down at the clean conference room carpet. Then he raised his eyebrows and leaned back in his chair—bringing a thin hand up to his chin and closing his mouth—laughter trailing off as his eyes opened wide and stared straight ahead at Mark.

INTERVIEWER: Well he was a medicine man with the world's largest pharmacy all around him I wonder if he discovered a-a-a mix of herbs that he could ingest and stay awake all the time and never sleep but let's get back to-to-to your paramour your daughter's mother did she have a name?

MARK: If she did I never knew it—never knew any of their names—like I said before.

INTERVIEWER: You were in love with this woman and you didn't even know her name? And-and-and you spent every night with a man in a tiny hut this medicine man this-this-this spiritual leader of sorts and you never got his moniker either?

Mark gripped the arms of his chair—flexed the knot of jaw muscles on one side of his face—molars pressing together inside his mouth with nothing to chew. Then he brought a hand up and rubbed the smooth skin around his chin—close shave and moisturizer making his fingertips slip.

The famous journalist kept looking at Mark—little smirk on his wrinkled face—one of his heels bouncing up and down underneath his chair.

Mark glanced down at the printouts back in the famous journalist's hands—wondering again what they said—all the research that must've been done on him—condensing his whole life down to a few sheets of burnable paper.

MARK: That's what I said.

INTERVIEWER: Yes and that's why we so desperately wanted to talk with you so-so-so intensely wanted to hear from you to fill in these apparent gaps in your story. It's incredible the tortuous conditions the-the-the sheer isolation they subjected you to just incredible and for you to stay sane and to escape with your two young children in tow is just hard to fathom.

The famous journalist set the printouts down and leaned forward—trademark pose again with his elbows on his knees and his hands coming up to his chin—frown now forming on his face with a furrowed brow to match. He breathed deep and exhaled for a long time.

Mark did his best to maintain eye contact with the older man—distracting himself as the silence settled in by studying the man's face—well-trimmed eyebrows and the surprising lack of nose or ear hair.

INTERVIEWER: So I think there's more to the story there are things that you're not telling me that-that-that you haven't told anyone yet and I just want to help you get those things off your chest.

MARK: You're just trying to help me—that's what this is all about? Why I'm here?

The famous journalist was gesturing now as he prepared to speak—spreading his arms wide and sitting as erect as possible without either standing up or falling forward. Mark did the opposite—shrinking back with slouched shoulders and head down. He began to smile, though—mouth closed tight as his body bounced a little with a silent chuckle.

INTERVIEWER: Yes, Mark. Yes, of course.

CHAPTER
THIRTEEN

FACT

T HE RAIN HAD STOPPED BUT MARK KNEW THE NIGHT WAS not yet over—knew the sun had not yet made its way back around to the eastern horizon. He listened to the trees dripping and the sloshing river just outside their makeshift hut—eyes still closed after something had woken him up. He sat there and listened for a while—hunched over his sleeping children underneath the propped-up raft—the woman pressed against his side with an arm draped over their daughter. He thought about the name he'd given her earlier that night—May—a smile forming on his face as he began raising his head and opening his eyes—stretching his legs slowly so not to wake his children.

Water suddenly slapped the soles of Mark's bare feet— then receded back into the darkness as the loose sand pulled away from his calloused heals—the water coming again a few seconds later but with more force—splashing over his toes and reaching up his shins—receding, regrouping and returning but this time the black, rippling river was pushing onto his lap and waking Mondo—shifting the heavy raft above their heads—disturbing the thin layer of leaves and bark the woman had laid over the logs while they slept.

Mark held May above the water and leaned forward—letting go of Mondo and grabbing one of the driftwood paddles he'd used to prop up the raft.

"Get out!" Mark yelled.

The woman was already standing—pulling their daughter from his arm as he struggled against the rising water. Mark gave her their now-crying baby and watched her duck out from under the raft—grabbing Mondo by the arm as she began pushing her way through the rising river—leaning against the strong, surging current. He kept watching her as he ran his hands along the logs—frantically searching for the ropes that tied them together. The woman slipped after just a few steps and Mondo nearly went under—May wailing with her toothless mouth open wide—tiny body held just above the violent river.

Mark felt the raft drifting away as he watched the woman and his children—tracking the slow movement of the dark figures toward shore—tiny breaking waves shining in the moonlight all around them. He slid out from underneath the logs and finally found a place to grab hold of the tightly wound ropes. The river was rising every moment and he watched the woman struggle to find her footing—dragging his screaming son by the arm—holding his screaming daughter up near her chin.

Mark tried to pull the raft toward shore but the current was too strong—pushing the logs too swiftly downriver—finally taking him with it as his head went under and his legs continued kicking against the river's shifting bottom—frantic feet and toes curling into loose sand. The woman and Mondo and May disappeared each time he was forced under the chaotic water—when he was spun around by the strength of the rushing river and the weight of the raft.

"Go!" Mark yelled.

He twisted his whole body and kicked his legs—trying

to find something solid enough for his feet to push against. His head went under again but he kept hold of the raft—both hands twisted and tangled in the ropes and logs above his head—machete spinning and smacking against his forearms—pulling against the lanyard tied to his wrist—the black water swirling around him and rushing downriver—rising higher and higher—eventually leaving his feet unable to touch the sandy bottom.

He felt something hit his side as he fought for the surface—a downed tree branch or maybe a boulder tumbling in the current. It took the breath out of his lungs and he felt water going down his throat—arms flailing in the underwater chaos—one hand losing its grip on the raft. He felt the machete break loose from the rope wrapped around his wrist—tarnished metal and scarred plastic handle sinking and spinning—disappearing into the swirling darkness.

When Mark's head finally broke the surface of the water again he coughed and sucked in air—feeling his feet suddenly press down against the sandy river bottom. He was somehow still clinging to the raft—floating logs still pulling him downriver but he managed to keep them moving closer to shore—every step a struggle that raised his body another inch or two above the choppy waves. He looked back to where the woman had been struggling to escape the rising water—his children in her arms and her feet losing their grip. But he saw only jungle—violent floodwaters smacking against the trunks of trees.

He was still fighting with the raft as he scanned the shoreline—still coughing up brown river water—lungs still panicking to take in air. Eventually he managed to climb up the expanded riverbank and pull the raft a few feet into the trees. He yanked his hands out from the twisted ropes and crawled back to the water's edge—breathing hard but not coughing as much anymore. He scanned the shoreline again—looking for any sign of the woman—desperate to see the two tiny bodies he'd created—the two children he'd been forced to father—forced to make but not to name—not to rescue or to worry at all about.

"No," Mark said—dread, anger and exhaustion all in his voice—regret mixed in as well—as always. "No."

The blue-gray light of early morning was just beginning—river changing from black to brown—jungle green brightening as most of the stars had already disappeared.

Tears mixed with the dirty drops of water on Mark's face—his wet eyes looking upriver—wondering how far he'd floated as he struggled with the raft—watching the shoreline for movement—trying to guess where the current would have carried them if the woman had fallen—if she'd slipped in the mud and sand—overwhelmed by the rising, raging river.

Mark began to stand up once he had the strength—pulling his fingers and knees out of the soft, muddy earth—still looking for the woman and his children. He got to his feet and walked out into the river until the water was almost up to his waist—stood there and looked back at the wall of jungle—tangled vines and branches and the deep blackness between. The current pushed and pulled at his legs and he felt the sand around his feet shifting and drifting away. He scanned the brown surface of the river—ripples and small waves crashing over into white jumbles of bubbles and foam.

"Mondo!" Mark yelled. "Mondo! May!" He stood there—trying hard not to fall—scanning the water and both banks of the river—wondering if Mondo even recognized the name he'd given him yet—knowing how useless it was to yell his infant daughter's name—to yell anything at all, really.

A few minutes later he stepped backward out of the water—watching as a small tree slowly fell into the river along the opposite bank—roots flipping up and out of the ground after the current had eaten away the tree's anchoring soil. He scanned the surface of the water one last time—still searching for the children he feared were lost. Then he turned around—planning to walk upriver to where he'd last seen them—where he'd seen the native woman struggling as the violent water rose and rose around her legs—feet slipping as she held their daughter up around her neck.

The raft was there where he'd left it—flat on the ground among the trees. He stopped suddenly when he saw the woman seated on top of the rough-cut logs with Mondo and May on her lap—both suckling at her breasts with river water dappled over their tiny bodies. The woman sat there with her eyes closed—back straight with her head held high—never turning to look at Mark—her arms draped around his children—letting drops of water coalesce and drip down her face in jagged, speckled lines—calm and relaxed with one leg crossed over the other.

Mark ran to them and dropped to his knees—thud on the hard, wet platform of logs—the sudden jolt of his bodyweight causing both children to stop suckling. He cried uncontrollably and his body shook—sticky saliva and mucus oozing from his nostrils and the corners of his open mouth—rubbing Mondo's back and shoulder and placing his other hand on May's head—hair wet and curly under his palm.

Eventually he looked up at the woman—tears in his eyes distorting her image. He watched her pull the two children back toward her breasts and hold them as they went eagerly for more milk—Mark sitting there in front of them—his body finally beginning to calm after what seemed like a long time—his heart rate gradually slowing and the tears eventually drying from his cheeks. He watched them until Mondo and May both closed their eyes—air warming as the sun rose and lit up the highest parts of the jungle canopy—only dim, leftover light making it to the forest floor.

The woman finally turned and opened her eyes to look at Mark—staring at him without anger or fear showing on her face. She said something to him in a soft voice—seemingly aware her words would not be understood by the strange man who'd nearly gotten them killed. There was no scowl or grimace—no pointing or gesturing—no change at all to her facial expression. But Mark got the message she intended for him—the harsh words he knew he deserved—blame he knew he couldn't avoid.

The children slept once they'd had their fill of the woman's milk—Mark sitting there in front of them on the raft the whole time—the woman closing her eyes again but not sleeping—holding Mondo and May while they slept for hours—Mark watching over them—never turning to look up at the rising sun through the layered screen of jungle leaves—birds flitting from branch to branch above their heads—the river's violent push and constant, garbled sounds.

Mondo and May finally woke up around midday—Mondo stretching and looking around as he pressed his tiny body against the woman—May wriggling with her eyes still closed—searching instinctively for more milk. A few minutes later the woman opened her eyes and yawned—stood up without looking at Mark—without detaching their daughter from her breast—Mondo soon standing beside her—holding her hand and shyly glancing at his father.

"Where are you going?" Mark said as the woman turned and started walking away from the river—knowing there would be no answer—no chance of stopping her or changing her mind.

The raft seemed heavier now as Mark began dragging it after the woman—grabbing hold of the still-wet ropes and trying not to smash his fingers between the shifting logs. He was tired and his side hurt from whatever had slammed into him earlier in the swirling, chaotic river—nerves still shaky after nearly losing his children.

Mark was out of breath by the time he found the woman—sitting with her back against a tree and Mondo and May in her lap—playing and smiling and almost dry as the afternoon began with no sign of rain. Mark was sweating and his legs were trembling as he struggled through a few more steps before dropping the raft—having walked not far—just minutes and up only a slight incline away from the river—his feet unstable and his vision going dark around the edges.

He collapsed onto the rough-cut logs and closed his eyes—thick blood pounding through his head—breathing hard and deep and almost in rhythm with his heartbeats— bark and clumps of coarse rope digging into his skin.

Minutes passed. His breathing slowed and he opened his eyes—lying on his back and looking straight up into the trees—arms and legs spread wide with feet extending over the edge of the raft. He watched the center of the filtered sunlight move slowly across the sky—tiny specks of piercing warmth shooting through gaps in the chaos of branches and leaves—winding vines and bursting flowers—ripening fruits and drying seed pods.

More minutes passed—hours, maybe. His eyes closed

and he may have slept a little—hearing his children from time to time—laughing and playing—Mondo talking and the woman singing that same song—that rhythm he knew from the full moon nights—the bonfires and the tiny hut—Splinter always there with the charcoal lines tracing across his wrinkled face.

Eventually Mark felt strong enough to sit up. He blinked to clear his vision and then looked over at his children—both suckling at the woman's breasts again—quiet now—the woman's eyes closed and her head resting back against the tree—mumbling through the same song—voice lowered but still full and beautiful—breaking off each time she took in a slow, deep breath.

Mark stood up quietly and paid close attention to his balance—the muscles in his legs and the way his head felt. He heard the river behind him—strong and steady but not nearly as loud as it had sounded earlier. He looked down at his resting children and the sleeping woman—sitting there in the dirt with dead leaves and tree roots all around them—nearly naked and filthy and not at all ready for another hard night.

He turned and took a few careful steps—checking the height of the sun—trying not to make too much noise as he walked away.

Mark sat on a wide green leaf in the middle of the jungle—more giant leaves piled next to him—roofing materials for the night ahead—shelter from the incessant tropical downpours—himself and his children and the woman all huddling together under another makeshift roof.

He felt himself breathing—chest expanding—lungs

pressing out against his sore ribs—loose hair hanging down around his face and beard—empty eyes staring down at his shoeless feet.

He lifted one of the rough-skinned, dark purple pieces of fruit and examined it—several bundles more gathered in his lap—a lucky harvest he'd stumbled across as he wandered through the jungle. His fingers were now stained a deep red from the three or four he'd already peeled and eaten—struggling with his nails to cut through the tough skin. He felt weak and dizzy as he watched his sticky hand tremble—holding the small, dark ball with his fingertips.

The sun was dropping and he knew the day would end soon—drab light filtering through the thick canopy at a sharper and sharper angle. Some of the insects were already coming out to sing their evening songs and he knew there would soon be bats—stealthy, leathery wings zipping silently between the trees.

Mark sat there and thought about his children—waiting for the dizziness to pass—for the trembling hand to steady and for the sugars to reach his bloodstream. Then he would stand up—walk straight back to where he'd left them— bring them the fruit and the pile of wide green leaves—keep them alive and dry for at least one more night.

But as he waited the coming darkness and the still-there hunger began to wear on Mark—the dangers lurking in every tangled corner—disease-carrying insects and venomous snakes—flash floods and poisonous plants—all trying to keep them locked inside their suffocating jungle prison.

He still felt weak as his thoughts quickly went to food— conjuring his favorite dishes in his mind—dark purple bundles of fruit in his lap standing in for mashed potatoes and juicy Thanksgiving turkey—chicken parmesan and green bean casserole—cold beer and strawberry cheesecake.

He soon began to speak to his children as if they were sitting right next to him—filling their plates with savory entrees and perfect sides—trying hard to pretend—to push away the dark thoughts—to dream out loud—to pray for all their struggles to end.

He took turns telling Mondo and May about each dish he served—the way to cook each kind of meat—amount of butter and milk for the mashed potatoes—the way salt brings out flavors and how to make sure the dinner rolls were cooked all the way through.

He poured May a glass of apple juice and tucked a napkin inside the collar of Mondo's shirt. There was music in the background and tall, thin candles stood glowing above the homemade centerpiece—steaming platters arranged carefully by the mittened hands of proud cooks—overflowing gravy boat near Mark's plate—small brown puddle already dribbled onto the white tablecloth.

STORY

"Careful, May. Rolls are hot right out of the oven. You have to juggle it back and forth in your hands until it cools. "Look—like this."

.

.

"That's it—good job!

"Now I'll show you how to butter it. First you take your knife and cut right down the middle. Be careful not to let it break apart. Some rolls are worse about breaking apart than others—crumbly ones that are cooked too long or made with too much flour.

"Now here—smell this. Do you smell the steam coming out?"

.

.

"Now get some butter on your knife. Be careful because your knife's going to be hot still from cutting the roll in half. The butter's going to start melting and trying to slip off the blade."

"There you go. Spread it on the bottom half and then smash the other half down on top."

"It's good, isn't it?"

"Make sure you don't fill up on too many rolls, though. There's a lot of food here—lots of food. We'll have leftovers for weeks."

"Mondo, don't cut into the steak right away, OK? It needs to sit for about ten minutes."

"I know it's hard but there are plenty of other things to eat. Here—take some mashed potatoes. Do you want gravy?"

"Yeah, I know—that was a stupid question. Everybody wants gravy."

"Here, May. Dip that roll in some gravy. There you go."

"No, we can't have dessert until we finish our food. You have to eat your green beans, Mondo—can't just eat steak and mashed potatoes and gravy. I'll give you a piece of cheesecake once you finish what's on your plate."

.

.

"It's in the fridge. The strawberries are in a bowl next to it—whipped cream canister on a shelf in the door with the ketchup and mustard and mayonnaise—next to the carton of eggs I'll use to make breakfast in the morning."

SHOW

MARK: The woman—my daughter's mother—she was with us when we escaped. She was with us the whole time until we finally made it out—back to civilization.

The famous journalist relaxed his arched back—chest sinking and falling as he slowly leaned back in his chair. He brought a hand up to his temple and crossed one leg over the other—tiny smirk forming as his eyes never wandered from Mark's face.

INTERVIEWER: Did she insist on coming along or did you somehow invite her?

MARK: I convinced her to come with us—but she wanted to go—so both, maybe, I guess you could say.

INTERVIEWER: How did you communicate your intentions to her if you had no shared language I-I-I assume you had been planning your escape for quite some time?

MARK: I planned it out ahead of time—hid supplies and made sure I could steal the machete and grab my kids without anyone noticing. And like you said before, we had our own ways of communicating.

INTERVIEWER: Were you going to take your daughter either way—with or without her mother?

Mark nodded—eyes staring through the older man seated across from him—lips folded in on themselves—tight-mouthed as he remembered the second battle—the chaos and confusion—frightened women and confused children—warrior screams echoing through the jungle.

INTERVIEWER: How did it happen the-the-the sequence of events starting from the day you escaped?

MARK: All the men were in the largest hut at the center of the village. It was around noon and we hadn't gone hunting that day because it'd been raining most of the morning. All the kids were running around—chasing each other and sliding on the slick mud—laughing and shouting. I stood in the doorway of my little hut and watched my son playing with another boy—my daughter nursing in her mother's arms off to the side. The rain had stopped and sunlight was just starting to break through the clouds.

INTERVIEWER: It was just the perfect moment where everything fell into place and-and-and you saw your chance and you took it is that what I'm hearing you say?

MARK: That's right. I grabbed all the rope I'd stashed away—the machete and a few other supplies. Then I went and chased down my son—picked him up and walked over to my daughter and her mother. She knew something was going on—you could see it in her eyes. Our daughter was asleep and I looked down at her—some milk leaking out of her mouth around her little lips.

I put my hand on her mother's back and she turned and let me guide her into the jungle—walking fast and being as quiet as we could be. We just kept going the rest of that day—got to the river and followed it downstream until it got dark.

The famous journalist shifted in his chair—clearing his throat as he uncrossed his legs and leaned forward—elbows stabbing down into the tops of his knees and hands coming together in front of him. Mark watched the pale, puffy, soft fingertips tapping each other in the space between their two chairs—almost within reach. He focused on the older man's hands and the conference room carpet—avoiding the man's eyes—the black glass eyes in each corner of the little curtain-cloaked partition.

INTERVIEWER: Why did you say there was no one else with you when you escaped that-that-that you emerged from the jungle alone with your two children?

MARK: Because I loved her. I thought she was coming home with me—raise our kids together and get married—get a dog and a white picket fence and all the rest.

But when I turned around—when I knew it was finally over and we were finally safe—finally out of that terrible place—she was gone. She was just gone.

CHAPTER
FOURTEEN

FACT

MARK SQUINTED HIS EYES AGAINST THE BRIGHT SUN-light hitting his face—unsure how long he'd been asleep—head resting on the pile of wide green leaves he'd collected—bundles of dark purple fruit scattered around his legs—insects beginning to find the weak spots in the tough, thick peels.

A spotlight of the setting sun had somehow weaved its way through the tangled vegetation and now shined unobstructed over his thin body—Mark turning his head as he blinked himself awake—wondering where he was for a moment—where his children were and his daughter's mother—whether just a few minutes had passed or a few hours or maybe even an entire night.

He was alone—quickly on his feet and frantic to get back to the river—to the place he'd last seen Mondo and May. So Mark picked up the bundles of fruit and the pile of leaves—taking a moment to get his bearings before setting off through the jungle—weaving his way between the trees on calloused, shoeless feet—listening for the sounds of the flowing water—making sure each step took him slightly downhill.

He eventually found them at the base of the same tree they'd been resting against when he left—Mondo and May laughing and playing as the woman sang to them. He dropped to his knees and caught his breath—smiling at the happy scene playing out in front of him—night sounds just starting as blackness began to swallow the sky.

Mark set the bundles of fruit down in front of them and watched as the woman expertly peeled away the dark purple skins. While they ate he built a structure of dead and broken branches he found scattered among the decaying layer of leaves that coated the forest floor—leaning them against the tree and butting the raft up to its base. Then he draped the wide green leaves over the structure of soft, wet wood—testing its sturdiness and looking for gaps in the temporary roof as he worked from one side to the other.

The night already seemed old and well established by the time Mark finished with the makeshift shelter—tropical sun always dropping faster than he was used to—setting without the sweeping, slashing angle it had back home in Colorado. So in the deep jungle darkness he inspected the shelter and tested a few of the branches—adjusted some of the leaves as he spotted gaps—then ducked inside and sat on the raft across from the woman—infant daughter suckling at the woman's breast again with her little eyes closed.

"Here, Mondo," Mark said—holding a piece of fruit out to him. "Eat." The boy's mouth and fingers were stained dark red—sitting there next to the woman with his head against her arm—tired and uninterested in his father's offering.

The woman put her arm around Mondo—began softly singing the children to sleep—her pretty voice filling their small shack with music.

Mark sat there in the dark and watched his son begin to grimace and moan—hoping he was just cranky—hoping he wasn't coming down with some strange jungle sickness. Then he turned toward May and worried for her as well—hoping his daughter could still get milk from the underfed woman.

Mark listened to the woman's song and ate the piece of fruit himself—waiting until both his children were asleep—then turning to watch the jungle outside through the little doorway he'd made between the leaves and broken branches. Soon he laid his head down next to Mondo's feet—using his hands placed together as a pillow—adjusting his body on top of the uneven logs and coarse ropes of the raft—the woman still singing as he closed his eyes—still singing as he drifted off into dreams of other places and other times.

Mondo was sick the next morning—sweating and moaning—talking in a soft, pained voice to the woman—mumbled syllables she seemed to have a hard time understanding. There was no rain during the night and Mark looked up at the patchwork roof of wide green leaves—dry and still intact—glowing from bits of sunlight that were somehow piercing the jungle canopy.

Mark sat up and tried to keep thoughts of rain from overwhelming him—how much sicker Mondo might be if it'd stormed last night—what would happen if the dark clouds suddenly appeared later that morning or early in the afternoon—how best to keep his ill child dry and warm so he could be well again as soon as possible.

The woman soon started inching her way toward

Mark—careful not to wake their sleeping daughter as Mondo continued to moan quietly behind her. She motioned for Mark to take their baby—to carefully transfer May into his own arms. May shifted suddenly as he reached out for her—trying to find the warm body she'd been held against all night—eyes still closed as tiny sounds emerged from her puckered, infant mouth. Mark and the woman waited—kneeling in front of each other just inches apart—watching their daughter slowly fall back into a deep sleep—Mark finally taking May from the woman a minute or two later—cradling her in his arms and making sure to support her head.

The woman laid herself out flat on the raft as Mark slowly sat back with his sleeping infant daughter—watching the woman stare up at the green leaves he'd laid over the makeshift frame—stretching her arms and legs—fingers fanned and reaching—feet and toes flattening out and causing her calf muscles to flex. Mark watched her—waited and tried to be patient as Mondo moaned in a crumpled ball against the base of the tree.

Mark sat there for what seemed like a long time—inside the little shelter he'd built the night before—the woman still stretching in front of him—May still sleeping and his son in agony not six feet away. He lost his patience after having watched the woman for several minutes—twisting her body and bending her limbs—articulating each joint in every direction. He poked at her a few times with his toe before she got to her feet—bent down and lifted Mondo off the raft—carried him past Mark and out the little open doorway—sweat on the boy's forehead—both hands folded over his stomach.

Mark hoped the woman was just taking him to the river—replace the fluids he'd lost—maybe come across some medicinal plant she had knowledge of that could cure whatever sickness he had—just a stomachache, Mark told himself—too much fruit and too little of everything else.

May woke up an hour or two after the woman and Mondo had left the little temporary hut—after the sun had moved across the sky and nearly reached its apex—Mark anxiously following the bright glow as it slowly moved over the green leaves of the makeshift roof he'd built—waiting for his daughter to finish her sleep.

He looked down at May as he felt her moving and saw her eyes opening—blinking and staring up at him. He smiled—watched her and could think of nothing else as she studied the features of his face.

But once she was fully awake May began searching and diving toward his chest—instincts of hunger kicking in with the impatience of a fast-growing infant. Mark tried to give her his finger—tried to rock her in his arms and talk to her. But she soon began to cry and scream—tears being squeezed between her tightly shut eyelids—so he crawled out of the shelter as carefully as he could—ducking and measuring each step—shielding his howling child from the low-hanging branches and leaves—then hurried toward the river—not yet looking up from his feet but assuming he'd find the woman and Mondo there.

"She's hungry," Mark said—having found them resting against a tree just a few feet from the brown, flowing water.

The woman moved slowly—reaching up to take their crying infant. When Mark looked down he saw Mondo—asleep with his head resting in the woman's lap—still examining his son as he knelt and helped the woman position their screaming daughter—cradling the back of her head with one hand—unsure what to do with the other.

Once May settled down and began to nurse Mark stood up again and felt weak—sick almost even though he was relieved to see Mondo sleeping peacefully. His stomach churned and he felt dizzy and his hands trembled—body-weight shifting involuntarily between the balls of his feet and his heels. He managed to sit down as he tried to focus on not vomiting—not allowing his body to give up what little he had in his stomach—the fruit and the murky river water. He thought about the energy it would take to run to a spot far enough away—to contract all the muscles in his midsection.

After a few minutes Mark looked up at his children—Mondo in a deep sleep—dry and warm—May with her lips dancing over the woman's nipple—eyes staring up at her mother's face. He watched them and waited for the spell of nausea to pass—for his hearing to return to normal and for the shaking of his hands to stop—his vision to gradually come back into focus.

It was early afternoon by the time Mark got the raft dragged down to the river's edge. He dropped the platform of heavy logs onto the sand and stood there with his hands on his hips—panting and looking up at the sky above the flowing water—approximating the location of the sun—the distance it had travelled past its noon position.

"Once I find a paddle, we'll go," Mark said as he kept peering up at the sky—still panting—the woman and his children sitting against a tree a few steps behind him. "Machete's gone—food's all gone."

He dropped to his knees on the smooth, wet sand and

felt tiny waves splashing against his thighs—then cupped his hands and lifted water to his lips—watching his trembling fingers as they allowed most of it to slip away—telling himself it was just fatigue from dragging the raft—that his symptoms would soon subside—that the blackness at the edges of his vision would soon recede.

"I'm not dying, you know," Mark said—this time turning to address the woman—muddy river water dripping down his matted beard. "I'm fine—we're fine." He nodded as they looked at each other—both trying to believe that they'd all survive—all four of them—or at least the two children.

Mondo was awake now—trying to play with his baby sister in the woman's lap—waving his little hands in front of her face. Mark smiled as he watched them—kept breathing as deeply and slowly as he could—still working to push away the hunger and exhaustion—the nausea and the bad thoughts.

"We'll make it—we'll make it out of here."

Once he was able to stand up—to ignore his twisting stomach and pounding head—it didn't take him long to find a paddle. The flooding river had washed down numerous pieces of driftwood—had left them scattered all along the receding shoreline—gray, cracked logs left to rot—to wait for the next flood on the sand and mud. He found a piece with a broad, flat end that was around three feet long—dead wood still water-logged from being in the river.

"OK," Mark said—sliding the raft into the water over the packed wet sand. "Let's go." He held the raft steady by the ropes he'd looped and tied tightly around the logs—standing in knee-deep water—feeling the current already trying to push and pull him downriver.

He looked up at the woman and motioned for her to stand—to bring his children to him—to climb on top of the strange, floating platform that the strange, hairy man had made—to leave solid ground for the first time in her life.

She watched him and Mark could tell she was unsure—nervous and maybe even a little scared. Her eyes bounced between the raft, her daughter and Mark as she assessed the situation—returning to her calm and confident demeanor after just a few seconds—fearless as she'd always portrayed herself to be—the woman with the loud laugh and pretty singing voice—taller than most and older than some.

She stood up and walked in a straight line to the river's edge—holding Mondo's hand and keeping May pressed against her chest. Mark watched her and kept the raft steady—one edge bouncing against the sandy shore while the other floated freely in the brown water.

He glanced up at the sun and guessed they had at least four hours of daylight left—clouds gathering in the distance—some turning dark gray—Mark watching them as he began to worry about a storm bubbling up while they were on the river—the lack of shelter—passing a blind night soaked and cold—bobbing helplessly in the muddy, black water—May and Mondo getting sick or their raft overturning.

"Maybe we'll stop tonight," Mark said as the woman tested the raft with an outstretched foot. "Build another shelter and stay dry—let the kids sleep." He watched the woman as she inched her way forward—unsure of the water and the strange craft of logs and braided rope. "Maybe we'll find some food—pork chops and some pasta—chicken fettuccini." He smiled at her and held out a hand—lifting her arm as she struggled to get herself and the children up onto the raft.

It started raining soon after they got themselves situated—the raft sinking a little under their shifting weight—the woman placing herself in the middle with Mondo and May huddled together on her lap—Mark behind them and up on his knees—driftwood paddle in his hands. The rain came down in small, regular drops and there was no wind—no debris left floating down the river and no sudden surge of floodwaters. Mark smiled as they began to drift out into the middle of the river—even though it was raining and the sky was full of gray clouds—even though they were skinny, hungry and the raft was nearly submerged under their collective bodyweight—allowing even the smallest waves to wash over the logs and splash against their skin.

"We're moving," Mark said as they began to float with the current—raindrops making myriad little dimples on the river's brown surface.

He turned his head from side to side—checking both banks—watching trees and sandy stretches of shoreline as they slowly drifted past. He smiled again and felt his body lifting and filling—coming alive as blood seemed to reach deeper into the muscles of his legs and arms—each breath coming more easily as he allowed himself to hope.

It rained all afternoon—consistent, medium-sized drops—no wind to blow them around and no lightning or thunder. The woman stayed huddled over Mark's children the whole time—wet hair matted to her head and parted down the middle. Mark watched May's tiny hand slip between the woman's arm and side—delicate fingers stretching and playing across the woman's back. He listened to Mondo making noises and talking softly to the woman. Mostly, though, he watched the river and the sky—kept their little makeshift raft away from shore.

Late that evening—as Mark began looking for a place to exit the river for the night—the rain suddenly stopped and the sky cleared—then sunset colors spread quickly across the dissipating clouds—first few stars just starting to show in the east. Mark kept paddling—steering most of the time with the piece of driftwood used as a rudder. He wondered if he should still find a place for them to camp—to put a roof over Mondo and May and maybe even try to build a fire—find something for them to eat if he was lucky—if he had the strength, the courage and the moonlight to walk any distance into the dark jungle.

Weighing his options as they drifted downriver, Mark felt the emptiness of his stomach again—the idleness of his whole digestive system as he allowed his mind to wander once more to food. His body was exhausted from the afternoon of rain and the little waves constantly splashing against his legs—the paddling and steering—the worrying.

"How are they?" Mark said—leaning forward and pulling on the woman's shoulder.

The woman leaned back and let him see Mondo's face—lips moving up and down over small teeth as he mumbled and smiled—his hair wet but not nearly as wet as the woman's. May was suckling at the woman's breast with her eyes closed—hands exploring and fingers testing their movements.

Mark could feel the woman shaking under his hand—shoulder quivering but not violently—consistent vibration his eyes could not see. He looked at the woman and saw that her eyes were closed—face studded with raindrops that were leaking down out of her hair—her head swaying with the easy, regular motion of the raft. She did not sing as she often did when it wasn't raining—when she had Mondo smiling on her lap and May drinking her milk.

"We're going pretty fast," Mark said. "We've covered probably ten miles already—at least." He turned his head and looked out over the river—rippling, muddy water shoving past them—moving slightly faster than the raft. Then he looked up and saw the full moon just starting to rise over the treetops—its yellow face reflecting off the undulating surface of the water.

Mark didn't look down again until Mondo began to whine—fussing against the woman's chest—trying to find a comfortable position with his eyes closed—his legs dangling down over the woman's knee. May stirred but stayed attached to the woman's breast—her eyes opening wide—searching for the source of the cries she was hearing.

"Let's keep going," Mark said. "The moon's out—doesn't seem like it wants to rain—river's calm." He nodded his head and looked as far as he could downstream—wall of trees a few hundred yards away where the river made a sharp turn.

The woman was staring up at him when Mark looked back down—stronger it seemed without the swaying head or shivering shoulders—her eyes steady and calm with no tears forming. She did not blink and eventually he looked away—busying himself with the driftwood paddle as he scanned the surface of the river.

Eventually the woman spoke—still twisted around to stare up at his face—pronouncing words they both knew he wouldn't understand—his two children held in her arms. But Mark didn't acknowledge the sound of her voice—trying to act like he hadn't heard her—like she could have been speaking to someone else—or maybe not even making any noise at all.

He continued scanning the river and both banks—darkening walls of tangled vines and jungle trees. The sunset colors were nearly gone from the sky now and the moon was rising quickly—more and more stars becoming visible—tiny dots of light wavering in whites and pale yellows.

Soon the woman turned back around to face forward—huddling over Mondo and May with her back to Mark. He knelt behind them and worried about how quickly rain-clouds could appear overhead—how long it would take him to paddle to shore. He thought about the woman's warning two nights prior when the river flooded and nearly carried them all away—about the possible meaning of the strange words she'd just spoken to him.

Mark sat back on his heels—floating down a wild jungle river on a makeshift raft in the middle of the night—his two half-native children in front of him—cradled by the native woman whose milk was keeping them alive. He watched the woman's back—little hands and heads fidgeting around her sides. His own hands still gripped the driftwood paddle—loose hair hanging down around his face and beard—eyes heavy with sleep and hunger.

He held out his hand and watched his fingers twitch in the moonlight—dirt and river water and jagged, broken nails—tanned, tough skin. He felt weak and dizzy but didn't have the urge to vomit this time—slowly setting the paddle down across his thighs—dead wood scraping against his thin legs.

Insects were still singing their mating songs and he watched bats flit silently over the raft—stealthy wings flapping as they went from one side of the river to the other. Mark thought about his children and waited for the dizziness to pass—for the shaking hands to steady—for whatever strength he had left to reach his arms and to trickle down into his fingers. Then he would paddle and steer them down the river as they slept—piloting by the light of the full moon a raft he built with his own hands to rescue his children—to save himself and to give them all a simple, safe and perfectly boring life.

As he waited the darkness and the still-there hunger began to wear on Mark—the dangers lurking in the black water—in the jungle and in every moment spent struggling to escape. He sat there with his feet folded underneath him and began to obsess over food—driftwood paddle across his thighs standing in for chicken piccata and baked potatoes and a cheese-stuffed meatloaf—caesar salad and bacon-wrapped dates—cold beer and chocolate chip cookies.

Mark spoke to his children as he filled their plates with food—real food that he knew was not there. But he tried to pretend and to push away the dark thoughts—to dream out loud—to pray for his children's struggles to end. He told them about each dish he served—the way to mix all the ingredients together for chocolate chip cookie dough—amount of butter and sour cream for the baked potatoes—the way to squeeze lemons through a strainer so you can throw away the seeds.

He poured May a glass of apple juice—tucked a napkin inside the collar of Mondo's shirt. There was music in the background and candles on the table—steam rising from the chicken—cheese oozing and spreading from cracks in the base of the meatloaf.

STORY

"Just like Thanksgiving—whole table full of food right here—even had to set up one of those cheap folding tables for the cheese plate—the vegetable platter and the fancy cured meats with names I can't pronounce—all the snacks—might even need another one for the desserts."

.

.

"When I was a kid we'd always do that for Thanksgiving—set up an extra table in the living room for the chips and crackers—olives and pickles and those little weenies smothered in barbecue sauce. My father had a lot of brothers and they'd all be in front of the TV watching football—beers and snacks and their wives would be yelling at them to slow down—to not get too full or too drunk. My mother, your grandmother, was always the loudest."

.

.

"It'll be a smaller group once we make it back—less

people to eat all this food—just my sister and her kids, probably."

    .

    .

"We'll carry the food to the table—baked potatoes and corn on the cob—steaks with chimichurri sauce."

    .

    .

"Those Thanksgivings when I was a kid—every year my mother insisted on lighting a bunch of tall candles around the centerpiece—leaning over the table with a lighter as the food was brought in—then dimming the lights until it was hard to see.

"My father would always wait until everyone was in their seats—watching us all as we passed around steaming side dishes and filled our plates. Then after everyone was settled in—drinks filled and napkins placed in laps—after us kids finally stopped fighting with each other—my father would stand up and there'd be this dull yellow light everywhere from the candles—him clearing his throat and making a big show of it. Everyone would stop and look up at him—stop talking and you'd hear serving spoons being placed carefully back into dishes. Then he'd start saying grace—reciting the little speech you could tell he'd written out and practiced delivering at least a few times in front of the bathroom mirror. Once he was finished he'd lean over the table and start carving the turkey—rattling off some stupid jokes while everyone watched him and waited for their portion."

    .

    .

"He always gave me the first piece—big slice right off the breast with the skin still on it—crispy brown and slimy and salty underneath. He'd look at me and wait until I said thank you—then he'd go on carving the rest of the turkey. Everyone would be talking and laughing—but I'd just sit there and look at my plate with my mouth watering—my first piece of Thanksgiving turkey—almost too pretty and special to eat."

.

.

"Then someone would plop a spoonful of mashed potatoes down in front of me and I'd snap out of it—start making faces across the table at my cousins—begging for someone to pass the gravy boat and the rolls."

.

.

"It'll be like that when we get home. After dinner we'll sit around the living room playing games—board games like Monopoly and Scrabble. Maybe your grandmother will have some big sheets of paper and an easel so we can play Pictionary."

SHOW

INTERVIEWER: So where did she go this native woman you'd fallen in love with I-I-I mean did she return to her people to the village or-or-or was she possibly taken into custody by local authorities?

MARK: I don't know.

The famous journalist threw his hands in the air—falling backward at the same time into the soft padding of his chair—printouts rising out of his lap in a creased, jumbled stack still pinched between his soft fingers. Mark lowered his eyes and watched the older man's polished shoes come off the ground a few inches—then drop back down with a thud—timed to coincide with a sarcastic huff from his already open mouth.

INTERVIEWER: How can you not know I mean this is the woman you loved the-the-the woman you had a daughter with how is it possible that you just couldn't find her all the sudden as if she'd disappeared into thin air I-I-I mean how does that make any sense?

There was a stain on the conference room carpet—barely visible on a section of the thin white cords that snaked away in repeating rows. Mark focused on the stain as he shook his head and shrugged his shoulders—no other acceptable answer coming to mind for the man across from him—for the hordes of viewers sitting at home on their couches—sipping their sodas or their glasses of wine as they watch him two or three weeks from now—bowing his head in anguished silence.

He sat there and continued examining the stain—wondering how it had gotten there—how long ago and under what circumstances—spilled cocktail at a wedding reception, maybe—maybe a dropped hors d'oeuvre during a corporate dinner party.

INTERVIEWER: Let's go back to the beginning of your escape when you took your son and your daughter and your daughter's mother and you fled into the jungle now-now-now once you reached the river what happened?

MARK: We followed it downstream until it got dark. Then I found a spot to make camp—high enough and far enough from the river so we wouldn't get caught in a flood in the middle of the night. I built a shelter and we slept—or they slept. That would be more accurate.

INTERVIEWER: And the woman, your daughter's mother, was she scared or hesitant at all? Did you ever worry about her leaving or-or-or somehow alerting the tribe as to your whereabouts?

MARK: No. She was braver than I was most of the time—took care of the kids and kept them calm—sang to them and played with them and put them to sleep—helped me find fruit and the giant leaves I'd use to put a roof over our heads every night. I think she was determined to help us get out safe—get to wherever we were trying to go—determined to make sure the kids survived.

The famous journalist nodded—an elbow propped up on the arm of his chair—splayed fingers pressed against his cheek and chin. He flapped the printouts against his leg with his other hand and kept nodding—staring and not talking until Mark looked away.

INTERVIEWER: Let's take a break.

Mark stood up and followed the famous journalist through the parted black curtains—trailed a few feet behind him as they left the conference room and walked out into the hotel lobby. They passed the front desk without talking and without looking at each other—Mark behind and to the side—a little surprised at how fast the older man moved.

INTERVIEWER: I'm going to take a piss. Then we'll go across the street to the park.

The famous journalist looked back but never stopped walking as he spoke. Mark stood near the automatic doors and watched him stride into the bathroom—needing to go himself but not wanting to follow the older man inside for some reason.

So he lingered there in the sunshine streaming in through the glass doors—then paced back and forth between the hotel's main entrance and a forgotten corner of the lobby where payphones had once been installed—empty counters with offset, dimpled holes still visible on the wall through layers of white paint.

INTERVIEWER: Beautiful dry day like today must make you glad to be back—to be out of that tropical humidity once and for all.

MARK: It's nice.

They walked through the automatic doors and stood next to each other on the sidewalk—both squinting as their eyes adjusted to the bright sunshine—breeze blowing across their faces as people walked by in front and behind them—bikes and cars and loud, lumbering delivery trucks gliding over the smooth surface of the road.

INTERVIEWER: Some people go into the woods or up a mountain to find calm or tranquility or whatever but I like this—the madness and chaos with the whole damn world buzzing by—chasing its own tail in a tight little circle around me.

The famous journalist smiled at Mark—popping up on the balls of his feet with hands on his belt—elbows jutting out away from his body. Then he hurried down the hotel steps and across the busy street—stepping confidently over the brightly striped crosswalk—little yellow lights in the pavement blinking to alert oncoming traffic in both directions.

Mark followed the older man but lagged behind—cautiously waiting for the cars and trucks and busses to all come to complete stops.

INTERVIEWER: They always stop I've crossed this street a thousand times.

The famous journalist was standing there on the other side of the busy street—yelling back across with hands on his waist again—smiling as he waited for Mark to join him at the entrance to the park—strollers and skateboards and leashed dogs populating the sidewalks—dark green patches of grass covered in a few spots by picnic blankets.

They started down a path that ran perpendicular to the street—rising over a little hill with leafy branches fanning out overhead—shaded benches evenly spaced—small placards riveted to their gently sloping backs—dedicating each one to a departed friend or family member.

INTERVIEWER: Our stories are more important than we are, you know. We're nearly always too stupid to learn anything from our own experiences but we can and very often do learn something from the experiences of others.

MARK: So you're just trying to help people? That's what you do for a living?

INTERVIEWER: Yes, Mark, I am. I'm trying to help them learn from your incredible story to-to-to glean some sort of knowledge or understanding from what you've been through—the whole story of what you've been through—and apply it to their own lives.

MARK: That's very generous.

The famous journalist stopped—turned toward Mark as a trio of women pushed strollers full of sleeping, pacified children around them. Mark stopped and peeked under the brightly-colored sunshade of one of the strollers as it passed—messy hair and clear, glimmering slobber leaking down to the collar of the child's cotton shirt.

INTERVIEWER: It is generous and-and-and I know what you're thinking, Mark, but just because I happen to get paid to do it—happen to get paid quite well these days and-and-and just because I happen to get myself invited to fancy parties and award shows on a fairly regular basis—it never boils down to simple greed for me, Mark—never.

Mark watched the three women as they walked away—one laughing quietly with a hand covering her mouth—a joke having been whispered between them as they carefully navigated a crack in the sidewalk—every movement slowed and every word muted so they didn't wake the children.

INTERVIEWER: Look at me, Mark. Look at me.

CHAPTER FIFTEEN

FACT

Mark stayed awake all night—talking softly to his sleeping children—dozing off only as the full moon began to set—his head dipping forward—his eyes closing but never for more than a few seconds at a time. He used the driftwood paddle as a rudder and allowed the current to carry them downriver—dark water with a thick band of moonlight shining across its rippling surface.

The woman seemed to sleep the entire night as she crouched over Mondo and May—curling her arms around them and allowing both to drink her milk as they pleased. Mark watched her ribs as she breathed—pushing out and stretching the skin of her back—knots of vertebrae running down the center. He listened to her cough and clear her throat a few times during the night—listened to the soft baby sounds of the daughter they shared—mumblings from Mondo as his young mind raced through dreams.

All night he scanned the dark riverbanks for any sign of civilization—an electric light or metal roof—raising his eyes from time to time to watch the moon and the stars slowly sweep across the blackness above their heads—attempting at one point to find the constellations he'd learned as a boy but unable to locate any—unable even to keep his head tilted back for more than a minute or two at a time.

"Almost time for breakfast," Mark whispered—still working hard to keep himself awake—still fixated on food.

The woman had woken up in front of him and raised her head to look around—moon and most stars now gone—sky quickly turning gray and blue.

Mark breathed deep through his nose and fixed his eyes downriver—stomach turning over on itself—vision starting to blur around the edges. He gripped the driftwood paddle and felt his hands shake with weakness—closing his eyes as he waited for his strength to return—hoping this would not be the time he passed out or vomited—startling his still-sleeping children and tipping them all off the raft.

"I'm OK," Mark said to himself—only mumbled sounds making it out of his mouth. "I'm alright." He sat up straight—opened his eyes and began scanning the banks of the river over the woman's head—eyelids drooping as the morning light suddenly dimmed for a moment—body and mind demanding sleep but another part of him pushing—pumping blood and adrenaline to keep all parts up and running—awake and alert and alive. "Almost home," he said—blinking and shaking his head. "We're almost home."

Mark began to paddle a few minutes later as his strength slowly returned—letting the piece of driftwood slip down into the river—then pulling against the weight of the water with his quivering arms—repeating the motion slowly—shimmering droplets sometimes splashing over his thin legs.

Soon the sun was fully above the horizon in front of

them and Mark raised his head—closed his eyes and let the warm, bright rays strike his face—burning into his delicate eyelid skin. He continued paddling—steering when he needed a break—always managing to keep them in the middle of the river. The sky was clear and blue now—brown water moving through dense green walls of jungle—birds all awake and singing their morning songs—going from tree to tree in search of food or love.

Mondo began to stir not long after the sun had risen above the tops of the trees—warming the boy's skin as he sat up on the woman's lap—wrapped in her arm with his cheek pressed against her chest. Mark watched him as he yawned and stretched—arms and little hands and fingers unfurling—dipping down to the surface of the water. He could see his son's curly hair—dry and shining in the sunlight.

"How'd you sleep, Mondo?" Mark whispered—unsure whether May was still sleeping or not—hidden as she was in the woman's other arm.

Mondo turned his head and peeked around the woman—probably just to see who was talking, Mark thought—doubting his son recognized his name just yet—his bright, curious eyes busy studying his father's face. Soon, though, he lost interest in the strange man at the back of the raft—turning instead to the woman's breast for his breakfast.

"Hey!" Mark screamed— trying to clear his blurred vision so he could watch for a reaction—blinking hard with his raised, flattened hand shading his eyes—desperate to confirm what he thought he'd just seen along the riverbank.

Mark did not understand the words yelled in

reply—sounds coming across the closing gap of water between the man's aluminum boat and their makeshift raft. He tried to listen more closely—elation and disbelief causing him to shake as tears formed in his eyes—adrenaline surging through his starving veins—worn-down body and exhausted mind close to their limits.

"Hey!" Mark screamed again—the only thing he could push out of his mouth—lower jaw chattering—trembling hands barely able to hold onto the driftwood paddle.

The woman sat up straight and pressed the children hard against her chest—holding them as she'd done all night just above the water that lapped against her bare legs.

The sun was bright and harsh now—angling upward in front of them as they closed in on the wooden dock and long boat—a man standing with a foot on the edge of each—seemingly dumbstruck and unsure what to do—cotton shorts and shirt and wide-brimmed hat shading his face and shoulders—rubber sandals on his feet.

"Hey!" This time only a tiny, mumbled sound came out as Mark tried to paddle—weak strokes barely helping to push them along.

He raised one hand and waved—then used nearly all his remaining strength to lift the paddle out of the water and swing it wildly above his head—nearly dropping it onto the woman and his children—drops of water raining down on them from the long piece of driftwood.

Soon they were floating up next to the man's gray aluminum boat—Mark making frantic, feeble strokes again with the paddle—smile on his face as the man leaned toward them with a coiled rope in his hands—eyes wide and searching—mouth open in disbelief.

The woman scooted away as their raft bumped into the boat's stern—turning it in the current and nearly tipping them over—Mark's children pressed and screaming against the woman's chest.

But as the edge of the raft lifted out of the brown water, Mark grabbed onto the aluminum boat and stopped its momentum—countering the woman's weight and over-powering the pull of the current—somehow raising himself up at the same time to reach the rope held out by the man. He looked up into the man's eyes—shocked at the site of Mark's beard and emaciated body—small piece of cloth and coarse rope wrapped around his waist—his wild, desperate eyes and the terrified native woman with him—clutching two small children on the far edge of a raft made of rough-cut logs.

"Thank you," Mark said—smiling up at the man as he tried to say something else—tried to answer some of the questions the man obviously had but the words refused to form—muscles twitching uncontrollably throughout his throat and mouth—his arms shaking—hands cramping as he clung to the man's rope and struggled to keep the raft from floating away—strange combination of exhaustion and exhilaration pouring tears down his weathered cheeks.

Mark pulled himself into the man's aluminum boat—falling over the side with one arm holding desperately to the makeshift raft—the woman just beginning to shout something in the strange language Mark never came to understand. He raised himself up onto his knees and looked at her—her head tilted toward the man with the cotton clothes and the rubber sandals—pleading eyes trying to tell him something—strong voice raised over the fearful wailings of Mondo and May.

The man said something back to her in his own language—look on his face showing that he hadn't understood the woman's words—her language somehow not related at all to his own—spoken by a prehistoric tribe probably no more than fifty miles away—hidden inside an untouched patch of jungle for thousands of years.

Mark reached out and grabbed Mondo by the arm—pulling and turning the raft as the woman tried to speak again to the man. She hesitated to let go of the boy—crying along with his half-sister ever since they first saw the boat and the dock and the man with the odd clothes and the strange things hooked onto his feet—tightening grip of the woman only confirming his fear and distrust—increasing the ferocity of his toddler screams.

The woman kept talking as Mark took Mondo from her and dragged him into the boat—kept her eyes on the man who'd just found them drifting out of the jungle. But Mark could tell the man had given up trying to understand the woman's words—still in shock over the wild strangers he was pulling from the river—mouth open and eyes darting as he helped hold the makeshift raft against the side of his aluminum boat.

"Come on," Mark said—reaching out for the woman with one hand as he fought to keep Mondo still with the other—their eyes meeting as Mark watched the expression on her face start to change—fear still showing but receding as she became more confident—more steady as she relented—realizing once again how futile it would be to continue her protests.

Mondo kept trying to get away from his father—away from the strangeness of the man now standing above him—the hard gray boat and the wooden dock somehow suspended above the river. At the same time May was screaming against the woman's chest—searching for comfort amid all the commotion.

"It's alright," Mark said to the woman—wagging his fingers and nodding his head.

As Mark continued trying to coax the woman off the

raft, the man tried to speak to him—standing in his swaying aluminum boat above the strange scene he could barely believe. Mark did not acknowledge the man at first—keeping his hand held out for the woman to grab—fighting with his terrified son at the same time. But the man continued trying to talk to him—repeating the same words over and over.

"American," Mark finally said—hoping to provide a quick answer as he glanced up at the man—squinting and blinking his eyes against the sun.

He didn't wait for a response or to see the expression on the man's face—turning back immediately to the frightened woman and resuming his finger wagging—eye contact and head nodding to persuade her to leave the raft—to step out of the wild and into the civilized world—his daughter held securely in her arms.

A few seconds later Mark felt the man pulling on Mondo—still talking as he took Mark's writhing son from his arm and climbed up out of the boat and onto the dock—sandaled feet slapping down on the wood planks in a quick, practiced motion—Mark's screaming, naked, half-native son over his shoulder.

The woman looked up at them—glancing over Mark's head at the man struggling with the boy she'd kept alive throughout their journey—not her son but still a child of hers. Then she looked back down and met Mark's eyes as she grabbed his hand—pulling and scooting herself toward the near edge of the raft—toward the aluminum boat and wooden dock—the whole rest of the world.

"That's it," Mark said. "Careful."

The woman was unsteady but doing her best to be brave—May still crying as her tiny, helpless body was jostled between the woman's chest and flexed arm. Mark saw the makeshift raft begin to lift and flip—far side coming up out of the water as he tried to keep the near side from sinking—the woman's weight now on the edge of the last round log. She leaned and rolled onto her back and Mark grabbed her under her arms and pulled with all his remaining strength—lifting with his shaky muscles so the woman's back would clear the edge of the man's long boat.

Mark fell backward with the woman and May on top of him—their raft of rough-cut logs splashing and rocking as it spun away from the aluminum boat—current pushing and pulling it downstream—floating high in the water now without the weight of four desperate passengers.

Mark was breathing hard as May cried near his ear and the woman's weight pressed down on his chest—held them tight anyway and waited—breathed and felt the violent swaying of the boat as it slowly started to calm—heard the man trying to talk to Mondo as they waited above them on the wooden dock.

Once Mark felt strong enough he sat up while the woman scooted back and tried to calm their daughter—reached for the man's outstretched hand and pulled himself out of the boat—turned on the edge of the dock and pulled the woman up with May still pressed to her chest. Then they all stood up and began to follow the man away from the river—aluminum boat bobbing gently in the rippling, sparkling water—alone as it swayed against the pillars of the wooden dock.

Mark took May from the woman as she paused to examine the wood planks beneath their feet—such a familiar material used in such a strange way—suspended path over the muddy river—somehow keeping them elevated and dry.

Once on solid ground Mark took Mondo's hand and they

followed the man up a hill—cleared patches of grass carved out of the forest where nature had been tamed—managed in a way Mark was more familiar with. He looked at the man's clothes and down at his sandals as they walked a few steps behind him—Mondo at his side and May in his arms—feeling all the cuts, scrapes and bruises covering his body—the sore muscles and the foggy exhaustion in his mind—feeling how weak he was as he examined the healthy skin and thin layer of fat on the backs of the man's arms.

"We made it," Mark said with tears forming in his eyes—breaths coming fuller and deeper than before.

He carried his daughter and held his son's hand—kept following the man up a well-worn path that meandered through the clearing—grass beaten down and clipped short by unseen livestock—trees here and there for shade.

Mark stopped suddenly and looked back to check on the woman—saw her falling far behind as she studied the new landscape—as she turned to inspect again the dock and the boat and the wide brown river—every step careful and unsure—weaker and more scared than he'd ever seen her.

The clearing kept rising as they walked away from the water—up a hill bisected by a straight line of trees. Soon they came to a barbed-wire fence—the man holding open a homemade gate for Mark to walk through with his two children. There were houses beyond with unpainted wooden walls and metal roofs—trees full of mangoes and oranges and a little garden where two women crouched—digging and scraping in the red-brown dirt.

Mark stepped forward onto the packed earth of the

village—saw chickens chasing each other and barefoot children doing the same—men smoking cigarettes as they leaned against the houses where front porches would be—faces turning toward him—leery as they spotted the near-naked stranger and the two young children—curious and some looking fearful or even angry, Mark thought.

A few older women were the first to approach—emerging from the nearest house in floral dresses and aprons—brightly colored sandals on their feet. First they looked down at May—compassion on their weathered faces as Mark held his whimpering daughter.

He felt Mondo clinging to his leg and glanced down as the women slowly gathered around them—his son's curious eyes looking at all the new things—similar to his former village but still very different—foreign to him even though there were children playing and there was dirt and trees and men were talking together in groups.

"She wants milk, I think," Mark said. "Her mother—" He turned and looked back at the line of trees—the barbed-wire fence and the gateway he'd just walked through.

The women were slowly coming closer—a tightening circle of mumbled words he did not understand—gentle hands and motherly stares. Soon a few of them started shouting toward one of the houses—loudly calling out what he somehow knew to be a woman's name. He held tightly onto his daughter as numerous soft fingers began attempting to soothe her cries—wrapped an arm around his son as the scared boy clung to his shriveled, quivering leg—wrinkled faces bending down toward him with smiling, thin-lipped mouths.

The shouting continued and Mark stood there waiting—watching for his daughter's mother to appear at the now-closed gate.

A few minutes later Mark was stepping up into one of the houses—sitting down as directed on a small mattress near the open doorway—allowing a younger woman to take his daughter from his arms—his son still clinging to his side—still terrified—still alive and breathing and hungry and tired.

Mark watched the younger woman sit in a flimsy plastic chair and pull down the low-hanging neck of her thin cotton shirt—watched her bring May to her breast as she cupped the back of his daughter's tiny head—Mark sitting there on the thin mattress as May tried to suckle—loose, matted hair hanging down around his filthy face and beard—his eyes heavy and his stomach turning over on itself.

He looked down at his hands and watched his fingers twitch—dirty skin and the jagged, broken nails. He felt weak and dizzy again and wondered how much longer he could stay awake—how long it would take May to get used to milk that was not her mother's—how to get Mondo something to eat and drink.

Mark sat there and waited for the dizziness to pass—for the shaking hands to steady—for his daughter to stop fussing and his son to stop being scared.

Soon one of the older women came in through the open doorway with two plates of food—another with two plastic cups and a pitcher filled with a cloudy yellow liquid. Mark tried to raise his hands but they would not lift off his lap—fingers unable to spread—muscles unable or unwilling to flex.

The older women dragged plastic chairs over and talked softly to Mondo—words he did not understand as he clung to his father's arm—slowly opening his mouth and taking food held out to him on a metal spoon—rice and beans and his first taste of bread.

As he watched his son eat Mark heard May's cries soften and then change to hums. He looked up and saw her tiny hands exploring the younger woman's thin cotton shirt—her curious eyes staring up at her new source of milk.

Mark watched his children eat inside the darkened room—daylight slanting in through the open doorway—freshly swept wooden floor beneath his bare feet—body begging to stretch itself out on the thin mattress. He felt a deep peace coming over him—his children finally safe inside a dry house with plenty of food—all the terrible jungle dangers gone to yesterday—passing further into memory every second and with every step away from that place. He sat there with tears forming again in his eyes—warm plate of food now being placed in his steadying hands—cup of juice being poured from the plastic pitcher.

Mark began to speak to his children—talking over the gentle whispers of the women in the room. He tried to pretend and to push away all the bad memories—to dream out loud—to pray for his children's futures. He talked to them about going to school and summer vacations—two weeks off every year around Christmas and New Year's.

A thunderstorm began to rumble outside—clouds now dimming the angled block of sunlight shining through the open doorway. Soon raindrops were hitting the metal roof above their heads—at first just single drops smacking down between Mark's spoken words. He sat there holding the full plate of food he'd been given—metal spoon resting untouched between piles of rice and beans—still talking to Mondo and May as the rain steadily increased—his daughter still suckling—eyes closed now and soon to fall asleep—toddler son already on his second plate—hunk of bread half-eaten in his dirty little hand.

By the time the heavy rain started—the deafening, shattering sound coming through unfiltered from the thin metal roof—May was asleep in the younger woman's arms and Mondo had finally finished eating. But Mark was still speaking to his children—words drowned out by the midday storm—language still foreign to all ears but his own. As he spoke the older women stood up and took the uneaten plate of food from his hands—helped him lay his body down on the mattress—positioning Mondo close by his side and covering them both with a sheet and blanket.

Mark's vision was starting to blur with tears and exhaustion but he kept talking—resting on the floor of a barebones house at the edge of the civilized world. He even laughed once or twice at the dreams he was building—imagining his children ripping open presents in their warm, flannel pajamas—Christmas music playing in the background and flames dancing in the fireplace—snow gently falling outside.

STORY

"It'll be snowing in the morning—surprising everyone since it wasn't in the forecast. You'll both wake up early and run downstairs to the living room—Christmas tree all lit up with presents underneath—full stockings hanging over the fireplace. You'll check the plate of cookies you left out and the glass of milk—for Santa. Or maybe you won't even bother and you'll just start tearing into your presents."

.

.

"Me and your mother will come stumbling down the hall—your new mother or whatever you end up calling her—step-mother. I guess you should just call her mom or mommy or whatever."

.

.

"One of us will make a pot of coffee and the other will get something quick going for breakfast—cereal or oatmeal for you two and maybe some toast for us. We'll all have messy hair and we'll be wearing our warm, baggy pajamas—wrinkles everywhere from tossing around in our beds all night."

.

.

"We'll have a rule that you can't start opening your presents until me and your mother sit down with you in the living room. I'm sure we'll take our sweet time in the kitchen with the coffee and everything just to torture you—one or both of you running in from the living room every couple of minutes—begging us to hurry up."

.

.

"It'll be snowing outside. I'll get a fire going in the fireplace and when you two are big enough you can pass out the gifts and the stockings. Your mother will have the camera going—recording everything and cracking jokes she knows will be on the video forever."

.

.

"We'll sit there in the living room and watch you open your presents—watch the fire and the snow and then turn on a Christmas movie. I'll go to the kitchen and make you each a cup of cocoa—something else to eat if you're still hungry."

.

.

"You'll eat and drink your cocoa with those tiny marshmallows floating on top and you'll play with all your new toys—throw the packs of socks and underwear we got you to the side—rummage through your stockings and wonder how Santa could fit through the chimney."

.

.

"Pretty   soon   you'll   both   fall   asleep   on   the floor—wrapping paper and cardboard boxes all around you. I'll get up and sneak over—cover you both with blankets."

.

.

"More wood—more wood for the fire. More food—bacon and eggs and biscuits and pancakes."

SHOW

INTERVIEWER: How about we start the whole thing over, Mark? What do you say we go back in there and-and-and just start the interview from the beginning?

They were alone on the path now—in the shade of large, interlocking branches overhead—sounds of the busy street humming softly in the background. Mark looked at the famous journalist—makeup caked on his face more visible in the filtered sunlight. He saw the desperation in the older man's eyes—the pleading expression that was either genuine or an extremely well-practiced façade.

MARK: Sure.

The famous journalist smiled and slapped Mark on the shoulder—tilted his head back and looked up at the branches—grinning still as creases in the soft skin of his neck stretched open—revealing pale valleys that had evaded the makeup artist's applicator. Mark watched him and wondered what it was like to see yourself on TV every week—to live as a character with a mask and costume but still use your real name.

INTERVIEWER: We'll finish our walk first.

The two men started off again down the path—emerging after a few silent steps into direct sunlight. They eventually came to a playground and Mark followed the older man to a bench near the monkey bars—two children climbing and grunting as they reached fearlessly for each handhold—two others quietly watching off to the side.

INTERVIEWER: I bet you were a little daredevil like those two when you were a kid—climbing on everything and testing yourself—testing boundaries.

MARK: I was actually pretty cautious—careful—more like the two little spectators over there.

INTERVIEWER: Did you grow up here in Denver?

MARK: Never lived anywhere else. Well, I guess that's not really true—not anymore.

The famous journalist laughed—crossed his legs toward Mark and rested an elbow on the back of the bench. Mark sat there and kept watching the monkey bars—one of the two cautious children climbing up and grabbing the first handhold—reaching for the next but never allowing his feet to leave the top rung of the ladder—too scared to swing free above the ground.

INTERVIEWER: You know I've spoken to people who don't believe you ever lived with that tribe. They say all you did was hide out somewhere and have a couple kids with prostitutes or something like that. They think this is all a scam a-a-a made-up story.

MARK: What do you think?

Mark turned to look at the famous journalist—children laughing and chasing each other around the playground—sunlight reflecting off the older man's white, gelled hair.

INTERVIEWER: Either way would work for me—just need a good story for my audience—a good, believable, impactful story. You see, Mark, people have a deep need to hear something amazing that really happened—even if it didn't—or even if only part of it did.

They sat there in silence and watched the children for a minute or two—toddlers going down the big metal slide on their parents' laps—multiple games of tag circling the playground—herds of strollers being loaded and unloaded.

Eventually the famous journalist stood up and started walking back toward the hotel without saying a word—Mark waiting a few seconds before following him down the path. By the time they reached the street Mark had caught up to the older man and they marched through the crosswalk side by side—glancing at the decelerating traffic as the little yellow lights blinkered in the pavement.

The two men walked through the lobby of the hotel and back into the dark conference room—production staff standing around in groups—headsets dangling around some of their necks. The young assistant Mark had seen earlier came rushing over with a cup of coffee for the famous journalist—handing it to him just as they entered the little partition through the parted black curtains—bright overhead lights still shining down—cameras still stationed in each corner.

INTERVIEWER: This cup is somehow worse than the last one. Somebody please remind me to fire that girl after we're finished here.

Mark sat down in his chair as the famous journalist huddled with the cameramen—handing one of them the cup of coffee he'd only sipped at once. Mark watched them and waited—wishing he'd used the bathroom out in the lobby—wondering how much longer he'd have to spend answering the older man's questions—wearing his uncomfortable shoes with makeup on his face and bright, artificial lights beating down on him.

Soon the famous journalist sat down and crossed his legs—smiled at Mark and propped an elbow up on the arm of his chair. There were no printouts in his hands and he seemed more at ease—more relaxed or maybe just acting more relaxed so Mark would give him what he wanted—give him the story he needed for the overhead microphones and the glass-eyed cameras.

INTERVIEWER: So what are your plans now that you're home, Mark? What are your plans for your children?

MARK: I'll need to get a job, I guess.

INTERVIEWER: What'd you do before all this what-what-what was your vocation?

MARK: I did different things—always wanted to go to

medical school or be a photographer but one thing or another always seemed to get in the way.

The famous journalist smiled—closemouthed smirk and a nod.

Mark thought he could hear the whirring of the cameras—buzzing of the lights. He looked around at the black curtains and thought he saw them gently waving as people walked by on the other side—hushed conversations taking place among them—trying to find gaps or inconsistencies in his story—speculating about how many untruths he'd already told.

He looked at the older man across from him—waited for the next question but the famous journalist was silent—nodding still with that smirk on his face—raising his manicured eyebrows slightly—prodding Mark to continue unprompted.

MARK: I'd like to start dating again—meet someone—finally find the woman of my dreams, I guess—give my kids a mother.

I want to make sure Mondo and May go to a good school—a safe school. I want to take them to Disney World and the Grand Canyon and Yellowstone and New York City—Paris and Tokyo and anywhere else they want to go. I want to tuck them into bed every night and give them everything they want for Christmas—throw them huge birthday parties at Chuck E. Cheese's.

I want to save up enough money so they both can go to any college they want—study hard and get good jobs— give me a bunch of grandkids to play with when I'm an old man. Already I'm worried about becoming a burden— needing them to drop everything and take care of me once I reach eighty or ninety. I want to make sure that doesn't happen—that I'm taking care of them until they don't need me anymore—then I'll be gone and they'll have only good memories of me—remembering all the trips and holidays and how good a father I was—how much I loved them.

I guess I'd just like to make all our dreams come true—theirs and mine—that's all.

INTERVIEWER: That sounds wonderful, Mark—just wonderful.

Dear reader,

Thank you for reading **mark**. Please rate and/or review it anywhere and everywhere. Also, keep an eye on my website, AdamDarby.com, for news on upcoming releases or to contact me directly.

Again, thank you for reading,

Adam Darby

*Read the first chapter of **THE RIVER SNAKES** on the following pages. It's an action-packed crime novel set along the Missouri River—full of young love, intergenerational conflict and drug trafficking.*

Enjoy!

1

THE BOY DUCKED DOWN BETWEEN THE NEATLY planted rows and watched the two men—half a cornfield from where they stood—same distance from where he'd left the pickup. The men were on the top of a levee about a quarter mile away—the boy watching them through the swaying leaves of the short, dark green plants—watching them motion with their arms and kick the dirt as they spoke.

The sun was shining and the day had been hot since before noon—little breeze blowing across the field but not strong enough to cool the boy down—sweat soaking through his shirt—pesticide mixture he'd been spraying now sticky on his arms and the back of his neck—hand sprayer sitting on its side behind him—nozzle spurting milky white liquid onto the dirt. It was humid as it always was that time of year—more humid down between the rows of corn where he was crouching.

The boy watched the two men argue for what seemed like a long time—then watched as the man on the right

pulled a pistol from behind his back and started to raise it—
the other man then reaching out grabbing his arm—keeping
the pistol pointed down toward his feet. He saw the unarmed
man jump before he heard the gunshot—then looked more
closely and saw a little cloud of dust rising at the man's feet—
then heard another shot and then another—soon able to see
a red dot forming on the unarmed man's thigh—beginning
to droop and drip down his blue jeans. The boy saw the man
turn and start running down the side of the levee—heard a
string of gunshots and then saw the unarmed man trip or
collapse and start tumbling down the levee—raising dust
and leaving small divots in the dirt as he went.

Crouching even lower beneath the long green leaves the
boy lost sight of the fallen man—looked up at the one with the
pistol still standing there at the top of the levee—his shaded
face staring down at the man he'd shot—eventually taking
off his cowboy hat and wiping his forehead with the sleeve
of his shirt—then releasing the empty clip into his hand and
putting it in his shirt pocket—the boy still watching him as
he pulled another clip out of a pocket in his blue jeans—as
he pushed it up into the pistol. The boy tried not to breathe
as he watched the man standing there staring out over the
large, flat field—tried not to move as the man scanned the
straight rows of corn—the little patch of still-thriving weeds
where the boy was hiding—watching the man shake his
head before turning around and walking toward the river—
descending the other side of the levee.

Once the man was out of sight the boy tried to calm
his nerves—taking deep breaths as he shifted his weight
around—taking his hat off and running a hand through
his sweat-soaked hair—his feet tingling from crouching so
long—his knees stiff.

"What the hell," the boy mumbled to himself several
times—moving to a seated position in the dirt—using his
hat to swat at a pair of flies.

The boy kept watching the top of the levee—wondering if the man with the pistol would come back and do something with the body—wondering if he could make it to the pickup without being seen—wondering if the man had somehow spotted him already. He kept reaching down into his pockets for his cellphone—remembering each time that he'd left it in the pickup—parked on a little hill in a stand of trees at the opposite end of the field.

The boy sat there in the dirt and tried to think—watching and waiting for something to happen—hiding in the middle of the cornfield as the little breeze made the corn leaves sway and clack together—as the humid, heavy air wrapped around him.

Several hours passed with the boy still sitting there—too scared to move—sitting there sweating as the sun slid down diagonally in front of him—dimming as it got closer to the horizon—dropping until the first sunset colors started streaking across the sky—the boy looking up at the pinks and purples—finally starting to relax when he heard another gunshot—only one and he was pretty sure it came from over the levee. He raised up onto his knees but had a hard time seeing anything in that direction with the sun in his eyes—cupping the bill of his hat and pulling it down low over his forehead—not seeing anyone as he did his best to scan the levee.

The boy waited there as the light continued to fade—as clouds of mosquitoes began to appear and buzz around his ears—eventually getting to his feet but still crouching down—grabbing the hand sprayer and gathering the hose so he wouldn't trip—waiting and listening—watching the levee as the pesticide mixture made a sloshing sound inside the little tank.

"Guy probably killed himself," he said.

The boy raised up—stood there above the waist-high corn—the sun turning orange with half of it already below the tops of the cottonwood trees lining the river. He held the hand sprayer in one hand and adjusted his hat with the other—scanning the top of the levee before turning away—running toward the group of trees where the pickup was parked—holding the hand sprayer out a little away from his body so it wouldn't bounce against his hip—taking long strides so each footfall landed between the rows as he pushed his way through the corn. At the edge of the field he finally stopped to catch his breath—turned and looked back toward the levee but didn't see anything.

Soon he was running again—on through the mosquitoes and a few fireflies—able to hear the cicadas that were starting up. The pickup was down a little dirt path—parked next to a honey locust with clumps of thorns sticking out of its bark.

The boy ran through the little stand of trees—coming to the pickup from behind—tossing the hand sprayer over the tailgate as he continued on to the driver's side door—then squeezing the handle and pulling it open—breathing hard still—sweat dripping down his neck—causing his shirt to stick to his skin.

There was a man sitting in the passenger's seat—brown mustache above his pink lips—cowboy hat on his head— sitting there talking on the boy's cellphone. The boy looked down and saw a pistol in the man's lap—then watched the man hold up a finger like he was nearly finished with his call—sounding lighthearted as he spoke into the phone—bit of an accent that didn't quite seem natural. The man seemed completely at ease—like he and the boy were old friends who'd spent the whole day together—not at all concerned about the pistol in his lap or the dead man at the foot of the levee.

After a second or two the boy took off running in the direction of the highway—another quarter mile along the dirt path to the blacktop but he only got a few steps from the pickup—all the sudden feeling a sharp pain—still trying to run but his body soon refused to move—paralyzed some-how as he stumbled forward—trying to look back over his shoulder but unable to turn his head.

The boy knew he was going down—knew he couldn't stop himself from falling forward—but he wasn't conscious when he hit the ground.

WHEN THE BOY STARTED WAKING UP—HOURS OR minutes or days later—he could hear someone playing mu-sic off in the distance—or maybe close by—playing some-thing that sounded like a flute—high-pitched notes played in rapid succession. Later he'd find out the instrument was called a penny whistle.

The boy's eyes were half closed and he was only half-way back—listening to the penny whistle play on—notes becoming more distinct as the seconds ticked by—his eyes soon opening—seeing a few stars and little gray clouds in the sky—wiggling his fingers and toes—his arms and legs. Then the pain started coming from a spot around his right shoulder blade.

"Hello, Seth," the man said—standing a few feet away with the penny whistle held up in front of his chest.

"What?"

"Let me finish—then we'll talk."

The man raised the penny whistle to his lips and start-ed playing the song from where he'd left off—Seth blinking up at the blurry figure—waiting for his eyes to focus. It was hard to see much of anything in the dark—barely able to tell he was looking at the same man he'd seen in the pickup—average height—maybe a little skinny—wearing blue jeans and boots.

Seth watched the man blow into a metal pipe and shuffle around to the music he was making—watched him from flat on his back on the dirt path—the man making two circles around him before coming to the end of the song—then holding his arms out like he was quieting a crowd—the penny whistle in his left hand—eventually folding his arms into his body as he slowly bowed—finally standing up straight again after what seemed like a long time—turning and looking down.

"Seth."

"Who are you?" Seth said as he raised himself to a sitting position—still not ready to try standing.

"I am a man you're going to drive to Kansas City."

Seth didn't say anything—just watched as the man twirled the penny whistle in his hand.

"We better get going," the man said. "Do you have any hand sanitizer, Seth? I couldn't find any in your vehicle."

"It's not mine," Seth said. "I can't drive you anywhere."

The man tucked the penny whistle into his back pocket as he quickly closed the distance between them—putting a foot on Seth's thigh as the boy tried to shuffle backward—then putting his other foot on Seth's chest—somehow keeping his balance as Seth's back slammed down onto the dirt path. Seth felt the sharp pain from his shoulder blade—then felt the man's fists punching down on his face—connecting several times as Seth's vision went black again—relieved when he felt the man quickly jump off his chest—when he saw the blurry glint of the penny whistle as the man pulled it out from his back pocket—when he heard him start playing an even faster song than the one before—hopping away into the darkness.

Seth looked around for the man as he tried to stumble to his feet—taking a long time just to get to his knees—then putting one hand on the ground as he pushed himself up—planting the soles of his boots on the ground and grabbing his knees with both hands—the man still out there some-where playing the penny whistle.

Seth turned and tried to run—this time back toward the cornfield and the levee—getting just beyond the tailgate before he felt a sharp sting in his right hamstring—thinking at first he'd been shot as he waited to hear the sound of the pistol firing—hopping a few steps on his left leg—then falling forward onto the ground—raising a cloud of dust in the dark.

"Get up, Seth," the man said—suddenly nearby. "That one's not nearly as strong as the one I put in your shoulder."

Seth lay there with his face in the dirt—listening as the man opened the passenger's side door of the pickup—as he hopped up into the seat and shut the door. Then everything was quiet.

Seth propped himself up on his elbows—feeling like he might vomit—feeling blood and saliva dripping from his face onto the dirt—pain in his shoulder blade still but now his hamstring hurt more.

After a few seconds he reached back and pulled a dart out of his leg—blinking the tears out of his eyes so he could see the bloody tip—thin shaft and the brightly colored feathers.

www.ingramcontent.com/pod-product-compliance
Lightning Source LLC
Chambersburg PA
CBHW071241300726
48975CB00002B/509